MY NEIGHBOR
JOHN

Dear Janet,

Blessings to you!!!

Paul M. Feinberg

PAUL M. FEINBERG, PhD

ISBN 978-1-0980-1916-7 (paperback)
ISBN 978-1-0980-1940-2 (hardcover)
ISBN 978-1-0980-1917-4 (digital)

Christian Faith Publishing, Inc.
832 Park Avenue
Meadville, PA 16335
www.christianfaithpublishing.com

Printed in the United States of America

It is the glory of God to conceal a matter; to search out a matter is the glory of kings.
—Proverbs 25:2

ACKNOWLEDGEMENTS

Writing this book has been an experience in and of itself. It began as a joyful embarking on a journey which I wanted to share with many people of faith, people not of faith, and the uncommitted. As I look back over the time it took to bring to a "conclusion" what I had hoped would be a pleasant story with some solid principles which could potentially give hope and/or guidance to those searching for a personal resolution between their faith and what scientific discovery and study outside of the Bible were saying to them, I realize just how difficult the process actually was! In fact, it was at least as difficult as was writing my doctoral dissertation! Difficult and wonderful at the same time! Many have stuck by me the entire time, enthusiastic for the project and believing that it had the potential of being meaningful. Others have prayed for me, and supported me during these years, encouraging me to keep on. And for all of these things I am very grateful.

I would especially like to thank my wife Sofia Mercedes who always supports me in virtually anything I set my hand to and who provided specific suggestions for the telling of "My Neighbor John", my mother Nancy Feinberg who was a constant source of encouragement and the first person I remember in my life to tell me that I must never be afraid of the truth, my sister Susan Meli who believed in the project from the very beginning, and my sister Jill Stueck who made it physically possible in more than a few ways, always generous to a fault!

I would like to thank my mentors who have put up with me over the years: Pastor Leslie B. Flynn of Grace Conservative Baptist Church, Pastor Hank Beukema of Grace Conservative Baptist Church, Dr. Paul E. Toms of Park Street Church in Boston, Dr. Robert

Schuller of the Crystal Cathedral Ministries, Dr. Robert Cornuke of the BASE Institute, Dr. Chuck Missler of the Koinonia House ministry and the Koinonia Institute, and Pastor Miche Maniguet, formerly of Hydewood Park Baptist Church. Thank you gentlemen for your kindness, patience, and willingness to minister to me at so many different times and ways! I am still amazed at the grace of the Lord Jesus in blessing me so extensively through each of your special ministries when it came to nurturing me in the faith. Of these seven men, so influential to me throughout my time here on Earth until this point, only two are still "Earth side". To each of these persons I say "Hey, you're amazing! Let's do some more exploration!" To those who have changed their address to a celestial residence, I say "I miss you all and love you immensely. Thank you for all you have given to me to help me with my walk here on Earth!!!"

I would also like to acknowledge John and Kerri Coppola, Michelle Peters, Dr. John Anton, Gil and Rose Hernandez, and Antonis Nicolaou. Thank you all for your prayers, encouragement, and friendship over the years!

And thanks to Jay Tintle, Julie Garbowsky, and Max Kleiman-Lynch of Jay's Cycle Center of Westfield, NJ for the wonderful products which they sell and for the "instruction" I received as to what constitutes a "hot" bicycle by modern standards! I'm grateful for the time Max spent with me in learning about the details of the equipment during the summer of 2018 and also for the gracious permission from Jay, the proprietor, to use the establishment's name in the book. Finally, I am grateful to Julie for her wonderful hospitality and encouragement when I met her and Jay the following year! It's always more than a treat to meet a brother and sister in the Lord, especially in doing a project like "My Neighbor John"!!!

I am grateful to both Mr. Scott McLaughlin, Literary Agent and Ms. Taylor Birk, Senior Account Manager both of Christian Faith Publishing, Inc. Their encouragement proved to be a great source of strength to me during the process of publication and their advice, explanations, and recommendations invaluable to me in trying to follow the correct path to the publication of "My Neighbor John". They have been true friends to me and I remain indebted to them for their shepherding me through this journey. I hope this will be the first of many projects with them!

Most of all, I would like to thank the Lord Jesus for this assignment. I hope that He is pleased with it ultimately and that He will use it to bring more children into His Kingdom in the time remaining. With this book I wanted to help make known the special ministry built upon His foundation and which He established for me in my life. As my wife and I have said more than once, if one person comes to faith and can point to this story as having played a small part, it was well worth the time!!!

To those reading the book and searching for answers, please keep searching for the truth and never forget to live by it, to apply it to your life. It will in fact bring you into the light! Note the many wonderful resources cited throughout the chapters and be encouraged to follow up on those things which were the most intriguing to you at the start, but don't let up until you find the resolution to these and the other answers for which you have been searching in your life. Get ready for a true adventure!!!

CHAPTER 1

A RECORD OF SIGNIFICANCE AND A TIME WARP BACK TO CHILDHOOD

"I am writing down the events that have had a profound effect on my life and that happened during the early age in my own development. I believe that these are still significant for both present and future service for God Almighty—and because this record may one day encourage others who read it. Right now I am about to embark on another task of service nearly identical to the one that I undertook when I was only eight years old, more than a decade away from the present time. Perhaps it is needless to say among those who know me as a friend that I am still very excited and even exuberant about all that happened back then, and my heart is still full of hope. Ironically, there was a time when my outlook was so different, one of at least partial bewilderment or even desperation, knowing that I was facing an imminent, overwhelming battle that threatened to severely rearrange my world—and not for the better—or so I thought. Of all things, I was battling a paradigm (and all of the emotions of those people who were invested in it). And even immediately after those events, I battled a seemingly overwhelming tragedy.

"That first battle actually threatened to severely upset my world view and even to displace the role of faith in my life. And now, all these years later, I am facing once again an extremely 'similarly themed' battle onstage, in full view of people needing to know things. What is different now is my view and attitude toward demonstrating a faithful perception of, first, the Scripture and then how science can serve one's true pursuit of knowledge. Long ago the first battle took place locally, drawing people from my own childhood community, involving my church, my school, and even my neighborhood. Now I face a similar one, taking place on a stage in an auditorium on a college campus. In each venue, that from the past and that of the present, a review of the formative older events might just play a pivotal role in pointing a person toward the light.

"I was overwhelmed the first time for sure. The potential consequences of what surrounded me I understood well, even at that young age. But thanks to God's wonderful grace, delivered through my neighbor John, that was not how things were to end. In fact, this might just be one of those cases in history of a victory in the face of the enemy when the odds might certainly 'promise' to go against you since so much of what was on trial was to be evaluated by the local community, initially only armed with the 'commonsense measure' of today's world."

Samuel put his pen down and thought for a moment. In another moment he picked it up and added, "I will try to relay as accurately as possible the events that did occur, however I acknowledge that there certainly could be errors of omission, since I am only one person and there were many involved. May dear God, guide me so that all of the critical information will be put down for His Glory!"

Samuel felt more satisfied that he openly "acknowledged" that other details might show up from other sources later, to be brought into the account for people to consider and assess. He did not want to pretend that his account was exhaustively complete, only complete from his point of view. This was at least part of John's lesson for him after all... But we'll get to that later.

SAMUEL AT AGE EIGHT

So much had happened in the last three months. First, there had been normal life that included school, specifically his fourth-grade class. The first time the problems Sam experienced occurred when he was in the spring term. There had been homework, friends after school, chores, hobbies, television, church on Sundays, and his cherished times of visiting John Barzeb, who ran the local fishing supply store down near the lake that abutted the town. Truthfully, Samuel regarded John as his best friend, making any excuse possible to walk over to John's store after school or ride his bicycle there on the weekend. Sometimes he would tell his mother that he was doing a report on something within the realm of John's expertise, tailoring the voluntary aspects of school assignments according to the stories—or even things linked to the stories—that he would hear from John. To him John was the wisest human being he ever met; and he loved listening, pondering, and discussing any and all aspects of what he deemed came from John's unique wisdom.

A double blessing soon entered his life when he found out that John was teaching the fourth grade Sunday school class at his church beginning in two weeks! Now his time would be naturally expanded without the need for him to come up with connections to justify visits to John and his wonderful store.

Oh, that store! He loved going into the store and learning about all the wisdom behind the "art of fishing." Although he fully acknowledged fishing as a sport and a recreational endeavor, talking to John had shown him that there was an active thought process behind catching fish. John had told him that he had been blessed to have learned to fish in grander waters while a boy, although in the beginning of their relationship he never told him where. John's father had also owned a fishing business, only in this case it was based upon catching fish directly instead of supplying equipment. John had said that his labors were not recreational at all, but truly necessitated by the need for his family to eat, barter, and, in so doing, allow others in the community to eat. To John fishing was an activity that needed to be understood, respected, and perfected as much as possible for the simple matter of survival; however, in his heart, John said, he always knew that God would protect him and his family, giving them sustenance if they put in a full honest effort.

Fitting this description, Sam had imagined a picture of an obscure local fishing business somewhere in the southern United States, maybe off the Louisiana Coast. He had tried to Google every variant of "Barzeb" on the computer to see if he could find out more about John's father or about the family business if it still existed in some form. According to Samuel's mother, John appeared to be about in his mid-fifties, so it was possible that his father could still be alive. Sam couldn't find anything without more detail about the family but resisted asking John more about this because he didn't want John to think he was trying to assess the size or strength of the family business in case it was truly small, maybe embarrassingly so. His questions were confined to specifics only—fishing equipment, techniques, sizes of the largest fish seen in the catches of the past, etc.

John had told Samuel that after the war he wanted to come to quieter waters, allowing him to carry on with his life in a community where he could serve an active part again. He had said that his father had shown him and his brother that pattern long ago, and he wanted to emulate it as much as possible in his own life. Good old Bolton Landing, New York, was where he ended up living now.

Although he never told Samuel the details, John's brother had died many years before, prior to the Vietnam War, which Samuel assumed John had come out of to return to fishing. Aside from an occasional mention of something learned or experienced by him and his brother, John almost never mentioned the details of his and his brother's deep friendship. Samuel knew that it had been one of deep caring, because Samuel had once seen the tears in John's eyes well up during the telling of one of his family vignettes where the two boys had travelled to a town with virtually no travelling cash, both confident that there needs would be met by God. The tears had come when he astounded young Samuel by saying that their needs were more than met! Initially and out of respect, Samuel decided that he would not ask about his brother in order to "protect" John from ever feeling bad, where Sam could help it.

CHAPTER 2

A GROWING FASCINATION WITH SCIENCE

Samuel had always loved science. At eight years old, he especially loved learning about the space program and following the projects that the National Aeronautics and Space Administration (NASA) was always orchestrating or in which they were participating. One day he still hoped to be able to fly on the space shuttle (or whatever hopefully would replace the space shuttle orbiters) to the International Space Station, or station Alpha, as the NASA team called it. The first time he ever talked to John about science was on a summer night when they were looking through his telescope together. John had come over for dinner, and they were in the backyard afterward, looking up at a beautiful star-filled sky. Sam asked him about how far away one of the stars was, and he said probably at least six light years away. He didn't understand this answer of light and time at first and asked him about it again for clarification. John said that he was referring to a distance, but that it was expressed in terms of the amount of time it took for light to travel from the star to the Earth. He said it was on the order of just over thirty-five trillion miles! Hearing this, Sam was more than a little surprised. John always had a way of framing things in such fascinating terms!

John's astronomy lessons always gave Samuel a thirst to learn everything he could about the universe. John had told him that scientists had established that the farthest stars were between thirteen billion and fourteen billion light years from the Earth! He guessed that would make them seventy-eight billion trillion miles away or something like that. Wow! Sam then immediately asked John a follow up question: "How long would it take to travel out to a planet around the farthest star?"

"Hmm," he replied. "Probably if you used a spaceship that could travel at twice the top speed of the space shuttle, you would be looking at over one trillion years!"

Sam could hardly believe that! He then asked how long it would take to visit the star they were looking at. John's answer shocked him again.

"Oh well, probably if you could travel a good one hundred thousand miles per hour in a spaceship, maybe on the order of six to seven hundred million years!"

Sam's heart sank. "Then how would we ever colonize space?" he asked.

John could see that this problem of time bothered Samuel. Instead of launching into some negative discourse about the limits of time, he said, "But, Sam, you don't even know what new technologies will be available in the future for space travel."

Sam still wasn't happy. Instead, he replied, "Even if we could get to warp 1, the speed of light, I bet you're still talking over one million years! How can we ever explore the universe in our lifetime with these kinds of limits on our speed?"

John smiled at this. He said, "What if we learn how to fold space and could step from one end of it to another instantaneously?"

Sam had to admit to himself that the question caught him off-guard. John had told him that "When dear God created the universe, it was with careful planning," which to Sam meant that there were many things that still had yet to be discovered. That surely made sense. Then John did what he would later do quite often—he amazed Sam. This time with a fact so out of the ordinary that it made him want to discover it sometime in his life and use it to become the smartest scientist in the world.

John looked at Sam and then said, "Sam, have you ever heard of Rabbi Maimonades of the twelfth century?" He shook his head no.

John continued, "According to his study of the book of Genesis in the Bible, he had determined there to be ten dimensions, only four of which were knowable. These include length, width, height, and time! The interesting thing is that quantum physicists today tell us the same thing from their theoretical models and experimentation. You and I still have no idea how any of this will work out to revolutionize space travel and exploration. So let's not jump to any negative conclusions! It's a big universe, and if dear God wants it to be colonized by us, it will be."

Truthfully, Sam's basic sense of innate optimism returned in force! He responded, simply saying, "Wow, John! That sure is cool! I bet you that this is exactly what future spaceships will do…travel in other dimensions! Maybe that's what a real 'warp drive' would do like in *Star Trek*! Do you think so?"

John replied simply, "It may be. One thing is certain, I don't think we will ever get bored exploring this beautiful universe that the Lord created!"

This was something else that Sam hadn't thought of. But John was right. Dear God had to create everything, so therefore he knew all the details before he put them into his creation. It was only right (and even scientific) to try to perceive all these amazing things (including "amazing distances") through the eyes of dear God. Immediately, he began to wonder about the vastness of space and how dear God could create all of it in such amazing detail! It sounded exhausting!

Sam simply said to John, "Do you think that we'll ever be able to learn enough to travel the full breadth of the universe?"

To this John responded, "Right now there is so much to focus on about the human race getting right with God in this corner of the universe that I wouldn't begin to know…but if that's your calling inside, Samuel, keep pursuing it!"

Oh, how the young boy loved John! Never willing to squash his hopes or dreams and always encouraging him to actively look to see more openly and deeply and to always maintain an air of hopefulness…always keeping dear God (as he was fond of referring to the Lord) in mind in all things.

CHAPTER 3

A QUESTION IN AN EARLY SEARCH FOR TRUTH...AND A HEARTY APPROBATION

Well, it all seemed to start with that sermon titled "Trusting the Lord's Word: A Focus on How the Bible has been Revealed through the Lens of History" on June 7 at the church. Samuel's parents sometimes let him go with them to the adult part of church. This was one of those special Sundays, the beginning of a new series of sermon topics that the pastor liked to introduce from time to time to keep the times of worship for the congregation interesting, exciting, or both. Since Samuel's mother knew how much he enjoyed hearing about the Bible and archaeological discoveries or historical connections she let him know about the plan and suggested to him that he just might like to join her and his dad instead of Sunday school for that series of messages. Samuel had to make sure to remember to ask John if it would be all right to miss his Sunday school class, just to make sure John wouldn't think that he didn't like going to his class! As he recalled, John only smiled at him and told him to "enjoy it and make sure you tell me all about your favorite parts!"

The minister, Pastor Gregg, actually had done a really wonderful job of talking about the foundation and trustworthiness of the biblical account. He spoke of the precision found in the Greek texts used for the Gospels and other New Testament accounts. Samuel was literally blown away when the pastor linked the account in Daniel 9:25 of the Tanakh precisely with the triumphal entry of Jesus recorded in the New Testament! He spoke of how the angel Gabriel gave Daniel a mathematical prophecy of the Messiah's coming to Jerusalem, which was literally fulfilled to the day during the Palm Sunday entrance to Jerusalem by the Lord Jesus after 173,880 days! Samuel found such a fact exhilarating! He couldn't have been happier that his parents had asked him to come for the sermon!

Samuel was so excited by this that he could hardly contain himself. Only the fear of missing any word of the sermon kept him from asking his mother and father questions. The pastor then ended his examples by talking about the likely location of the real Mount Sinai. He went on to compare the rediscovery of Jabel Al Lawz by adventurers Robert Cornuke and Larry Williams in the late 1980s with the traditional location for Mount Sinai in Egypt. He talked of the discrepancies of the traditional location with the biblical account and then showed some amazing pictures of what was thought to be the real mountain in Saudi Arabia. Once again Pastor Gregg showed the "needs of the landscape" according to what was recorded in Scripture. Samuel pondered thoughtfully the implications of massive flocks of animals, perhaps one million Israelites, the term "lands end," the Egyptians being drowned in the mighty ocean, and even the references to the "Bitter Springs of Marah" and the "Oasis of the Seventy-two Palms," etc.

At the end of the service, Samuel sat there awestruck. He thought about the Bible's precision in its description and being able to take this venerable book (or books, as the case is, actually) as completely accurate as written. The next week Pastor Gregg said he wanted to share more treasures of the biblical text that seemed to be "hidden in plain sight," and Samuel was wishing he could go into a time machine right then and there to begin relishing every word! And then it occurred to him… "Hmm, each word is precious…each significant…" As his eyes glanced over the church sermon bulletin, he noticed the Scripture quotes of the day: Matthew 16:27–28, Luke 9:26–27, Matthew 24:34–35, and Matthew 5:18. He began reading them out of the church pew Bible in the holder on the seat back ahead of where he sat. In a few minutes his mother and father smiled as Samuel immediately got up and began walking up to the pastor still holding the Bible open to the last of the Scripture verses he had been referencing. His father smiled to his mother and said, "Uh-oh, here we go again!"

Pastor Gregg saw Samuel in his determined walk toward the pulpit and smiled. He thought, *If only the rest of my congregation were as thirsty for the Truth as this lad is… Hope I can answer his questions…* Quickly, Pastor Gregg prayed a silent prayer.

"Pastor Gregg?" asked the little man.

"Yes, Samuel?" asked the kindly minister.

"I loved your sermon today and wanted to ask you a question about this Scripture verse…" said Samuel, gesturing to the verse from Matthew 24. "How could Jesus's words disappear? What does that mean exactly?"

"Well, actually, Samuel, it says that Jesus's words will never disappear until all has been fulfilled," replied Gregg. "In fact, it's not only his teachings but how his actual words and how they were recorded are extremely important!"

"So that links to the next verse, Matthew 5:18?" asked Sam.

"Exactly, Samuel. Everything which is breathed by God is precious and is not to be neglected, abused, or truncated. God's Words will never pass away because they are too important, too holy, and He has established their continuity," Gregg continued.

"Continuity?" questioned the boy.

"Meaning, the actual words live on!" replied the pastor.

Samuel just nodded and smiled, thinking, *I'm sure glad they are "edit proof."* He was thinking of the last corrected essay he got back from his language arts class. "But, Pastor Gregg…," continued Sam.

Immediately, Gregg thought, *Oh no, here it comes…*

"The first two verses listed for today seem to be referring to the same thing that Jesus was saying, but they are not exactly the same… How can that be if Jesus's words will never pass away?" asked the inquisitive boy.

"Well, Samuel, the thoughts are what is being reported in the best Greek that the respective writers knew. In other words, they wrote down what they remembered in the best summary possible, based upon their individual experiences, recollections, and Greek-writing skills. You can see that the meanings as we read the English essentially line up just as we would expect them to line up," Gregg explained.

"I think I see Pastor Gregg—they wrote down their own experiences and then those words are the ones which are protected from passing away!" Samuel chimed in.

"My boy that is possibly the best explanation I think I have ever heard!" Gregg smiled.

Samuel was off like a shot back down the aisle to his parents.

CHAPTER 4

AN EXCITING SERMON, A DISTURBING PRAYER, AND AN ORDER OF SCHOOL DETENTION GIVEN TO AN ELDER!

It was now a week later, and this seemed like one of the best days of Samuel's entire life! It was Sunday, just before church, and he was positively ecstatic with the prospect of another sermon like the previous week with a presentation of more amazing truth about the Bible. He couldn't wait to tell John about both of the sermons (even though one had yet to be heard) and planned on running right to him after the pastor dismissed everyone! This was a wonderful day indeed! That is, it certainly felt like that until the final prayer was led by one of the members of the congregation, Mr. Allen, one of the remaining farmers in the community. Sam liked Mr. Allen but didn't interact much with him. Allen always volunteered to help out with church events like the spring and fall barbecues, the summer picnic, the Christmas party, the Easter Egg hunt, and a few other events that everyone always enjoyed. He even told a few jokes every now and then, some actually not that funny but always delivered with a smile and a good-natured wink. Everyone knew him and regarded him with friendly respect. It was because of this that Sam couldn't believe what he heard that morning in the final prayer.

Mr. Allen walked up to the front of the church and over to the microphone as Pastor Gregg moved toward the first pew. As the congregation stood to pray, Mr. Allen began the prayer with, "Dear God, we know that you didn't create the universe with a big bang…" Samuel was dumbfounded. Was Mr. Allen not aware of science? The big bang theory was an amazing theory that seemed to be in line with the creation account in Genesis! Why was he saying this? What was he telling everyone what the real truth was? And all this coming after so splendid a sermon talking about archaeological discoveries confirming the biblical account! Samuel felt crushed, disappointed, and angry all at the same time. And that is when he prayed silently to the Lord, "Dear God, I am confused and need your help to understand all of this. Please tell me the truth, dear Lord. I don't ever want to be wrong about you. Amen."

Once the prayer was finished and the congregation dismissed, Samuel got up quickly to move out from the pew and begin his run straight to John's classroom. His mother and father were surprised by his abrupt outbreak of energy and asked him if anything was wrong. He only said, "Everything is wrong… I have to get to John!" As soon as he entered the aisle, he bolted from the sanctuary.

John was putting away some of the materials from his Sunday school lesson when Samuel burst into the room. John looked seriously at him and said, "Something wrong, Samuel?"

Samuel replied quickly, "Yes, John, everything is wrong!"

"Okay then," John said as he sat down at one of the tables, "tell me."

Samuel relaxed somewhat now that this friend, upon whom he had determined was the only one who could help him, had now actually focused on him and his problem.

"At the closing prayer in the sanctuary just a few minutes ago, Mr. Allen said that he knew the Lord did not create the universe with a big bang! Why did he have to say that in a prayer? I don't want to pray a lie to God. But, John, is he right? Are all the scientists wrong? Does it mean that people who love science are really going against God, err, um, dear God?"

John smiled, noting that Samuel remembered to respect the Lord by adding "dear."

"Well, Samuel, I see you have had your first introduction to a 'difference among the brethren!'" As he paused, he seemed to think back over his years of Christian fellowship. He sighed, then said, "Samuel, you will find as you grow up that seldom is there no difference of opinion, even among the saints. Mr. Allen is simply trying to be faithful to his principles as he prays with a complete heart in spirit and in truth. He wants to make a stand for God, and to him that means that believing in something that goes against God is not acceptable in any form. He wanted to include the entire congregation in his rejection of blasphemy. To him, modern-day science has come up with a picture of the creation of the universe that doesn't require God to be present at all. That is what the big bang theory is to him, an explanation of the universe that doesn't require God to be present!"

Samuel's gaze never left John as he countered with, "But the big bang theory doesn't exclude dear God's creation of the universe! Where does he think the explosion came from? The theory is only a testimony based upon the discovery of the motion of the galaxies away from each other and the background radiation! It doesn't say that God did not create the universe!"

John smiled again and said, "Relax, Samuel! Mr. Allen probably hasn't thought about the details behind this theory, let alone read any serious publication describing it. Just because he feels threatened by the theory, doesn't mean that it is necessarily blasphemous or evil… I would say more than likely he isn't bothered by the idea of galaxy movement or background radiation anyway. I would assume he is more uncomfortable with the age of the universe being assumed to be over thirteen billion years!"

"I'm bothered by all of it, Mr. Barzeb," came a voice from the classroom door. "It don't make sense to me that the universe should be changing at all! The Word of God says that God doesn't change, so maybe that means His universe doesn't change either! But you are right about one thing, though… I am greatly bothered by anyone trying to tell me that the universe is thirteen trillion billion gazillion years old when the genealogies of our Lord and Savior show clearly to me that it's around six thousand years or so!"

John looked over at Mr. Allen and smiled, hoping to diffuse the situation as much as possible. He then said politely, "Mr. Allen, young Samuel here is a junior astronomer and wants to grow up to be a NASA scientist. I was telling him that you were defending what you thought to be right from a standpoint of faith."

"Well, that's certainly true!" replied Allen.

John continued, "Sometimes a person's courage to take a stand can be misunderstood by someone considering the situation from a different perspective."

Again that seemed to alleviate some of the sharpness in Mr. Allen's demeanor.

"Yes, I think that does make sense, John," Allen replied again.

"I assume you're here to make sure that everything is okay with young Samuel?" offered John.

"Err, yes, I saw the boy run out of the sanctuary after my prayer and thought something must be wrong. I asked his parents, and they told me that Sam was upset, but they didn't know why. I came to see what the trouble was." Allen looked over at the boy, who looked at him questioningly. "Everything okay now, Samuel?"

"I guess so," said Samuel. "We have a difference of opinion, is all..."

Allen seemed to bristle again. "No, Samuel, not a difference of opinion. You have not yet matured enough to grasp the authority of the Bible, and you have a lot more maturing to do!"

The last sentence was said so loudly that Sam actually caught his breath. But then suddenly, a louder voice was heard in the room.

"That will be enough of that, Mr. Allen!"

Shocked, both Samuel and Allen turned toward the end of the table to see John rising. His voice was loud, stern, and nonnegotiable. Gone was the conciliatory nature of only a moment ago.

Both Samuel and Mr. Allen would have continued staring a while longer, but John continued, "I think it's time we had a meeting with the pastor immediately. Samuel, I will see you later. Mr. Allen, join me now at the pastor's office!"

With that he strode forcefully out of the room, not waiting for a reply from the farmer.

Samuel again was dumbfounded. He didn't know what to say and didn't want to be left standing in the room with Mr. Allen alone, so he ran for his life. This time, however, he felt a certain glee over the hope of vindication in his spirit. He loved the Lord; and no one, he hoped, was going to tell him that science was getting in the way of that. As he cleared the exit door of the church, he glanced behind him to see Mr. Allen leaving the room purposefully toward the direction of Pastor Gregg's office.

CHAPTER 5

THE ESCAPE, THE GUILT, AND AN ACCIDENTAL EAVESDROP

Samuel took off out the door, grateful for being able to make it to the unconfined freedom of the sunshine outdoors. People were still walking to their cars or beginning their walks home, completely unaware of what had just transpired. As far as he knew, neither John nor Mr. Allen had ever been involved in a disagreement or misunderstanding, certainly never an argument. Now what had just happened would ruin everything, disrupt the peace of the church, and, for all Samuel knew, the whole community. The real problem, Samuel now realized, was that he had caused it.

He paused and then groaned as he contemplated this last thought. He didn't want to have done that. Maybe everything he had gotten upset about simply wasn't that important. He didn't want to cause strife among the members. He didn't want the elders of the church to think that he was disrespectful. He truly didn't think he was...at least normally. Mr. Allen accused him of ignorance, or at least a lack of maturity, and not accepting the authority of the Bible. He had not treated him as if Samuel was being disrespectful of him, but instead of dear God. And Samuel truly hadn't intended to be seen in that way! Oh, all was ruined! Why couldn't he have just gone to Sunday school with John that morning? Why couldn't he even have just stayed home to do some Bible reading or something else special for Sunday?

As he raced past the side of the church at top speed, he was suddenly stopped in his tracks by these last thoughts literally just under the windows of the pastor's office. He looked up and noticed that the windows were open. He then gathered himself to continue on home and started walking away, more slowly this time. Just a moment before he wouldn't have been able to hear anything because of the increasing distance from the windows, he heard clearly the words, "What's the meaning of ordering me to the pastor's office, John? Just who do you think you are talking to?"

At this Samuel broke his pace and stopped again. Immediately, the details of the predicament returned to his mind. Mr. Allen had been so mean. John had then intervened strongly, practically ordering him to the pastor's office. For all of Mr. Allen's indignation, however, Samuel had never ever witnessed John being petty with anyone. If John had done this, it must have been for a good reason. Without realizing it, Samuel slowly drifted back toward the window, listening.

Inside he heard Pastor Gregg say, "Yes, John, what is going on here? I don't understand such abrupt and seemingly discourteous behavior on the part of one of my elders in the church!"

John met his gaze directly and then said, "Mr. Allen has committed a very clumsy and foolish act toward one of our own upstanding youth, and I wish to bring it to your attention for his immediate admonishment and correction."

The way he stated it was not with malice but with thoughtful expression and yet quiet urgency. This was not how Mr. Allen took it, however.

"Who do you think you are calling a fool? Whatever your differences are with me, John, you need to show the proper respect for your elders! I'm sixty-five years old. I'll have you know—"

"Mr. Allen," John said loudly, "if respecting church elders is on your mind, I'll request the same of you now. I am at least ten years your senior!"

At this, both Mr. Allen and Pastor Gregg stared at John in shock! Neither had assumed him to be any more than middle fifties, in all likelihood, possibly early fifties because of his apparently good athletic condition.

Before either of them could say anything, John continued, "I have spent many hours with young Samuel, and I can tell you with much assurance that he is zealous for the Lord and completely respects and venerates biblical authority. Your accusation to Samuel of otherwise is unacceptable, Mr. Allen. Unacceptable and unwise. Despite the fact that Samuel is my friend, I feel strongly that your treatment of him in this way or of any of our youth in similar ways must stop immediately. It will stop here and now, or this congregation is finished. Our church community here and even among the brethren in this nation and around the world have too many important things to do without exasperating our youth and driving them from the love and devotion to the catholic church!"

Stammering a bit, possibly an after effect from the shock of learning John's apparent age, Mr. Allen responded, "I ain't said nothing about the Catholic Church and am even good friends with Father Richard..." Pastor Gregg interrupted him calmly then and said, "Bill, 'catholic' in this use refers to the universal church as in the Body of Christ." "Oh. Well anyway Samuel rejects the Word of God as recorded in the book of Genesis! He wants to be able to interpret it any way he wants so that he can maintain that interest in space of his without appearing to leave the Bible behind!"

"Nonsense!" John replied sternly. "I've spent hours with Samuel looking through his telescope and talking with him about God's universe. Nothing could be further from the truth! He loves God and is fascinated by His creation. He has not yet closed his mind to apprehending God's truth as it is revealed in nature. He holds the biblical account dear and wonders about it often. At the same time, he is fascinated by the study of astronomy and its foundational theory of the big bang. In my view, this is *exactly* where he should be at this age, not stymied into your own limited interpretation!"

"What do you mean by limited? Are you trying to say that I'm narrow-minded? *Why you...!*"

"*Gentlemen!*" Pastor Gregg interrupted loudly. "This is not getting us anywhere. I'm particularly shocked at you, John! You've never treated any of our elders in this manner before..."

John replied, "This is not a personal affront to Mr. Allen except that I am insisting that he refrain from any more rebukes of Samuel of such nature as what took place. It is not healthy for this church, nor is it healthy for the right kind of growth for the family of God."

"Now what makes you so sure of this, John?" replied Pastor Gregg more calmly now.

"Throughout my life, I have seen unhealthy ways of wielding 'religious conviction' without honest study, prayer, or contemplation of the Scriptures and their unfortunate results," John stated. "If you want a classic example from the public's domain of 'cultural examples,' reference the Spanish Inquisition and what was done to Galileo. Although I am not advocating the various ways that Galileo communicated his findings, I would like to say that his observations, theories, and conjectures of planetary motion were largely correct. He was slapped down hard by the Roman Catholic Church and put on the condemned list for hundreds of years. This has been seen as a mark of intolerance, even disgrace, on the part of the church ever since then. Who knows how many lost souls have been deterred from exploring the Gospel as a result of this. If there was any truth in what he said or wrote, I maintain that a Christian regarding such should contemplate the assertions of the speaker and check them against the Scriptures. This is what the Bereans did for our brother Paul. If there is no contradiction, then one needs to keep his peace in terms of condemnation. If one wants to question or explore honestly, it can be done calmly, respectfully, and decently. I am talking specifically among the brethren. We all should know what can happen in the world at large. Even in the outside world, it is possible for the "salt of the Earth" to engage people in a respectful manner, having kind regard for where they are coming from at the moment. Can you imagine Paul meeting with success in Athens if he started by condemning the Athenians' misdirected worship? Instead, he took a path of respect, being willing to engage them, beginning in a non-hostile manner at the level upon which they were found as they stood outside of Christ. Or imagine our Lord condemning the Samaritan woman at the well before he engaged her in conversation, knowing already the history of her 'sinful' life.

"Even if you begin within a legitimate community established in truth, we should not face the risk of mistreating—or worse—any member at the hands of those who fail to control their emotional outbursts and vocal condemnations. My own brother James died for his belief and faith in the Lord Jesus Christ because of such worldly reactions to the Truth. He was killed by people who believed they were committing a religious act! In this church, I am determined to point it out so that does not take place!"

Both Pastor Gregg and Mr. Allen kept staring at John as they took in what he was saying. Both of them were extremely curious and even fascinated about this newfound knowledge concerning their fellow church member. At the same time neither of them wanted to question him about any of it at the moment...not until this crisis was over.

"So what you're doing to Mr. Allen wouldn't count as an inappropriate reaction?" offered Pastor Gregg.

To this John said, "The Word says in the letter to the church at Colosse, in the twenty-first verse of chapter 3, 'Fathers, do not embitter your children, or they will become discouraged' and again in the letter to the church at Ephesus in the fourth verse of chapter 6, 'Fathers, do not exasperate your children; instead, bring them up in the training and instruction of the Lord.'"

John then continued, "My reaction to Mr. Allen is appropriate in that it is not a personal reaction. It is a reaction that is appropriate and right for the church. It is appropriate for the proper training of our children here and in all parts of the church. By exasperating our youth and speaking such words of dismissal and disregard, we will risk losing this generation and cutting off the healthy growth and contribution of these vital seeds for the Lord. Has either one of you contemplated what Samuel must be thinking right at this moment? If not, then you should start right away."

"I was just trying to help Samuel to get a correct view of the creation as it is recorded in the Good Book!" said Mr. Allen emphatically. "I wasn't trying to slap him down, just correct him!"

"By telling him that he had not yet 'grasped the authority of the Bible' as you put it and that he had 'some maturing to do,' you completely disregarded his joy in the Lord, assumed him an outsider because of immaturity, and rejected any notion of a spiritually healthy interest in science. The combined effect of this will not be to Samuel's benefit, the benefit of the youth within and outside the church, the catholic church's benefit, or this community church's benefit," John replied.

"Is that what you said Bill?" asked Pastor Gregg.

"Yes, pretty much," replied Mr. Allen in a more subdued voice.

"Then perhaps John has a good point we should learn as a church," said Pastor Gregg.

"I suppose, but I still don't like the notion of a 'big bang' creating anything!" Allen offered.

"I don't agree with it either, my friend, but at the same time I don't want to slam the door in the face of those who are contemplating repenting and asking the Lord Jesus to be their Savior and Master. That is more important by far! In all likelihood, young Samuel will grow into a more sophisticated appreciation of our Lord in time and reject all errant notions leading away from God," comforted Pastor Gregg.

"Excuse me, Pastor, but I'm not sure we are all on the same page here," John replied.

"Please don't tell me that you disagree with what I just said, John," said Pastor Gregg.

"Before I respond to that, I would like to quote our Lord again in the tenth chapter of Mark, verse 15, 'I tell you the truth, anyone who will not receive the kingdom of God like a little child will never enter it.' With all due respect due Ravi Zecharias, I believe we need to 'recapture the wonder' here. Whether you believe that the theory put forth by Dr. John Matther is on the right track or not is really not at issue. The issue for the church and its ministry to the world is to proclaim the Gospel. Salvation is solely through Jesus Christ, the only Name given under heaven by which men are to be saved. My Bible does not have a footnote that salvation requires a belief in a literal six-day creation. Given the state of scientific research and the fact that our college-bound youth, like it or not, will be exposed to this research, it behooves us to be more contemplative and less forceful in assertions of 'blasphemy' and let the careful study of the Scriptures enlightened by the Holy Spirit guide our beliefs about such scientific theories. What is paramount for a Christian to do with regard to this matter is to consider it through the lens of Scripture. If there is not a conflict, then a scientific theory may be part of the revelation of truth by nature. Even if proved false later, it will not have the calamity of having functioned as a stumbling block for those searching for the Truth."

"But, John, don't you believe that the Scripture says clearly that the Lord God created the Earth in six days and rested on the seventh?" asked Pastor Gregg.

John replied, "I believe that the ancient Hebrew tells the Truth about the creation in the first chapter of Genesis. I do not maintain that it is necessarily six twenty-four-hour time periods, which are the days."

"You've got to be kidding, John!" snapped Mr. Allen.

"Not at all," replied John.

"But looking at the Genesis account—" started the pastor.

"I'm aware of what many have written regarding this account, Pastor Gregg. I'm also aware that many are unfamiliar with ancient Hebrew as well."

"So now you're telling us you read ancient Hebrew, John?" queried Allen.

"Read it, speak it, and write it, Mr. Allen," replied John.

"So what do you believe, John?" asked Pastor Gregg.

"Pastor, I believe that what I am saying here pertains to the overall meaning of what is being communicated as opposed to the precise rendering of the individual Holy Words spoken by our Lord. I'm talking about an attitude, an approach even, toward understanding new ideas, new research, and new discoveries. With regard to the creation account in Genesis, I am simply saying that one should withhold judgment of what the account precisely says without a full consideration of the ancient Hebrew language."

"So where does that leave us, John?" asked Pastor.

John paused for a moment in apparent contemplation. Before he answered, he seemed to shake his head yes, as if in acknowledgement of some silent suggestion. He paused another moment and exhaled slightly. Then he looked at both Pastor Gregg and Mr. Allen and said, "It leaves us with an opportunity for a church-wide debate to be carried out in the sanctuary in front of all the congregation. For starters, I will represent the view that it is acceptable and even desirable to contemplate the big bang theory among other things in science, as a possible means of interpreting the Genesis account. You, Pastor, will take the view that it is not correct based upon the biblical revelation."

"A church-wide debate?" offered the pastor, shaking his head thoughtfully. "I'm not sure instigating a fight among the church—"

John intercepted him. "Not a fight, Pastor, but an exposition about two different ideas… It may foster a division of opinion, but if done in the right spirit, it will foster our congregation making a careful survey and exploration of the Scripture in order for them to understand the Truth… It will be as if they were… Bereans!"

"Maybe that's just what the doctor ordered, John," offered Pastor, satisfied at the proposal's wisdom.

To this John replied, "Maybe not just a doctor, but the Great Physician."

Just outside the window, upon hearing this, Samuel couldn't believe it! He was now excited again! He was ready to burst with excitement. He started off at top speed again, only this time it was with joy! He couldn't help shouting, "Thank you, Lord Jesus!" as he took off down the path.

CHAPTER 6

A Fresh Burst of Energy, the Arrival Home to Mom and Dad, and a Visit from Pastor Gregg

Samuel burst through the front door and ran straight into the living room. He was greeted by his parents immediately as they simultaneously said, "Samuel! We're so glad your home!"

He stood there looking at them bewildered for a moment, trying to catch his breath.

His mother immediately added, "Your father and I were so worried when you ran out of the sanctuary because we didn't know what was wrong—"

"Are you all right now?" his father interrupted, desperately wanting to cut to the chase.

"Oh yeah, Dad," replied Samuel. "I'm finer than fine!"

At this admission, both his mother and father realized that their son had a changed manner about him. Only this time it wasn't upset they perceived but joy and excitement. They loved watching their son learn to enjoy his discoveries and were both grateful for this turnaround of emotion.

"Then please tell us what happened, son, since you never did during your dramatic exit at the church," his father continued.

"Well, Dad, I went to tell John about what Mr. Allen said during his prayer... It was hard for me to think that I had been so wrong in my thinking about the big bang in our astronomy studies. I wanted to ask him if he thought it was wrong too. Then Mr. Allen came to check up on me—"

"Mr. Allen came to check up on you, Samuel?" his mother couldn't help confirming.

"Yes, Mom. He noticed me running from the sanctuary also and wanted to find out if anything was wrong, I guess."

His mother then added, "That kind man! Mr. Allen has that wonderful quiet way of concern for everyone in the church. He once—"

This time it was Samuel who interrupted. "Mr. Allen told me that I didn't grasp the authority of the Bible and that I had some maturing to do..."

"Allen said that?" his father said incredulously. "Samuel, I hope you don't believe that! I know your diligence and enthusiasm for learning the Word of God. It's nonsense for him to even comment on that part of your life given your limited exposure to Allen!"

"Thanks, Dad. John wasn't happy about it either!"

"So you found John?" his mother said.

"Yes, Mom. I ran straight to his classroom, and he was still putting away Sunday school materials when I got there."

"Well, what did he say, Samuel?" his father asked.

"He pretty much ordered Mr. Allen to be quiet and to follow him to Pastor Gregg's office. He seemed pretty angry with Mr. Allen."

"Really?!" his father said. "So what happened then, Sam?"

"Mr. Allen followed John to Pastor Gregg's office, and I ran outside away from all of them to get away from the battle."

"You don't look upset now," his mother said.

"No, Mom, I'm not. At first, I felt so guilty that I had started this thing over astronomy and that maybe it was selfish after all. But as I stopped outside the church, I became more upset as I thought about all that had happened. I must have stopped without realizing it right under Pastor's office windows. Just as I was about to run home, I heard Mr. Allen start yelling at John..." Samuel paused now, knowing his parents wouldn't be pleased that he eavesdropped. "I'm sorry,

Mom and Dad, but I couldn't help but stand there and listen to John as he started to teach both Pastor and Mr. Allen."

"We understand, son, you were quite honestly overtaken by the circumstances and we don't blame you," his father replied.

"Dad, John is so smart when it comes to Scripture! Did you know he is at least ten years older than Mr. Allen? Did you know he speaks, reads, and writes ancient Hebrew? Did you know that—"

The front door bell rang, interrupting young Samuel's recount of the events at the church.

Mrs. Bodden opened the door to see a smiling Pastor Gregg.

"Hello, Mrs. Bodden!" the pastor greeted.

"Why, hello, Reverend Gregg!" she replied. "We were just being filled in by Samuel of the events that happened after this morning's sermon."

Perhaps only a little sheepishly, Pastor Gregg smiled and then in somewhat of a reduced voice said, "Well, that's why I came by. I understand that there was a slight altercation between young Samuel and Mr. Allen and wanted to make sure that everything is all right with Sam."

"Won't you please come in, Pastor," replied Mrs. Bodden.

As soon as he had greeted Samuel and his father and was seated down with a glass of lemonade in his hand, Pastor began by saying to Sam, "Samuel, I hope that you are not feeling badly about what Mr. Allen said to you at the church."

"No, sir," Samuel replied.

"Perhaps you could tell us what Mr. Allen said to Sam, Pastor?" Mr. Bodden added.

Pastor Gregg cleared his throat and then said, "It seems that Mr. Allen wasn't very open to the idea of the big bang theory and likened young Samuel's believing in it as essentially ignoring God's Truth in Scripture. Although I don't pretend to understand all the implications of this theory, I do not want to lay a stumbling block in front of Samuel as he grows up in the church."

"So how was it left then, Pastor?" asked his father.

"Well now, that is the most remarkable part of it, Arthur. It turns out that John Barzeb was most specifically upset by Mr. Allen's approach to 'corrective mentoring.'"

"Corrective mentoring? What is that?" continued his father.

"Essentially, John felt that Mr. Allen rebuked Samuel too harshly...actually needlessly, even rudely, asserting that he himself had good knowledge of Sam's love of the Lord God and His Ways," replied Pastor Gregg. "He also had some advice for me in terms of future practices with regard to 'corrective mentoring' condoned in the church, both our own here locally and with regard to the church worldwide."

"So what happened ultimately? I mean how was it left between the two of them? John and Mr. Allen, that is," Mr. Bodden continued the query.

"Well, that's the funny thing, Arthur. John has suggested a friendly-natured church-wide debate over the acceptability of the big bang theory where he will represent that it is acceptable, and I will represent the opposite view."

"You're kidding, Pastor Greg! Why initiate a church-wide fight?" replied Mrs. Bodden incredulously.

"That's initially what I thought too, Ruth. However, John seemed to be full of good advice this morning and told me that such a topic, if discussed in the right spirit, would actually foster the spiritual health of our congregation in doing a careful survey and exploration of the Scripture in order for them to understand the Truth. He maintains that it could potentially turn out to be as if they were... Bereans! To tell you the truth, I think he's absolutely right about that. It's also funny that he should suggest this since I was at a prophecy conference earlier this year where someone had mentioned the training they experienced with the online Berean Fellowship started by Chuck and Nancy Missler at Koinonia House. Apparently they were very committed to learning all about the Scriptures from a careful study of each book of the Bible and the fellowship continues that great mission of training servants of the Most High in that way. I wonder if John belongs to that or if he's heard about it."

"Wow," said Mrs. Bodden. "Something like that can be very useful and instructive for our church...really help us to go about learning and proving the Word."

"And the Good Lord knows we could do with a lot more of that at our church, even as far as its own pastor is concerned!" replied Pastor Gregg humbly.

Samuel smiled at this. "When will the debate take place, Pastor?" asked Samuel.

"We put it on the calendar for the first Sunday of August to give us enough time to prepare," said Pastor Gregg.

"I can't wait!" cried young Samuel.

"I'm glad you approve," replied Pastor Gregg.

"I do, Pastor...and you know what?" asked Samuel.

"What?" replied Pastor Gregg.

"I'll bet you'll still like John a lot, even after you lose, I mean!" stated Samuel quite frankly.

"You seem to have a lot of faith in your friend, Sam," replied Pastor Gregg good-naturedly, ignoring the innocent slight.

"That's easy, Pastor," said Sam. "John knows lots about the universe...about everything really." Then as if suddenly realizing he might have sounded rude or condescending, Samuel added, "Don't feel bad, Pastor, John is a lot older than you!"

Pastor smiled at this. He then added to the amazement of Sam's parents over a second glass of lemonade a few of the wonderful tidbits of knowledge he had gathered about their family friend that morning.

John was, after all, apparently in his mid-seventies and still feisty and sharp as a tack. Pastor thought to himself that he had better get used to the idea that it was not necessary for him to win the debate on details alone, but only necessary for him to earnestly endeavor to impart the more powerful lesson to his congregation of learning to bear each other in love, always comparing all things that are new and unfamiliar to what might be revealed about them in the Scriptures. He hoped he could set a good example at least.

CHAPTER 7

HOSPITALITY, A PECULIAR FISHING TECHNIQUE, AND THE ADOPTION OF A STUFFED BUNNY

The next day after school, Sam walked directly to John's fishing store. After Pastor Gregg left the previous day, Mom and Dad asked him to stay home with them, relax, and think about all that had happened before running over to John and allowing him to quietly relive the details about the initial conflict with Mr. Allen and any potential misgivings he might still have to sort through. Based upon his own experience with the whirlwind of thoughts that initially began to consume Sam shortly before the time spent under Pastor Gregg's windows, he completely understood. He also wanted some time to sort things out himself about the bigger issue prompted by Mr. Allen's prayer. That way he could focus on the questions that he wanted to ask John, based upon all that he had heard and experienced.

Samuel hoped that John was not angry with him. He also hoped that John would not have any misgivings about what he had begun within the church. Sam appreciated the fact that sometimes people were content to live quiet lives, not rocking the boat so to speak. In defending Sam, John had taken center stage at the church and even severely risked ending any kind of good feeling between him and Mr. Allen. Oh, how Sam hoped John would not be angry with him! In fact, this was so much on his mind, he didn't even focus on the other questions he had decided were the best to ask John as a follow-up to the incredible information he had revealed about himself in Pastor's office.

When Sam reached the long gravel road that turned into the woods from the highway, he noticed how wonderful it was that this special place of business was literally shielded from the world at large. A modest sign of black letters on a white board read "Barzeb's Fishing Supply" and was posted on two legs to the left of the driveway. Only those on a "fishing mission" might determine to continue down the long drive, nearly a quarter of a mile distant from the road to the actual shop. John's business was situated in a beautiful log cabin, painted dark brown and located at one end of the local lake. His full property actually encompassed a good portion of the shoreline, extending at least a quarter mile in either direction of the shop along the lake and then back up to the road from the shore.

John loved the view that this location afforded and welcomed anyone who wanted to come and enjoy it, even noncustomers. He always insisted that being a good neighbor meant proactively looking after the needs, both mental and physical of the people with whom you shared a community. "Mental" also meant "emotional" to John. And this is why he had some Adirondack chairs, wooden benches, and even a few barbecue grills set up along the shore for others to drop by and enjoy! Oftentimes he'd bring out some lemonade or coffee and cookies for his "guests" to make sure their short sojourns were special! In addition to this, he had expanded the remains of an existing dock to include not only a large enough slip for his own boat, a Boston whaler, but three additional slips as well. He figured that if a "crowd" of boating guests wanted to enjoy his small hospitality, they should have a place to park their boats! More often than not, however, people from the town loved to come in from the road and walk out the length of the dock and sit down to watch the view or even to fish from the plentiful supply that always seemed present in the lake.

The cabin that John built had stood for at least twenty years, built shortly after he had come to town and acquired the property. It actually was a rebuild of a former abandoned cabin that had probably served in times past as a pavilion of sorts for the local town. At that time it lacked nearly everything a modern domicile would need to have in order to be considered by most to be fully functional. John had seen its potential however, according to Sam's parents. He had worked diligently on the cabin's restoration, putting in plumbing, refurbishing the floor, supports, and a new roof. He even expanded one end of the cabin to house a stockroom as well as three additional rooms for his living quarters. One room was used as his bedroom, one was his kitchen, and a large room served as his living room, complete with a stone fireplace and an amazingly comfortable couch with complimentary armchairs. The unusually long kitchen area was actually divided into two spaces separated by a thin divider. Behind the divider was John's workroom, complete with workbench, tool racks, equipment stands, drawers, a small painting booth, and blueprint holders. The man sure liked to keep busy! The funny thing was, you would never know that so much of the cabin existed behind the front store showroom. He had also erected a large garage and work bay a good fifty feet away from the main cabin in the same materials used for the house construction. Although John normally put his car away in the early evening, Sam had never had an opportunity to explore inside this area.

John wanted his "fishing supply showroom" to also be a place of dreaming or imagination for those who had an interest in fishing. To him, fishing was more than a vocation, and even an art form besides. When one walked through the front door of the shop, they became immersed in a series of tasteful and neat displays depicting the joy of fishing. Instead of fluorescent lighting, John had opted for a series of natural lamp lights placed at strategic intervals throughout the store. Net rigging decorated the aisles and ceiling. Among the poles, tackle boxes, lures, hooks, nets, boating supplies, and the usual accessories of any fully-stocked fishing supply store, there were models of boats; birds; and, of course, fish; various paintings of fishing ventures; boats; serene settings on lakes, rivers, and seas. He had also laminated and framed local maps depicting ideal fishing and camping locations in the surrounding one hundred square miles, just to save people a lifetime of preliminaries.

As Samuel approached the cabin store, he noticed some activity on the lake out of the corner of his eye. He turned his head in time to see John casting a net into the lake from the dock. It was a fairly large net, probably at least seven or eight feet in diameter if fully extended. John held the net over his head and, with a broad spinning motion, threw it into the shallow water. Sam watched as the net hit the water and then sank down immediately into the lake. Intrigued as to why the net went immediately down into the water as opposed to not floating on the top of it first, at least for a while, Sam found himself walking toward John on the dock.

After he had taken five steps in that direction, he was greeted with a "Hi, Sam!" from a joyous little girl and her mother who were sitting on one of the lakeside benches enjoying the view. Surprised at first, Sam greeted back. "Hello, Melinda! Hello, Mrs. Ortega!"

Sam had met Mrs. Ortega about a year before when she had first come to town. She was a single mother whose husband had been killed during his military service in Iraq only eighteen months before. She had become nearly destitute, unfamiliar with the language, let alone how to claim the benefits due her as a young military widow. She decided that she wanted to raise her daughter in a quiet community and had moved from New York City with no more than a backpack and suitcase. Samuel had supposed that she insisted on keeping one hand free just to hold little Melinda's hand. Fortunately for her, she had met John immediately as she departed from the bus. According to Mrs. Ortega, John had found them lodging, bought them a meal, and introduced her to the owner of a local restaurant who was a good friend of his and whom he had known as a customer of his shop for more than five years. Before she went to bed that night, Mrs. Ortega had a job, a full belly, a safe place to sleep, and remarkably, a complete answer to her silent prayers!

Now, more than a year later, Mrs. Ortega actually worked part-time in the evenings at that same restaurant, saving carefully out of each paycheck toward her own dream of restaurant ownership. To add to the variety of the town's dining fare, hers would be the ultimate establishment for Mexican cuisine. During the day, she ran a wonderful little taco stand by the public waterfront, bringing a unique delight to the snacking itinerary of the locals. Sam's parents made a habit of treating their family to those delicious tacos whenever they visited the lakefront. In fact, it had become a family tradition for them as well as for many other families in the area.

Melinda was about four years old now and doing quite well in nursery school. She had long curly black hair and big brown eyes that seemed to always smile at you. She seemed to giggle with joy to accompany nearly half of everything she said, capturing every heart in her vicinity. Samuel thought she was the cutest little girl in the world and always loved the attention she lavished on him. He had even parted with his savings from his allowance one day to buy her a big stuffed rabbit that he saw her looking at in the toy store. Samuel had come in to the store to purchase a model airplane that he had been saving for over the past few months. Just before they left the store, he heard Mrs. Ortega encourage Melinda to remember to mention the stuffed rabbit when she asked Santa Claus for a Christmas gift in the coming week.

To Sam's horror, one of the other, older local children ran up to the same stuffed animal a few minutes later and commented to her brother who had just then joined her how they should buy the rabbit as a joke gift for their grandfather who was having trouble keeping his garden from being consumed by a local rabbit family. As soon as they ran off to ask their mother for money, Sam grabbed the rabbit, went to the cashier, and soon headed out of the store with the rabbit safely concealed in a bag to put it away for safekeeping. He absolutely had no idea how he would give Melinda her rabbit, let alone explain how he knew about her Christmas wish, but he was determined to do whatever he had to in order to make it hers.

On Christmas day, his parents let him bring the rabbit over to Melinda in a big decorated box just after breakfast. Feeling awkward, Samuel forced himself to get on with his task and rang the doorbell. When Mrs. Ortega opened the door and saw him standing there with the big box, she smiled and invited him in for a cup of cocoa. She was just beginning to tell him that Melinda was happy to hear that the rabbit she saw in the toy store was able to go to live with his family in the country… She was a little sad that she wasn't able to say good-bye to him and had wanted to give him a bag of carrots for his journey... As they walked into the living room, Sam saw little Melinda sitting on the floor in front of the coffee table carefully putting the finishing touches on a picture of a rabbit getting off a train in front of his family of rabbits outside of their bunny hole. He noticed that she had made sure to draw a bunch of bright orange carrots in a basket being held out to the rabbit coming home.

Samuel immediately became excited and said, "Hello, Melinda! Merry Christmas!" She returned his greeting with a, "Merry Christmas, Sam! Do you want to see my picture?" Before he could even answer, she said, "It's a picture of Peter Bunny going home to live with his family in the country!" She giggled. Sam bent over the picture and examined it for all its wonderful details. Suddenly, he said to Melinda, "You know, Melinda, I heard that Peter Bunny realized that he needed to stay out this way in order to work and send home extra carrots to his family... They love carrots, you know."

Melinda looked at him carefully, paying full attention to his words.

Continuing, Sam added, "In fact, I even met him this morning when he was getting on the train!"

Melinda smiled at this and asked incredulously, "You did?"

Samuel continued still. "Yes, and he said to give you this." At which point he held out the large box.

Little Melinda's eyes brightened hugely in wonderment, accompanied by a big smile!

Samuel gave her the package and said, "He said you should open this right away!"

Melinda took hold of the box and then looked at her mother to see if she was watching. As their eyes met, Mrs. Ortega encouraged her. "Go ahead, honey, open your gift!" Wrapping paper was carefully torn away to reveal a box that curiously had holes punched in it. Little Melinda looked up quizzically at Samuel, who smiled at her and said, "Hmmm, I wonder what that's all about!" As she opened up the cardboard flap, she discovered a furry brown dome with two projections on either side that seemed be folded downward, deeper into the box. She reached her little hand into the box and touched the soft fur of the rabbit's head and carefully pulled it upward.

"Peter Bunny!" she screamed in delight. "I'm so glad you came back here to live!" She pulled the stuffed bunny all the way out and hugged him tightly to her chest, kissing him repeatedly on his furry head. "This is the greatest Christmas ever!"

Sam didn't notice it, but Mrs. Ortega, with a tear running down her cheek, was silently thanking the Good Lord for yet another miracle in her life. Melinda amazed Sam even more as she threw one arm around his neck and gave him a big kiss on the cheek! "Thank you for bringing him over to me, Sam! I will take good care of him forever!"

Sam and Melinda were now friends for life. And this friendship would extend to Mrs. Ortega as well.

Now Samuel looked at both of them in the bright sunshine and said, "It sure is nice to see you both Mrs. Ortega!"

"We also love to see you, Sam," replied Mrs. Ortega. "Melinda always enjoys her times with her 'boyfriend'!" Samuel blushed at this. Seeing his light shade of red, Mrs. Ortega said, "Don't worry, Sam, she truly loves you and just wants to distinguish you from her other playmates in a special way!"

"You mean she really calls me her 'boyfriend'?" Samuel asked in earnest. Seeing the little girl examining him closely as he was speaking, he forced himself to smile and say, "I'm honored, Melinda!"

At this, Melinda's face lit up with another smile accompanied by a joyful giggle! She gave him a huge hug and a kiss on the cheek after this, and Sam returned the favor.

"I love you, Miss Melinda!" he said. He paused for a split second and then added, "And you too, Mr. Peter Bunny!"

"We love you too, Sammy," she replied.

"Melinda and I were doing our usual walk together and just visiting, telling John about our cousins who are planning to come and live with us in the United States early next year. It turns out that they're fishermen too, even once had a supply shop all their own before things became all unsettled in their country. We wanted to see what John thought about their prospects at resuming that kind of business up in this neck of the woods, maybe over by Shumway's Lake closer to Albany."

"Hello, Sam!" called John from the dock.

Samuel looked up in surprise, having momentarily lost himself in the greeting of Mrs. Ortega and Melinda. "Hi, John!" replied Samuel, feeling joy spread throughout his whole body at this friendly and even enthusiastic greeting. *He's not mad! Oh, how God is so good!* Sam thought. John wasn't mad at him, and it was just like than old times with the event that had only occurred twenty-four hours ago! "What are you doing, John?" asked Samuel.

"Oh, I am trying out an old technique that I once learned from my own father in the 'art of fishing.'"

"He reminds me of a bullfighter tossing his cape!" said Mrs. Ortega.

"The only thing is that the fish don't come running for me, Mrs. Ortega! They run in the opposite direction!" replied John good-naturedly.

"How do you get the net to sink down in the water so fast, John?" asked Sam.

"Why don't you come over and have a look after I bring up the catch," replied John. As he said this, John pulled a line attached at a vortex of lines connected at the center of the net's outline under the water and which Samuel had not noticed before. As he pulled on this line, the net enclosed around the fish that had been swimming within its zone since it was plunged into the water. This caused the net to be drawn closed like a sack, which John then pulled out of the water. It must have caught about one hundred fish, which Sam could see! Samuel had seen nets used to capture fish that had been brought up individually on line but had never noticed a net this big serving to bring up such a multitude of fish!

"Wow, John," said Samuel. "I can't believe you caught so many!"

"Well, in days gone by, Sam," John said, "we had to catch enough fish to feed both our family as well as to sell in the market. Nets are a good way of amplifying your efforts to extend to the whole community who needs to eat."

Samuel then noticed the answer to his own question. The net appeared to be ringed with little weights that acted to "pull" the net down with them as they settled through the water to the shallow bottom. "How smart," stated Sam in matter-of-fact tone.

John looked at him and smiled, noticing that he had answered his own question. He then added, "This is an old technique that my brother and I learned from our father growing up on Lake Genesareth. It is very effective when a school of fish comes your way!"

Samuel made a mental note that Lake Genesareth should now serve as another clue to learn more about his friend John. He then remarked, "It looks like a great technique to get supper for many days!"

John smiled again at this and said, "And in order for this to make it onto the supper plates of a lot of folks in this town, I had better get these guys into some ice and into the truck for a ride! If I make it to the market in the next twenty minutes or so, these guys might actually be the supper of some of our townsfolk tonight!"

"On that note then, John," said Mrs. Ortega, who had walked over by now for a better view, "we had better leave you to your work... Come, Melinda!"

Melinda smiled and picked up her bunny, saying, "Come, Peter, it's time to go!"

"We hope to see you both again soon," Mrs. Ortega said as they began to leave.

Both John and Sam said their good-byes to the mother and child and waved. To Melinda's delight, John tossed a "Good-bye, Mr. Bunny" after them as they walked, for which he was rewarded with a big smile from Melinda! Samuel then saw John begin to load fish into buckets sitting on the dock. He followed suit and began loading the fish into more of the empty buckets. He soon discovered how heavy a bucket could be under the weight of several fish! When they had finished transporting each of the buckets out by John's pickup truck, they emptied them into the ice coolers he had waiting there already half-filled with crushed ice.

Once loaded up, John climbed into the driver's side and said, "Thanks for the help, Sam!"

"No problem, John," replied Sam. "I was hoping I could visit with you for a while before supper."

"Perhaps tomorrow would be better Sam since I have no idea how quick this will be once I take the catch over to the fish market," said John with sincere apology written all over his face.

"That's okay, John. I mainly just wanted to come by and thank you for defending me yesterday," said Samuel.

"That was my privilege to do that, Sam. I think you will be quite surprised when you learn what dear God has opened up for us as a result of the little conflict with Mr. Allen!" John added. "Why don't we meet back here tomorrow and we'll strategize how to best handle the wonderful opportunity that has now come up!"

"Wonderful opportunity?" asked Sam.

"Yes, Samuel, whenever we have the occasion to minister to the body of Christ and encourage our brethren toward healthy growth, it is a most definite and wonderful opportunity! And as a result of our differences with Mr. Allen, the whole church can participate in a spiritually healthy debate, which may very well end up in new appreciation for the authority of Scripture and the proper reliance upon it and even more wonderful evangelistic opportunities throughout the community and beyond! Don't you agree?"

"I guess so, John. But truthfully, I was aware of the debate but wasn't sure you really wanted to go through with this just because of an argument between me and Mr. Allen," said Sam a bit sheepishly.

"Samuel, open your eyes and look. Mr. Allen's own preclusion of members of this community is now exposed before it could do any real damage to anyone. Your interest in astronomy brought this to light. Now the church can examine the issues at hand and compare each participant's testimonies and compare them to what the Scripture actually says… This will be very much like the Berean community, which was described in the book of the Acts of the Apostles in the Bible. It is the best way for all of the brethren to learn about and test new ideas and teachings."

"You think this will turn out to be a blessing then, John?" asked Samuel.

"It already has, Sam. We have stopped a clear oversight already on the part of Mr. Allen, and as the entire church will soon learn, we have pointed up a very unfortunate tendency by many in the church today to separate those living by the truth into only two distinct camps by a wall that is becoming increasingly impenetrable by either side. And, Samuel, please see that it wouldn't have happened without your righteous enthusiasm for dear God's creation."

"Really, John?" replied Sam, this time with much more enthusiasm behind his question.

"Really and truly, Sam," answered his friend. "Come back tomorrow so that we can review our strategy of debate. And you know what, Sam? Why don't you bring along your friend Chris? He just might want to serve as your wingman!"

"Oh boy!" replied Sam as he turned around and ran home, again excited that he was a part of the future and potential wonderment that he sensed was about to unfold in his community—and not just him, his best friend from school also was to be included!

John sat in his truck and watched him leave, a broad smile on his face. Samuel didn't hear him say, "Lord Jesus, I thank you, my Master and friend!" He paused then and added, "Lord Jesus, thank you also for letting me show him about fishing! It seems a perfect place to get serious once again about ministering to the Body. In your Holy Name, Amen," and he started his truck.

CHAPTER 8

SOME SWEET LEMONADE, ANCIENT HEBREW, AND A JEWISH WITNESS

The next day came, and Sam was very excited to be able to walk to John's house this time with an invitation! Word had begun to spread at school about the upcoming debate, and his friends were all beginning to ask him questions. His friend Chris would be dropped off momentarily at John's store if all went well at his dentist appointment. As soon as school was over, Samuel started out immediately, almost neurotically afraid that if he delayed, something could get lost or change his plans! When he hit the long driveway to the fishing shop, he started to run, hardly able to wait for things to begin.

When Samuel, the "human locomotive," arrived in front of the cabin, there were Mrs. Ortega and Miss Melinda sitting with John enjoying some fresh lemonade that John had no doubt brought out for them. Before Samuel could even greet them, John called out to him and said, "Hello, Samuel! Come on over and have some lemonade!" Little Melinda bounded over to him and gave him a big hug. Sam smiled, seeing there was a glass full of ice all ready for him to join them. Any doubt that he was intruding now evaporated. John poured him a tall glass and gave it to a grateful Samuel still breathing a bit heavy from his run. Samuel said thank you, paused a moment to thank the Lord, and then took a deep draught of the cool, sweet drink.

"Mmm," he said. "This is so good!"

"Well, from the way you came down the driveway, I thought we better be ready to cool that engine down in a hurry!" said John.

Sam giggled at that, still holding the glass and drinking as John made his comment. He finished the entire glass and put it down on the picnic table. Immediately, John picked it up and refilled it.

"Now maybe you can enjoy this next one more deliberately," said John.

"Thanks, John," said Samuel.

"I was just telling Mrs. Ortega and Miss Melinda about our colorful Sunday experience."

"Oh, Samuel, I'm so happy John was there to defend you...," said Mrs. Ortega. "Had he not been there, who knows what kinds of bad things would sort of naturally followed... For once, the idea of young people disrespecting elders doesn't even enter into it!"

"Precisely, Mrs. Ortega," added John.

"John and I are going to plan the strategy for the debate, Mrs. Ortega. I really want to make it strong and helpful to everyone. I already told Pastor that I'd bet he would still like John even if he lost the debate to him," said Samuel.

At this both John and Mrs. Ortega smiled and laughed.

"Samuel, you really said that?" John laughed! "I'll bet that really brightened up an already stressful day for our pastor!"

Mrs. Ortega, still smiling, added, "Well, at least it showed the pastor early on what the honest view was by one of his church members!"

"I trust he took it well, Sam?" asked John.

Samuel started to redden, slightly realizing that he might have hurt pastor's feelings, then remembered his good-natured answer and smile. Fortunately!

"Yes," said Sam, "I think so. I told him not to feel bad since you were a lot older than him."

At this, Mrs. Ortega wrinkled up her eyebrows and looked at John questioningly.

"Well, at least in the sense of having pondered certain issues maybe," added John quickly. Then changing the subject, John said to his first two guests, "Well, Sam and I are going to have to get busy now, but would you like me to refill the pitcher before we go?"

"No, thank you, John," replied Mrs. Ortega. "Melinda and I are truly satisfied. We're just going to stay a few more minutes and then get on with a little shopping at the market."

"Well then, my dear friends, *Shalom!*" said John earnestly.

"*Shalom,* John," they both said back.

Just then young Christopher arrived with his mother. As Chris departed the minivan, his mother rolled down the window and asked, "What time will you boys be done here?"

Both boys looked at John inquiringly with open enthusiasm. John smiled back at them both and called back to her, "We'll probably be good if we can have two hours today if that's all right with you?"

She smiled, waved, and then backed the car up the driveway and out.

"Come, Samuel and Chris, let's go to the living room," said John.

At this, both Samuel and Chris followed John in earnest toward the side door of John's cabin.

"*Shalom,* John?" said Samuel as they walked toward the door. "What does that mean?"

"It is a greeting of peace spoken in Hebrew, Sam. It is actually used as a welcome and a good-bye."

"Hebrew?" asked Samuel.

"Yes, Samuel. Hebrew is the language of the Tenakh, the Hebrew Bible. I think it's nice if people infuse it in some of their everyday speech with a positive reminder of how much we have gotten as a society from the Jews."

"Gotten from the Jews?" asked Samuel.

"Yes, Samuel. Do you remember what our Lord said about the Jews to the Samaritan woman at the well?" John stopped outside the screen door and waited for Samuel to answer.

Samuel paused for a moment and then thought. He responded shortly with a, "Yes, I remember, John! Jesus said that 'salvation is from the Jews' from John 4:22."

John smiled. "That's right, Samuel!" He then continued, "When people talk about Jesus as their personal Lord and Savior, they are speaking of their relationship to the Hebrew Messiah, who was predicted in the ancient Scriptures. It is important to remember that dear Jesus is very Jewish indeed!"

"That's interesting, John," replied Samuel, "because I don't really know anyone who is Jewish. Well, except for Phillip Cohen in our class. He is a very nice guy, but I don't really know him that well. He's usually very quiet in school."

"Well, not exactly, Sam," said John.

"But he is quiet, John," protested Christopher.

"Not about Phillip, Chris. I'm saying that you and Sam both have an active friendship with someone who is Jewish," continued John.

"Do you mean the Lord?" asked Samuel.

"No, Samuel, I was actually referring to myself."

"Really?" asked Samuel. "I thought you were a Christian, John."

"I am a Christian, but I am also born of full Jewish blood," replied John.

"Wow, John! I didn't know that. Were you always a Christian, John?" asked Samuel.

"No, not always, Samuel. I was blessed to begin my walk with the Lord at about the age of nineteen years," said John. "I was very dedicated to the nation of Israel and its independence prior to this. After the Lord Jesus bid me to follow him, I gladly gave up all things to work for him."

"John, I love the way you talk about your relationship with the Lord Jesus," said Samuel. "It helps me to realize how the Lord is someone who is always with me and leading us in our lives. It makes it sound like he really is there right along beside us."

"And He really is, Samuel. If you want to add to your own faith, think of how our Blessed Lord maintained a close relationship with His Father in heaven, who was invisible, constantly walking in faith and believing in His Divine Will. I can tell you for certain that the Lord did not waiver once from His walk with His Father. Not once. His life on Earth consisted of doing His Father's will and always seeking to please Him," said John.

"But, John, you sound like you actually—" Chris started to say just as the phone inside rang.

"I better get that," said John. "Come, Samuel and Christopher."

John led the boys through the back portion of the fishing shop past the main counter with the cash register and through the curtained archway separating his living quarters from the shop. Once inside, John picked up the ringing phone just before the third ring as Samuel sauntered over toward the dining table to the right of the living room, just before the entrance to the kitchen.

"Hello," said John, more of a statement than a question. "Yes, Mr. Newkirk, I'm sure I can help you with that list you faxed over earlier... Yes, of course, before Saturday. I should be able to have everything ready for you by late afternoon Thursday... Yes, that includes the special-order lures as well. I'm expecting those Wednesday... Friday? Well, that might be a bit of a problem unless you can get here before 4:30 p.m. sharp. I have to be somewhere before 5:00 p.m., so I hate to put you at risk of not receiving your equipment in time. Yes, Thursday is better. See you then." John hung up the phone and walked over to the table.

He saw young Samuel and Chris beginning to look through some of the material that John had begun to compile. John smiled at the young Samuel's fascination with a star chart and accompanying note section.

Cheerily, he began, "Well, my friends, I think the best way for us to begin is to start by clarifying our purpose for doing this debate. We then can begin to compile for ourselves a complete set of notes on the history of the church's view of the first six days of creation beginning, of course, with the Holy Bible, Genesis chapter 1." Samuel and Chris both listened intently to John as he continued, hearing him say, "I think a good overview of what Christians have basically believed about the creation story and about science in general is just what the doctor is calling for, but let's set up our main goals first.

"Samuel, since Chris was not in the sanctuary that Sunday when Mr. Allen began to pray at the end of the service, what did he say that so upset you?"

"He prayed saying that we knew that dear God did not create the universe with a big bang."

Immediately, Chris interrupted, "Get out of here! I know for a fact that John Matther, the scientist who came up with the theory, believes that God created it! Samuel and I talked about this before!"

"Yes," said John, "but Mr. Allen doesn't know anything about John Matther, or NASA, or current thoughts in astrophysics. Now, Samuel, after he joined us in our classroom, what did I say about the likely reason why Mr. Allen probably said what he said?"

"You said that Mr. Allen was trying to be faithful to his principles and that he prays with a complete heart in spirit and in truth."

"That's very good, Samuel! Do you also remember me saying that he wanted to make a stand for God and to him that meant that believing in something that goes against God is not acceptable in any form...and that to him, modern-day science has come up with a picture of the creation of the universe that doesn't require God to be present at all. That is what the big bang theory is to him, an explanation of the universe that doesn't require God to be present!"

"Yes, I remember, John," replied Samuel. "But is he right?"

"Well, boys, we want to make sure that we do no less than Mr. Allen in being faithful to dear God," stated John.

"What?" both boys seemed to say at the same time.

"We want to be able to make a case in a way that honors God and does not go against Him...that whatever it is that we are asking our brethren to consider is not against the Lord, the Bible, or the church. How important is it for us to make sure that everything we believe and tell others about is truthful or just the truth?"

Chris spoke up first. "It is very important!"

Samuel added, "You may as well not even speak if you can't be truthful. If any part of the big bang theory is not the truth, I don't want any part of it!"

John smiled and continued, "Boys, that is good to hear from you both. Did you ever read in the Bible what the Lord said in response to the Pharisee's question about what was the greatest commandment in the Law?"

Chris raised his hand as if he were in the classroom. "I know!" he blurted out.

John looked at him seriously and said simply, "Tell me, Chris."

"The Lord said to 'Love the Lord your God with all your heart and with all your soul and with all your mind.'"

"That is correct!" replied John. That response is recorded in Matthew chapter 22 verse 37. This is originally from the Old Testament in Deuteronomy chapter 6, verse 5. The account in Mark chapter 12 verse 30 gives a little more to what the listeners heard by adding, 'and with all your strength.' So what do you think 'with all your mind' means?"

"It means being sure of what we know about dear God! That we honor him correctly in the ways that he wants us to honor him!" replied Samuel.

"So we are to do it truthfully, that is in ways that honor him in accordance with the truth! There is no way to honor him with dishonesty, lies, distortions, or any kind of falsehood."

"But, John, scientific theories may not be the truth! So maybe it's not all right for me to believe in them. Is that right?" said Samuel with a worried look on his face.

John smiled again. "Wait a minute, Sam, remember also that much scientific understanding is based upon the best available theories which we find 'testable' in our world and which have not yet been proved false. That is basic to the scientific method. Only if we advance a theory which we know as false or which has been disproved would I say we are working against the truth!"

Samuel relaxed and said, "I see."

Chris then perked up and said, "I like testable theories. To me it's what my dad always says—the proof is in the pudding!"

"Well, I'm glad we are all committed to the truth and determined to not promote anything else," said John. "And one way of doing that, boys, is to open up our minds to what the Bible is trying to tell us! We also want to remember the second greatest commandment that was given to us and which dear Jesus spoke about in response to the question he was given, that we are to 'love our neighbors as ourselves.' We must be tolerant that not everyone is a Bible scholar but that they are no less valuable to dear God. If we believe in something that has come about as a means of careful Bible study and thoughtful consideration in view of scientific evidence, we may need to remind ourselves to be tolerant of those who have not yet made a particular connection. We still love them because dear God loves them and they are our brother or sister in Christ Jesus, but we do not attack them or demean them or insult them just because they reject our presentation of what we believe is the truth—even if they react the way Mr. Allen did toward you."

"But how do we do this, John?" asked Christopher.

"We present things carefully, in light of the Scriptures, and with a commitment to try to answer honestly any questions which our listeners ask… Remember, being a good listener is vitally important in bringing another person to accept the Gospel since there can be any number of questions they might ask based upon their own life experience! If they see us as sincere, they just might be inclined to consider that which we have to say."

John gestured toward a book on the table *Christianity and the Age of the Earth* by Davis A. Young.

"I want to explore these ideas in these books in a prayerful comparison to the Holy Scriptures and compare our thoughts to what has been said about the creation since the earliest times of the church continuing through to today. I have just begun to gather a few of my books together and think we should start with these." John pointed to two other books by themselves. "*Peril in Paradise* by Mark S. Whorton and *The Genesis Debate*, edited by David G. Hagopian. These books also outline the debate between the people who hold to a young Earth versus those who hold to an old Earth. I would like both of you to go through this one," John said as he held up another book with the title *God and the Astronomers* by Robert Jastrow. "This book was written by an astrophysicist who worked with Dr. John Mather, the Nobel Prize laureate, for his work on the big bang theory."

Samuel's eyes lit up upon hearing this; and he eagerly, but politely, took the book from John's hand.

John continued, "There is quite a bit here for us to explore in order to get a sense of what is being said or claimed and the Truth of what is recorded in Scripture. Our main purpose is not necessarily to prove one side over the other, but to show from example that neither side is necessarily mandated to be upheld for Salvation, that in fact both views have been held by Christians throughout the time of the church. We want to show that there is no perceived conflict between the inspired Word of God and what we have learned in observing nature."

"But, John," Chris interjected, 'if we are certain of what we are saying after studying the Bible and comparing it to science, why can't we just announce our beliefs?"

"Because, Chris," John answered, "even if you are 100 percent sure of what you are believing, if you present anything in a way that is disrespectful or which can be perceived as intolerant to our brethren, how successful do you really think you will be? Do you think that you will you bring anyone closer to considering what you have been blessed with in understanding?"

"I guess not, John," replied Christopher thoughtfully. "It's just that from what Samuel told me, Mr. Allen seems like he doesn't want anyone to think differently than he does even if he has no real idea about what scientists are saying!"

"Well, Christopher, I believe as Christians we must make every effort to live by the truth. In the account of dear Jesus with the Samaritan woman at the well in the fourth chapter of John verses 23 through 24, our Lord told us that dear God seeks worshipers who worship Him in spirit and in truth. In fact, in John 3:21, He tells us something remarkable about living by the truth: "But whoever lives by the truth comes into the light, so that it may be seen plainly that what he has done has been done through God.'"

Samuel then said, "That is so cool, John! If we continue seeking truth, we come into the light?"

"You're on the right track there, Samuel," John answered. "You must also remember to 'live by the truth' too! That means what dear God brings into your life clearly as truth should become a part of your worldview and affect any future actions on your part."

"Wow! So does that mean that if you are born in a different religion, you can still come into the light, John?" replied Samuel.

John thought for a minute before answering. He then said, "I don't see any qualifiers around that sentence, Sam. You may be surprised to hear what happened to some of our brothers and sisters who did this after they had been born into a different culture and practiced a different religion. The Lord's Word is trustworthy. I have observed in my life, however, that not everyone enjoys exploring new ideas, especially those which might potentially shake up their world-view! If this happens only to some within a church, it could lead, and often does, to a crisis in the congregation."

Samuel continued, "I guess, John, that you were trying to teach Mr. Allen about having the same consideration for me in exploring a new idea, right?"

"Exactly right, Sam! We must not be about extinguishing love within our fellowship! We must strictly be about enlightenment and edification of the entire Body of Christ, which means being patient with each other when we are pondering subjects which are complicated."

"I think I can do that, John," Samuel replied.

"I think you have always been considerate of other people, Samuel. My great concern for our church is that some people are so set in their ways that they are subtly driving others out the doors. Today's churches often see their youth go off to college and not return to the church until they get married, leading me to really question whether or not the elders truly want to do anything toward the health of the body of Christ."

"Really, John?" asked Chris.

"Well, let me put it this way. If you were comfortably exploring a topic of interest which seemed to have real biblical connections in a way that no one had ever made before and suddenly someone started screaming, 'Heretic!' at you before you could say a word to them, how likely is it that you would continue to attend that church?"

"I see your point, but still, if they would just give me a chance to explain…"

"Well, now you see why I 'ordered' Mr. Allen to the pastor's office. We must not ever let our love grow cold—even if one is self-righteously indignant, right or wrong!"

At this both boys giggled!

Picking up his Bible first, then picking up one of the books on the table, John then said, "We want to be able to show that believing in an older Earth does not necessarily compromise the biblical account and that people who believe in the likelihood of an older Earth based upon scientific observation can also believe the Bible to be the written Word of God and can also accept and believe in the Gospel as revealed to us in the Holy Scriptures. Those who believe in a young Earth can also continue believing this if their consciences lead that way, because they still believe in the Gospel of Jesus Christ. Since we have a month, we should try to get some detail assembled for our presentation and debate, going a bit deeper than usual for the benefit of everyone there, including ourselves. I will begin with these first books, and you two look through that one by Jastrow to see what you can find."

Immediately Chris picked up the book and started looking through the pictures and captions.

John's eyes looked straight at Samuel as he went over his plan with him. Samuel looked at him seriously and nodded his assent at each pause. Then John said something deeply significant before they even read a single line from any of the books.

"Now Samuel and Chris, let us pray to the Wonderful Lord for His Guidance and His Wisdom in our undertaking of this great enterprise. Let us pray to Him and ask for His Blessing upon our work, our interpretations, and, of course, upon our presentation and ministrations."

Samuel's and Christopher's eyes never left John's as they nodded their assent. John smiled again and then, taking the hands of both boys, closed his eyes and began to pray.

QUESTIONS, A CONFESSION, AND AN AFFIRMATION

They worked straight until 6:00 p.m. that first day. Samuel looked at his watch and was surprised by the time he saw. He asked if he could call his mother and, with John's urging, told his mother he would be home for dinner on time since John would drop him off. Chris had already left with his mother about twenty minutes before, leaving Samuel alone with John. Since they had at least another thirty minutes before they had to leave, Samuel decided it might be a good time to ask John about some of the things he had recently learned about his past.

"John?" asked Samuel.

"Yes, Sam?" replied John.

"Are you really older than Mr. Allen?" asked Samuel.

"Well, Samuel," John began, "I brought up that fact in Pastor's office because I did not want Mr. Allen to take refuge in seeming improprieties."

"Seeming what?" asked Samuel honestly.

"I didn't want him to hide behind some perceived violation on my part of not treating him with proper respect," said John carefully.

"Then are you really older than he is?" inquired the young boy.

"Yes, Samuel, truthfully I am quite a bit older. And even though I enjoy all of our conversations together very much, my friend, that subject is never one with which I am comfortable," replied Samuel's friend.

"Oh, sorry, John," continued Samuel, "I didn't want to offend you in any way."

"And you haven't," John soothed. "It's just that I don't want the age aspect to come in the way of the bigger things at hand here. If Mr. Allen is younger than I am, it doesn't mean that any viewpoints he has should be automatically dropped. It also doesn't mean that in living by the truth, anyone should need to yield to someone solely for the purpose of getting along by virtue of their age differences. We are after the truth ultimately, and in this case the truth will affect how we ought to live and function as Christians within a healthy Christian community when any subjects come up which can be potentially divisive. In other words, Samuel, that I am older or younger should have no bearing upon what was being discussed."

"Is it then all right to ask you how old you are, John?" inquired young Samuel honestly.

"Of course, it is," replied his mentor. "I am as old as my tongue and a little bit older than my teeth!"

Samuel giggled at the line he recognized from *Miracle on 34th Street* given by the Santa Claus, who was accused of being mentally incompetent.

"By the way, Sam, how did you know that I had said that I was older?" asked John now.

"Well, Pastor Gregg came by and brought it up after I came home Sunday," began Samuel. "That's how my family learned that you scheduled a debate. But..." Samuel broke off.

"But what, Samuel?" asked John.

Samuel stopped, not exactly sure on how to proceed.

"Samuel, please tell me what you wanted to say," said John encouragingly.

"I actually heard it before Pastor Gregg came to our house," said Samuel deliberately.

"Oh?" said John.

"Yes, John. I heard it as you said it from outside of Pastor Gregg's office window."

"I see, Samuel," said John seriously.

"It's just that I had stopped without realizing it when I was thinking about everything that had happened so fast! I was just about to leave when I heard Mr. Allen start yelling at you... I just couldn't leave then..." Samuel had been speaking while staring solely at the pile of books on the dining table. After he said this last sentence, he looked up, ready to endure John's disappointment with him, whatever form that might take. But instead of this, the face he saw was that of a smiling John, with a pleased look on his face!

Sam soldiered on. "I am truly sorry, John, for being so rude by eavesdropping—"

John cut him off with a loud but happy, "Nonsense, Samuel! From my view, you were being a good friend by sticking around to see what befell me! To tell you the truth, I wouldn't have blamed you if you had run all the way home and hid under the bed. I truly appreciate your concern for me, Samuel. But please know that I think that what needed to be said to both Mr. Allen and Pastor Gregg was said in that office. And please remember, Mr. Allen did something that I remain very much at odds with. There wasn't any way that I was going to let that remain hidden in the shadows of interpersonal relationships, never being resolved and continuing to do a full course of damage everywhere. It needed to be brought to light so that it could be corrected. Such acts as that which was done by Mr. Allen, when left smoldering and unseen and uncorrected, can do much harm to the love in the Body of Christ."

"You're not mad then, John," asked Samuel.

"Not in the least, Sam!" said John. "As I told you before, a great opportunity is now before us and we have to prayerfully and obediently do all that we can to help the Body of Christ learn and benefit from this debate."

"John?" began Samuel.

"Yes?"

"You talked about the benefit to the 'Catholic Church' during your meeting with Pastor Gregg and Mr. Allen," Samuel broke off.

"Yes, Samuel?" asked John.

"Well, I didn't quite understand Pastor Gregg's explanation. I thought we were a Baptist church?" replied Samuel.

"When I used the term 'Catholic,' Samuel, I was referring to the universal church in Christ Jesus. I didn't necessarily mean 'Roman Catholic,' although there are brothers and sisters throughout many churches in the world today," said John.

"Roman Catholics are also Christians, John?" asked Samuel.

John looked at him again seriously to make his next statement. "Samuel, if someone believes that Jesus Christ is the Son of the Living God and that He was sent to Earth in the flesh to die for their sins, that He was crucified, buried, and on the third day rose from the dead in the flesh for their justification, then they are saved and will inherit eternal life. They are part of the Body of Christ, indeed the Holy Catholic Church. They may also happen to be Baptist, Methodist, Presbyterian, Lutheran, Episcopal, Roman Catholic, Ethiopian Christian, Russian Orthodox, Greek Orthodox, and so on and so on," replied John.

"But doesn't some of what each of those groups believe differ from what we believe here?" asked Samuel honestly.

"That may be, Samuel. However, all who profess their personal faith in Christ as I just said are justified and saved. There are some groups to be sure who omit part or even all of what I just said and are therefore not Christians. These people are not yet saved. But those who are justified and saved will also undergo sanctification as part of living until the Lord takes them to be with Him. We may still make mistakes and sin; however, our orientation is completely different in Christ Jesus. Now we live unto Christ and He is our mediator before dear God. I don't expect we will be made perfect in this lifetime. Even our brother Paul did not claim to have been made perfect while he still was living on the Earth. Therefore, if someone gets the core of our faith right in his or her own life, then I claim them as a brother or sister in the Lord," said John. "The problem usually is that churches get contentious about a great many things, some of which are not that significant." John added finally, "I hesitate at saying 'not that significant' because I believe in the Word of God and am determined not to neglect any part of it, or even allow what I consider a direct misinterpretation of the Scripture."

"What happens to those who don't get the 'core' of faith right, John, or who get most of it right but make a mistake somewhere," asked Samuel.

"Well, the good news for them is what we already reviewed earlier. Our Blessed Lord said in the Gospel according to John in the twenty-first verse of the third chapter, 'But whoever lives by the truth comes into the light, so that it may be seen plainly that what he has done has been done through God.'"

"How does that relate to the core of the faith, John?" asked Samuel.

"It means, my friend, that if a human being continues to seek out God and learn His Truth without omitting any of it along the path, then he will end up before the Throne of our Lord and Savior, Jesus Christ," replied John.

"But they are not saved until they believe what you said?" questioned Samuel.

"Yes, Samuel, the essence of salvation is through faith, which is a gift of God. They need to believe on the Name of Jesus Christ and in his sacrifice and bodily resurrection from the dead by the power of God. It is not enough to believe in the 'essence' of his message or in some kind of distortion of the Gospel perceived by many as 'largely similar' to the original message. Our God is a God of Justice and a God of Mercy. He is a God of Love, and He offers salvation. Salvation is on His terms only, despite human teaching, which is inherently flawed," John replied. "If a person does not understand that dear Jesus is the Incarnation of God in human flesh, then how can he claim that his sins were paid for by someone who is not sinless? Only dear God is without sin. If our Lord was carrying any personal sin, which is not possible since it is outside His Nature, He would not have been able to take our punishment for us. We are saved through Him."

"Wow, John!" said Samuel. "I haven't ever thought of this all together. So people who are not in the Lord now but somewhere short of true faith need to keep searching for the truth?"

"Yes, Samuel," replied John. "But not just searching only, by also applying it to themselves and living by it. They cannot selectively omit anything that they are shown if they want to 'live by the truth.'

"Many people unfortunately don't even realize a small part of this," John continued. "The interesting thing about this is that it was written about by the Prophet Isaiah at least seven hundred years before our Lord was born in Bethlehem. It says plainly in the fifty-third chapter of Isaiah, verses 4 through 6 (NIV),

> Surely he took up our infirmities
> and carried our sorrows,
> yet we considered him stricken by God,
> smitten by him, and afflicted.
> But he was pierced for our transgressions,
> he was crushed for our iniquities;
> the punishment that brought us peace was
> upon him,
> and by his wounds we are healed.
> We all, like sheep, have gone astray,
> each of us has turned to his own way;
> and the LORD has laid on him
> the iniquity of us all.

"Literally, Samuel, we need to give up each of our 'own ways' and accept the Lord's Way. Remember what the Lord said to us. 'I am the way and the truth and the life. No one comes to the Father except through me' (John 14: 6, NIV)."

Samuel nodded in full acceptance of what his teacher had just said, appreciating it anew and at a deeper level than ever before. He found himself saying "Amen." At this, again John smiled at him.

Samuel thought back to the questions he had compiled from his time of "listening" under the window. He didn't know if he should bring this next part up or not.

"John?" he began.

"Yes, Samuel?"

"What happened to your brother?" asked Samuel.

John paused and then exhaled, forming a soulful smile with his mouth. He began, "My dear brother James was killed by people who were convinced he was being sinful in his convictions."

"Was he being sinful, John?" asked Samuel.

"No, he wasn't, Sam. In fact, he was my brother in the Lord just as you are my brother in the Lord," said John.

"Then why did they kill him?" asked Samuel again.

"Although I will not venture to judge those that committed this crime, I can tell you that it may have been over a matter that was a combination of religious contention, vanity, jealousy, and fear," said John.

"Which church were they from, John?" asked Sam.

"They were actually from outside the church, my friend," said John.

"That must have really hurt you?" said Sam.

"Oh yes, it was painful," said John, "for me and for our family, but the grace that the Lord gives is sufficient to get us through such difficult events."

"Your family, John?" asked Samuel once again.

"Yes, for me, my stepmother, and my father and mother among others in my extended family," replied John.

"You had a stepmother and a mother, John?" asked Samuel.

"Yes, in fact she was a very special woman, the mother of my dearest friend who asked me to watch after her as my own mother when he no longer could," said John, this time with a wistful smile.

"Then your father wasn't married to her?" asked Sam.

"Oh no, Sam," said John. "She lived with me in my home, and my father and mother lived in another place."

"You really are a good friend to many people, John!" said Sam encouragingly.

"And so are you, my young friend!" John smiled. "Anything else you want clarified?"

"Oh no...well...?"

"What?" again inquired John.

"You said to Pastor that you read, speak, and write ancient Hebrew," said Sam.

"That's right Sam, I most definitely do," said John.

"Where did you learn how to do that?" asked Sam in amazement.

"Well, Sam, that's almost the same as asking you where you learned to read, write, and speak English," replied John.

"You mean you went to school for that, John?"

"Remember I told you that I was Jewish. In the place where I grew up, at the age of thirteen, I was welcomed into adulthood and was trained specially for that day. It was in the school that I attended where I learned the ancient language. It took some years of study, but I learned it to the best of my ability, since I thought it was of great importance to the Jews everywhere. Don't forget that the original language of the Bible was Hebrew," said John. "In fact it was basically Hebrew for the Tanakh, also called the Old Testament, and Greek for the books included in the New Testament."

"Oh yeah, John, that makes sense," said Sam.

"Anything else on your mind, Sam?" asked John.

"No, I think that covers everything for now!" Samuel smiled.

"Well then, I think we've done a good day's work, young Samuel. What do you say we take you home for supper?" asked John.

"That sounds good, John! I am starting to get a little hungry."

"That's usually what happens when you start exploring the Lord's Truth in earnest! We get hungry for more!"

John then picked up his truck keys and walked over to the door and held it open for Sam. The screen door banged shut behind them as they walked over to the truck.

CHAPTER 10

NEGATIVE NEWS AND A SCIENCE TEACHER

By early the next week the local paper had run a short article covering the upcoming debate at the church, unfortunately headlining it as "A Scopes Trial to Begin Anew, This Time in the Church!" This caught the attention of many in the local community, particularly at young Samuel's school. On the last day before summer vacation, one of the science teachers at the school, Mr. Edmund, was quick to address Samuel with his thoughts on the matter.

"Young Samuel, why must you thrust science into the church in the first place?"

"Mr. Edmund, don't you think science and faith are both about truth?" offered Samuel in response.

"I believe that they both have their place, Samuel, but need not mix with each other. Throughout history much evil has been done in the name of religion whenever the religion was threatened by scientific enlightenment!"

Samuel looked at him in disbelief. He himself knew that to be an over-simplification. And it certainly wasn't going to solve the problems in the church either.

"But some of the greatest discoveries in science were made by Christians! Even by priests! Think what would have happened if those discoveries had never been made!"

Mr. Edmund didn't miss a beat and replied, "I'm sure they would have been made even faster by people with more clear minds had the church not positioned itself as a giant filter of sorts."

"You don't believe in dear God, Mr. Edmund?" asked Samuel.

"I believe in nature and reject the supernatural, Samuel," replied the science teacher. "Rational explanations are what interest me, young Samuel, not fairy tales."

Unshaken, Samuel looked back at him quite innocently and said, "But what will you do when you die?"

"I don't think it will matter too much. My body will return to nature and begin the cycle of living all over again," continued Edmund. "It's the way of things."

"But what about your soul, Mr. Edmund?" asked Samuel.

"My life is contained in this body, Samuel. It does not exist outside of it! One does not need to invent a Creator to justify our existence," countered Mr. Edmund.

"I'm glad there are other scientists who believe differently, Mr. Edmund. Dr. John Mather won the Nobel Prize for the big bang theory, and I've heard that he doesn't see things that way at all," replied Samuel. "Neither did his colleague Robert Jastrow."

At that statement Mr. Edmund became curiously silent.

Samuel's eyebrows went up in wonderment just as the bell to signal the end of the day, and school year, for that matter, went off.

11

A Chance Meeting with Pastor Gregg and a Mutual Curiosity Confirmed

It was always fun to Samuel to meet the church pastor by accident in public. Today's venue turned out to be in the supermarket.

"So how's the preparation for the debate coming, young Samuel?" asked Pastor Gregg.

"Just fine, Pastor," replied Samuel. "We've been getting together every day after school for two weeks already!"

"I'm sure that you're learning wonderful things in the process, Samuel!" said the pastor.

"Oh yes, I am, Pastor!" said Samuel. "It's fun to hear John translate the original ancient Hebrew while looking for the deepest meaning of the Words."

At that, Pastor Gregg remembered the remarkable claim by John made in his office the day of the conflict with Mr. Allen that, in fact, he could read, speak, and write ancient Hebrew. Not wanting to sound critical or doubtful of this claim but because he was truly interested, Gregg decided to see if young Samuel knew the origin of such a wonderful skill set. Trying to sound non-accusing and even casual about it, he said, "I wonder where John got such wonderful knowledge of ancient Hebrew?"

Samuel replied honestly, "John learned ancient Hebrew when he was studying in preparation for his bar mitzvah when he was thirteen years old."

"Really?" replied Pastor, truly interested. "I didn't know that John was raised in a Jewish family! I didn't even recognize his last name, Barzeb, as being of Jewish origin!"

"John always surprises me too, Pastor," said young Samuel with a smile. "He even showed me how to fish with a net two weeks ago!"

"You mean a net dragged from a boat?" asked the pastor again.

"Oh no," replied Samuel. "John did this with a net he twirled from the dock, but I suppose it could also be done from a boat too."

"Interesting," mused the pastor. "Did he mention where he learned that too?"

"He just said that was the way fishing was done in the old days or in 'days gone by,' is the way he said it."

"Do you know where he grew up, Samuel?" asked Pastor Gregg.

"No, but he told me the name of the lake where he used to fish with his brother, Lake Ge—I'm sorry Pastor, but I don't remember the name right now...but I did write it down to look up on the Internet."

"Let me know when you find out Samuel, I'd really like to know," said the pastor.

"You're interested in John's family too?" asked Sam.

"Yes, I am indeed. John now seems on a course of surprising me about quite a few things!" said Pastor. Seeing young Samuel's look of concern, he added, "Don't worry, Sam! He surprises me in good ways! I just am amazed at how often this has been occurring lately when I have known the man for more than a decade! Funny about that ancient Hebrew expertise though...," Pastor said, thinking aloud.

"What's so 'funny' about that?" asked Sam, somewhat defensive of his friend.

"Well, Sam, it's just that I was under the impression that twentieth-century Hebrew studies in preparation for the ceremony of bar mitzvah were not truly geared toward study of the ancient language in such detail as the knowledge which John professes to have. I'm

PAUL M. FEINBERG, PHD

sure he must have continued somewhere above and beyond the normal education in the study of Hebrew," added the pastor. "You sure you don't remember the name of the lake where he and his brother fished?"

"Why is that important, Pastor Gregg?"

"Well, it might give me a clue as to the background of our intelligent friend. Maybe he's from a special community where a higher level of education is prized? I'm just curious, that's all," said the pastor.

"Well, when I look at my notes, I'll let you know," said Samuel.

"Thank you, my good lad!" said Pastor Gregg. "You have a wonderful day now!"

"Bye, Pastor Gregg," returned Samuel. "I look forward to seeing you next Sunday!"

And with that, young Samuel headed for home.

CHAPTER 12

AN INTERESTING GOOGLE SEARCH

That evening Samuel sat at the computer and made sure to go to the Google website. He typed in "Lake Genesareth" and hit Enter. Immediately the following words came up on his screen:

> Did you mean: Lake *Gennesaret*
> **Search Results**
> Map of Galilee and **Lake Genesareth**
> Galilee and **Lake Genesareth** at the Time of Jesus Ministry.
>   www.circleofprayer.com/galilee. html-Cached-Similar
>   CATHOLIC ENCYCLOPEDIA: Sea of Galilee
>   6:1), otherwise known as "the sea of Galilee" (Matthew 4:18; Mark 1:16; John 6:1) or as "the **lake** of **Genesareth**" (Luke 5:1, and Rabbinical writings),
>   www.newadvent.org › Catholic Encyclopedia › T-Cached-Similar
> **Lake Genesareth**
> **Lake Genesareth** great largemouth bass and a loon sanctuary.

wikimapia.org/531111/**Lake-Genesareth-**
Cached

Further down the page Samuel saw other entries as well, one of which had biblical pictures:

Images for **Lake Genesareth**
Report images
Lake Genesareth, Oakland County, Michigan
Outdoors recreation info for **Lake Genesareth** and surrounding area in Oakland County, Michigan. www.goingoutside. com/**lake**/.../1047221_**Lake_Genesareth_** Michigan.html-Cached
Lake Genesareth—vaviblog
Aug 26, 2009...1926 November I also went to the **lake** of **Genesareth.** [1] There fishing is conducted just as it was in the distant past. www. vaviblog.com/**lake-genesareth**/-Cached
Lake of **Genesareth** | Facebook
Welcome to the Facebook Community Page about **Lake** of **Genesareth**, a collection of shared knowledge concerning **Lake** of **Genesareth**. www.facebook.com/pages/**Lake**-of-**Genesareth**/111287078899617-Cached
Lake Genesareth Guide | Ontario Canada
World Bay Community | Services, tips, weather, maps and attractions for locals, visitors and travellers. www.baysider.com/attraction/358694/ **lake-genesareth**-Cached

Samuel was surprised to see that the first entry actually read, "Galilee and Lake Genesareth at the Time of Jesus Ministry." He caught his breath for a moment and, as his eyes traveled down the page, noticed the various entry descriptions of "great largemouth bass," "loon sanctuary," "outdoors recreation... Oakland County,

Michigan," and then some kind of "guide" apparently for a place in "Ontario, Canada."

"Oh," Samuel found himself saying. It would make sense that John should have come from an area of great fishing. *I wonder which one*, thought Samuel. Samuel was soon confused with all the references. Apparently, it was safe to say that John was somewhere from the northeast but that could include Canada as well.

Something continued to nag at Samuel even though he thought he had made a considered conclusion. He realized what it was when he saw a caption under one of the entries: "There fishing is conducted just as it was in the distant past." This immediately reminded him of John and his method of net capture from two weeks ago.

Sam clicked on this entry and a blog came up that apparently was reporting a traveler's log from the year 1926. It also included a black-and-white photograph of fishermen in a boat with the caption, "Fishermen on the Sea of Galilee and distant hills of the Gaderenes, Palestine." (http://www.vaviblog.com/lake-genesareth/).

Samuel then thought, *Well, I guess he could be from the Sea of Galilee also! How cool is that!*

Sam soon went to bed, carrying with him his newfound knowledge.

And what a wonderful dream he had!

CHAPTER 13

A SIGHTING OF TWO MIRACLES, ONE ANCIENT AND ONE MODERN

Sam was once again on his way to John's cabin, contemplating all the wonderful things that had engaged his mind for more than two weeks. Again he decided to walk today, hoping to think through the many things he had been privileged to be exposed to during the preparation for the debate. He had enjoyed learning so much about the Bible's verses in Genesis and what so many scientists and even ministers had thought about them over the years. And as much as all this had meant to him, it was his amazing dream from the previous night that was foremost on his mind, causing him to ponder everything in a quiet, glad, and spiritually "enthralled" mood. What a state of peace his soul was enjoying!

In his dream he was standing on the shore of the Sea of Galilee, looking out onto the water at several fishing boats, very distant from shore. He didn't know how he knew it was the Sea of Galilee, but he had absolutely no doubt about what body of water it was. Suddenly, what had been a beautiful day quickly turned overcast and windy as a squall came down upon the lake. The waves grew to huge heights and, with the wind, tossed the boats wildly. Somehow Samuel then experienced a detailed view into one of the boats and saw a group of men, at least a dozen, actively, even frantically, scrambling around, adjusting lines, desperately trying to balance weight, some even trying to bail water as the boats appeared threatened to be swamped by the furious storm.

In the lead boat, however, one figure of a person was not moving around in panic but instead was apparently lying down in the stern of the boat, peacefully sleeping on some kind of cushion. Then he saw at least two of the crew run over to the sleeping man, who he assumed was the captain, and wake him with what appeared to be an urgent plea for advice or help. Samuel saw the man rise and stand in their midst, apparently looking out at the scene beyond the walls of the boat, watching as the storm threatened the tiny fishing boat flotilla. Samuel saw that all the other men in this boat had now ceased their frantic activities as they stopped to look upon the man who had been awakened and now appeared to be standing slightly apart from them. Samuel thought he then saw the man's arms spread outward forcefully, as if in making a firm declaration. His appearance was not as if he was making a plea, but actually issuing a decree or even a rebuke, with absolute authority as this figure of a man appeared to be standing firmly in the otherwise unstable boat. Immediately, the wind calmed, the waters settled, and the squall ceased. Then he saw the man turn to the others watching him, who had begun to cower away in apparent awe, putting their heads down or turning away from him in humility, but with gratitude and relief, some speaking quietly among themselves.

Samuel then knew it was dear Jesus calming the storm as recorded in three of the Gospels. Never before had he realized the severity of the event on the Sea of Galilee. None of the records of the event were very long in duration in their placement in the Gospels, just a very brief, matter-of-fact description of a dazzling superhuman act, witnessed by the men who travelled with the Lord. Samuel found himself with newly found appreciation of the event, almost as if he had been there to witness it himself, experiencing firsthand the miracle of the Lord Jesus. Samuel then made another realization: although the account of this miracle was not very long, it was so significant an event that it had made it into three of the four accounts in the New Testament. It declared firmly that the Messiah had control over the physical elements of the world and, Sam knew, the entire universe.

As he walked down the long road to John's cabin, these things were on his mind. Just before he could see the actual shore of the lake, something caught his eye in the woods to his left. It seemed to be some kind of fluttering papers being blown about in the trees and forest scrub. Samuel immediately turned off the road to retrieve the papers, always willing to do his part to keep the woods beautiful and natural whenever he had the power to do so. His meandering path among the trees brought him there in only a couple of minutes, positioning him on the other side of John's main cabin and garage.

As he bent down to pick up the rolling papers, he could see that they actually showed the current day's date. He was slightly surprised to see this, thinking that normally John kept the newspaper throughout the week in his home before throwing it into the recycling stack. These then he usually bundled up with string, keeping them gathered inside until the night before staging for the town's recycling pick-ups up on the main road.

Hmmm, Samuel thought, *maybe it belonged to one of John's frequent visitors—maybe Mrs. Ortega—who loved to come by and enjoy the peaceful setting.* He then dismissed Mrs. Ortega straight away, knowing that she too was careful to clean up wherever she had decided to sit down. Any picnicking items she brought with her were always carefully and even meticulously disposed of to avoid unnecessary despoiling of the beautiful lakeside, even subtly.

As Samuel gathered the fluttering newspaper pages, he now found himself coming down toward the lakeside from behind John's cabin and garage. In a moment he caught his breath suddenly as a scene came into his view that he immediately wished wasn't real. About 150 feet in front of him, just past the dock, was John and Mrs. Ortega bent over the inert figure of her beautiful little daughter Melinda! Mrs. Ortega was apparently administering CPR, bent earnestly over her little girl, trying to get her to revive. He noticed that Melinda appeared to be soaking wet and that John was kneeling directly by, ready to assist with whatever Mrs. Ortega requested in the emergency.

Suddenly, she jumped up and wailed aloud, "Oh no, please no! Not my baby! My life! Please dear God, help me! Please, John, please help me! Oh nooo!"

Samuel stopped in his tracks and dropped to the ground, watching, scared of the situation, unable to offer anything, afraid of what had happened and afraid he could not change what had happened! His wonderful little friend was dead! His heart broke for Melinda and for Mrs. Ortega. He also somehow felt terrible for John, who also stood by apparently unable to offer any more help than what had apparently been expertly rendered by Mrs. Ortega.

Samuel stifled his own cry as the tears welled up in his eyes. Oh, how terrible! He was speechless and didn't want to even intrude upon the scene, making one more person to detract from the tragedy on hand that had to be dealt with. He couldn't believe it. Oh, how everything a moment ago seemed to reflect the tranquility of spiritual bliss!

Suddenly, John, who seemed to be holding out his cell phone, spoke up and said to Mrs. Ortega, "Evelyn, I just called the ambulance on my cell phone, and they will no doubt be here any moment... But they will need to find the driveway immediately. Can you please run up to the entrance and direct them down to the cabin in case they cannot find it easily! I'll stay with little Melinda, but you need to make sure the ambulance can find us!"

To this, Mrs. Ortega, still sobbing, nodded and immediately turned and ran as fast as she could up the driveway to the road.

As soon as she was out of sight, John stood up quietly in front of the little girl's body. He bowed his head and prayed aloud, "Dear Lord Jesus, I beseech thee, as you did with Jairus's child oh so long ago, blessing me and my brethren to witness your gracious power, I ask in your Holy Name, to restore this little one to those whom she has been a blessing and who love her dearly."

Samuel was in awe of this entreaty to the Lord! Then unexpectedly, he heard John say, "Oh, thank you, LORD! May your Holy Name be praised forever! Amen." At once he turned to the little figure lying before him and squatted down, extending his right hand to take her little hand in his. Then he said, "Talitha koum!" Immediately, little

Melinda opened up her eyes and stood up. She smiled one of her big smiles at John and threw her little arms around his neck! John kissed her and held her to him as he looked up toward heaven and said with tears in his eyes, "Thank you, Lord Jesus, thank you, thank you! Amen."

Appearing on cue was the sound of an ambulance siren. Sam soon could hear the sound of its tires on the driveway to the cabin. It came to a screeching halt only feet from where John and Melinda stood now, her little hand in his. The doors of the ambulance flew open, and Mrs. Ortega came racing along with two medical technicians right over to the little girl and John. Melinda and John stood motionless as all this activity came bearing down upon them, just smiling at them with exuberant, but calm spirits.

Mrs. Ortega stared back in amazement at the vision before her eyes and then scooped up her baby, shouting, "My baby Melinda! You're alive! Oh, thank you, Merciful King of the Universe! Praise be to your Holy and Excellent Name forever and ever and ever!" Suddenly, she gave her precious child into John's arms directly and literally dropped to her knees and prostrated herself to God in full view of everyone. All could hear her cries of thanks and praise repeated over and over.

A miracle had occurred. A miracle such as recorded in the Bible. Dear God had literally rescued a child from the clutches of death and had also rescued a faithful woman from misery before Sam's very eyes. Samuel then stopped himself from moving over to the scene and offered his own thanks to God. He thanked the Lord and praised God for His wonderful mercy and love and the miracle that he had wrought through His own special power and majesty. When he finished thanking God, he looked up and saw that John was giving his explanation as to what had happened to Melinda after Mrs. Ortega had run to meet the ambulance. Sam only heard him say, "After you ran up the driveway, dear God had mercy upon your little daughter and woke her from her slumber!" Mrs. Ortega remained awestruck while the ambulance attendants didn't quite know what to make of the situation. They offered to bring the little girl to the hospital just to be sure she was okay, but Mrs. Ortega only thanked them and said she would follow up with their own doctor, asking them if they wouldn't mind dropping her off on their way back to the hospital. They all soon left together, the two paramedics relieved by the wonderful turn of events for Melinda, though not exactly sure of what had happened. They were at least pleased to be able to give the healthy-looking little girl and her mother a ride to their doctor instead of bringing a lifeless body to the emergency room!

Samuel crept quietly away as the paramedics, Mrs. Ortega, and Melinda got into the ambulance. He retreated back up the way he had come, the papers still clutched in his hand. Once obscured by the trees and brush, he made his way up to the road and quickly headed for home. From deep inside himself, he felt awe and a deep-seated peace and sense of thanksgiving. His life he knew was under the care of the King of the Universe. And he knew oh so firmly that death could never separate the King's children from the King. He commanded the universe, and He had the power of life and death. His was a Kingdom of Love. He is, always was, and always will be awesome. No ands, ifs, or buts. Now Samuel started to realize that maybe his dream from the previous night, seemingly showing him the actual events that took place on the Sea of Galilee nearly two thousand years ago, also showed him that regardless of the terrible storms of life that a person might find himself in, God is able to eradicate the storms even miraculously, bringing peace to the most violent storms—even in the midst of them!

Something else occurred to him then... God had actually allowed him to see the tragic loss of little Melinda and then her wonderful and amazing return from the dead. God had actually permitted him to see His miracle! This to Sam seemed almost unbelievably gracious! It was *believable* because Sam had witnessed it! Did God want him to tell anybody? As best as Sam could remember, the Scriptures recorded that in some cases, only some of the disciples were permitted to observe some of the miracles. He also remembered that the Lord sometimes seemed to not want the stories of the miracles spread around at certain times. Samuel knew that he needed to think carefully before he went around telling anyone what he was just permitted to see, actually literally blessed to see with his own eyes. He knew that he needed to respect and also better understand his truly awesome responsibility with which he had been blessed only moments ago! He needed to think it through.

CHAPTER 14

STARTING TO TAKE SOME TIME TO THINK THINGS THROUGH!

By the time that Samuel reached home, the phone was ringing in the living room. He half-suspected who it might be and quickly jogged over to the phone to pick up the receiver.

"Hello?" he said as he held it up to his mouth.

"Hello, Samuel?" returned the voice from the other side.

"Yes, hi, John!" Samuel said.

"I'm glad you're okay, my friend. We've had a little incident here this afternoon, and I just realized that you hadn't shown up."

"Oh, sorry about that, John" said Samuel. "It turned out that I needed to come home right away."

"Everything okay?" asked John concerned.

"Oh yeah, John, everything is just great."

"Are you sure? I thought you were excited about our work here, Samuel. You sure don't sound disappointed."

"Well, you see, John, I had so much on my mind today that I needed to come home and just think over some things."

"Is that why you needed to go straight home, Samuel?"

Samuel couldn't continue with the charade any longer. He just refused to lie to John.

"John?"

"Yes, Samuel?"

"I actually did go by your place first."

There was silence on the other side at first and then, "And?"

"Well, I thought you looked kind of busy."

"In what way, 'busy'?"

"Well, I saw an ambulance and Mrs. Ortega and medical technicians running toward you and Melissa by the dock. I just didn't want to get in the way of anything."

"Samuel, you're never in the way. Why didn't you come down and let us know you were nearby?" said John concerned again.

"Because it looked like big things were going on and I didn't want to mess anything up, I guess," said Sam, now uncomfortably.

"Sam, please don't ever feel like you can't come up to my place. If something is up, and I just can't afford one minute of time for you, I will tell you plainly. But please don't make such assumptions next time."

"Okay, John. Thanks, I won't," returned Sam more happily, knowing that he was probably not going to have to reveal to him just yet what he saw, giving him more time to think about the miracle.

"Will I see you tomorrow after school?" inquired John.

"Yes, John, right after school!" said Sam more enthusiastically.

"Well then, I suppose I'll spend some time here with Christopher on some related things and we can continue our preparation for the debate tomorrow. I will wish you a good evening, Sam, and hope I see you tomorrow. Please tell your mom and dad that I said hi!"

"Will do, John," replied Samuel.

"Goodbye, Samuel," said John.

"See you tomorrow," said Sam.

Samuel hung up the phone and decided that maybe he should go back on the Internet to check on something that he had heard at the dockside. As he started upstairs, he realized that he was still holding on to the newspaper sheets he had picked up in the surrounding woods by the lake. He opened it up again to see today's date. As he was about to close it, however, he noticed what appeared to be a woman's handwriting in the margin on the right side of the paper. Staring more closely, he saw that it was a short-numbered list of someone's "things to do."

Among the items on the list were "Call distributor and double the taco shell orders for the summer high school talent show" as well as "Make sure that special box order makes it to the nursing home." It was Mrs. Ortega's writing! She must have dropped it when Melinda almost drowned, actually did drown.

Now Sam had an actual souvenir from one of the principal people involved in the miracle he had observed. It would be interesting to follow up with Mrs. Ortega, but at the same time, she might not be one of the people to whom dear God wanted him to share. At the same time, however, she was principally involved in the event, thought Samuel. And she did need to get her shopping list back, right?

Sam was out the door again before he had spent a full ten minutes inside the house!

CHAPTER 15

A RECONNAISSANCE
WITH MRS. ORTEGA

By the time Samuel finished riding his bicycle over to see Mrs. Ortega, another fifteen minutes had elapsed. Samuel had taken the newspaper pages he had picked up with him in order to "return her list" and was hoping that there might be some sign forthcoming that he was supposed to talk with her about what he had witnessed. After ringing the doorbell three times, Samuel assumed that he had gotten there too early and that Mrs. Ortega had not yet finished with the doctor and little Melinda. As he was turning to leave, suddenly a taxi appeared, and both Mrs. Ortega and Miss Melinda emerged from the back seat.

"Samuel!" cried little Melinda.

"Hi, Sam," said her mother. "We've just gotten back from the doctor's office. I'm glad we didn't miss you!"

"Me too, Mrs. Ortega," replied Samuel. "I brought your list over for you...you must have lost it over by John's house since I found it blowing around the trees!"

"You brought my list, Sam? How thoughtful! I can't believe you found it!" said Mrs. Ortega.

"Me, too, Mrs. Ortega," replied Sam.

"Did you hear about Melinda, Sam?" she asked.

Sam simply said that he hadn't heard the story from anyone, which was technically true, and that he only noticed that an ambulance drove off from John's house shortly after he had rescued her list from the nearby woods.

"So what did happen, Mrs. Ortega?" he said finally as he finished relating the details, making sure that they squared with the description he gave to John.

After Mrs. Ortega sent Melinda into her room to find all the crayons necessary for her to continue her project from this morning, she turned to Samuel and spoke very softly about the events that unfolded that afternoon at the lake.

"Little Melinda was near the edge of the dock watching all of the fish swimming under the water while I was sitting on the Adirondack chair on the shore. I guess I should not have let her go so far from where I could pull her back, but I figured that I could literally jump halfway and swim to get her if anything drastic did happen.

"Suddenly, a wind blew my newspaper out of my hand toward John's cabin, and I ran to retrieve it. As John was coming out of the cabin to sit with me by the lake, he started asking me about doing a catering order for a family he wanted to entertain there. I spoke to him it seemed like for only a minute or two, but when I turned back, I didn't see Melinda. I called her name and ran toward the dock, looking up and down the shore for her everywhere. The water seemed so still, that I decided I would run along the shoreline to look for her, not thinking that she had actually gone under. As I was just about to run in one direction, I caught sight of her bunny on the dock edge where I had last seen her. I was very concerned now because at least ten minutes had gone by according to my watch since I had last seen her."

While he was listening, Samuel's mouth dropped open without his realizing it. He was experiencing again the severity of the circumstances that took place at the lake. He had been aware that somehow he needed to behave in a way as if he was hearing of the incident at the lake for the first time; however, his reactions still honestly portrayed his shock and concern as if he was going through the events for the first time.

Mrs. Ortega continued, "I ran to the dock edge, and when I looked, I couldn't really make out her shape beneath the water at

PAUL M. FEINBERG, PHD

first, but after another minute I noticed the cartoon shape of Mickey Mouse on one of her sneakers. She was literally lying at the bottom, face down with her leg caught under a submerged tree branch! I dove into the water immediately and hauled her up toward the surface as fast as I could, using the dock as an anchor to hold on to. John pulled her out of the water, and I followed, beginning CPR as soon as I heard no sound in her body and she did not respond to our cries for her attention. I was unable to revive her, Sam." Melinda paused, stifling a sob, her eyes watery.

"But then," she continued, "the next thing I knew, John had his cell phone out and told me that I needed to make sure that the ambulance would be able to find his driveway. Since I was at the point of desperation and since I had tried to revive my baby, I ran like a mad woman to the road in order to not lose my last hope of getting my baby back!"

Mrs. Ortega stopped for a moment and walked over to the kitchen to pour herself a glass of water. She took a swallow and continued, "And this is where things get both strange and wonderful, Samuel! I got to the roadside just exactly as the ambulance got there and jumped into the front seat with the two EMTs. We raced down the roadside as I told them that my daughter was a drowning victim pulled up out of the water only moments before and that I was unable to revive her with CPR. It was a strange thing, Samuel, because I had actually given the CPR lesson to one of the EMTs about nine months ago during the after-school CPR training course!

"As the ambulance stopped just in front of the last tree on the side of the driveway down by the parking lot, there were John and Melinda standing there, holding hands! I praise God for this miracle because I know that my little girl was dead the last time I had seen her body! Even after nearly fifteen to twenty minutes without breathing, the doctor says that there is no sign of brain damage whatsoever, nor anything else wrong with my baby! Praise God Almighty!"

"What happened then, Mrs. Ortega? Did John try CPR himself?" asked Samuel.

Mrs. Ortega answered, "No, Samuel. John simply said that dear God had mercy upon Melinda and had awakened Melinda from her slumber! I suppose that he might have done this while I was gone, but that was not the impression that I got. His explanation was wonderfully curious!"

Samuel quickly put in. "I saw the ambulance leave sometime after I got there. I didn't want to bother anyone since it looked like you were both busy with very important things! So I left for home. John called me later though."

"Oh well, he must have been worried that you didn't show up...and that would have meant that two of his delights had been in potential jeopardy during the same day!"

Samuel was all set to leave then, satisfied that he knew the whole story but disappointed that Mrs. Ortega didn't bring up any of the details that he had witnessed. He didn't really expect her to reveal anything more, based upon the fact that he had seen everything as it unfolded. He had hoped that John might have said something more to her after Samuel had left as Mrs. Ortega and Melinda were getting into the ambulance, but clearly he did not. Sam knew that he would have to keep this special knowledge to himself, at least for the time being.

"Well, I'm sure glad Miss Melinda is all right, Mrs. Ortega," offered Sam sincerely.

"Thank you, Samuel. I'm so glad you love her so much," replied Mrs. Ortega. "I truly felt as desperate as I've ever been, Samuel. Then this miracle came and set me at perfect peace."

"God is awesome, Mrs. Ortega" said Sam.

"You know, Samuel, one of the strangest, wonderful things about seeing Melinda with John when the ambulance returned was seeing the look on each of their faces...the same look in fact. A serene joy, almost quiet peace, but a deeply happy one... I really can't describe it."

Sam mused aloud then, "I wonder if the people that dear Jesus raised from the dead looked the same way?"

"That's very interesting, Sam," replied Mrs. Ortega. "It certainly gives me a new way to think about the Lord's healing miracles as recorded in the Bible."

16

Young Christopher's Personal Faith, Answers to Prayer, and Cool Bicycles

Young Christopher rode his decrepit bicycle down the path about five minutes after Mrs. Ortega and the ambulance left. John looked with concern at Chris as he fumbled with the hand brakes trying to make the bicycle slow down.

"Hi, Chris!" greeted John. "Looks like your vehicle needs a little maintenance there!"

"Yeah, it really does!" replied the boy. "My dad thinks it's probably better to put money toward a new bicycle than try to spend money on keeping this one working!"

"Well, that does make some sense, Chris. But if you can't use the brakes on your bicycle, I'd say it was an issue worth exploring sooner rather than later, don't you think?"

Chris looked at his bike and then replied, "I guess so, but it's just that I know that my father is trying to save up for a nice one to give me on my birthday. He says money is just a little 'tight' right now."

John looked over the bike and then said to the boy, "Well, I'll tell you what, since Samuel cannot be with us today, we'll have a little talk about some related things to our project, and then I'll do a maintenance check on your bicycle."

Chris looked at him gratefully and said, "Thank you, John. That is so nice of you!"

John smiled back and replied, "Remember, Chris, safety is a top priority when it comes to anything mechanical. To rely on the Lord is fine, but it's our responsibility to do everything we can toward the things we pray for or to help bring about His Will."

Chris nodded in agreement. "That's like a saying that I heard in Sunday school, 'If you pray for a job, the Lord expects you to read the want ads…'"

"Well said, Christopher," replied John as he pulled open the screen door to admit them both. Immediately, John went to the kitchen to get his pitcher of lemonade from the refrigerator. As Chris seated himself at their "preparation table," John made another trip, bringing back two glasses and a plate of brownies. Soon they were seated and enjoying their small snack amidst the books and papers.

After Chris had enjoyed his second brownie, John asked him, "So, Chris, what do you think of our ongoing program here as we prepare for the debate? Any thoughts or comments you'd like to share?"

In response, Chris replied, "Well, John, I find all of this study very interesting. I'm learning so many things which I can't imagine I would have learned otherwise, even at the Sunday school at my church!"

"Did you ever have an internal conflict with faith and what you have learned from the Bible or about science, Chris?" queried the sharp-eyed fisherman.

"Not really, John. I never had any reason to doubt my faith before—at least no one ever challenged me that way," replied the lad. "My faith always made sense to me. I understand that dear Jesus paid the price for my disobedience on the cross, and I accept the testimony of the apostles that He was raised from the dead. Only a sinless man could pay for my sins, so that tells me that He is the Son of God, without any sin at all. This makes sense in order to keep both righteousness and mercy alive."

John smiled broadly at this sincere testimony from one so young. "It's true, Chris, all people are guilty of sin and must be punished because of dear God's Righteousness. But it's wonderful to know that God still loves us individually even though we have sinned and has provided both the payment for our sins and personal forgiveness for each of us by the acceptance of His Son's payment!"

Chris continued, "And what happened to Samuel and what we are now doing has made me think a lot about being able to give good reasons for what I believe—at least the things outside Bible events."

"You're of course referring to the big bang theory and age of the Earth among other things I presume!" replied John.

"Yes, John, I am. I never realized that there could be so much hatred for science and scientific theory because of a person's religious beliefs, without even the hater's own investigation of whether or not science was actually supporting or denying their biblical beliefs."

"Do you believe that the big bang theory supports the Bible after all that we've looked at together?" asked John.

Chris then launched into a summary of the explanation he had been working on since they began their preparation for the debate.

"Yes, John, I do. The Bible says that the universe was created by God. That means it had a beginning. We've seen that so many people throughout human history who wanted to deny God pushed the 'steady state' theory that the universe is eternal without a beginning or an ending. This became one of their first assumptions and with which Christians had to contend. But after an examination of electromagnetic wavelengths and the Doppler effect and the discovery of background radiation, among other things, we see that such an argument is no longer with any merit. The universe had a definite beginning at a single point in time. No serious scientist even doubts this anymore. Scientific reasoning gave us the tools to see this clearly. It is a strong refutation of this argument made by those who denied the Bible or, worse, who denied God."

"So you are, to say the least, impressed with the way this discovery explains the universe?" responded John.

"Yes, John, I think it is readily seen by anyone who is honest about it," replied Chris. "Faith should not be afraid to incorporate those things which have taken place in our world. If it doesn't or can't explain them, then more study is needed. But I believe that evidence is always left behind for all real-world happenings! And just as in the documentaries you showed us about Dr. Bob Cornuke and the discovery of the real Mount Sinai or the one on the recovery of the anchor stocks of the Alexandrian freighter mentioned in the book of Acts, and it will always come out to validate the happenings at the right times and in the correct sequence."

"I like your way of thinking, Christopher," offered John. "Do you mind if I ask you a question?"

"Sure, John," replied the boy.

"What would you advise Mr. Allen to do in order to see more clearly some of these points you have made?" asked John.

"I'd advise him to pray to dear God for enlightenment," responded Chris.

John was pleased to note that, just as with Samuel, Chris was now referring to the Lord with the respectful "dear" in front of "God."

"Do you believe that dear God would answer a prayer like that?"

Chris thought for a minute and then said, "John, I think that this is such an important thing to ask, so I also believe that dear God will answer that prayer for him."

"Do you believe that the Lord answers all prayers, Chris?"

"I do, John, but you might have to be patient for the answer and be open to it coming in from a direction you don't expect!" responded the boy honestly.

"Could you give me an example of what you mean, Chris?" asked John.

"Well, let's say I prayed for a new bicycle"—he paused and smiled as he thought about it—"a Specialized Hotrock with eight speeds, a front suspension, black with silver trim, with rechargeable lights...and a bell, a JelliBell Twist. And then I received it a short time later, but not from my parents who couldn't afford it. Then, yes, I believe that is a definite answer to prayer. But if I do not receive it immediately, the answer may have been no. It doesn't mean that God has stopped loving me, but that it is not good for me to receive that kind of a gift now. But if I do receive it today"—he paused to look at the date on the paper—"say on June 30, the last day in June, and had asked the Lord for it on the twenty-eighth of the same month,

I should not ignore that fact! Let's face it, my prayer was answered!" Satisfied that he had answered John's question fully, he smiled and looked at John.

"So in conclusion, Chris, and please correct me if I'm wrong, from your point of view, we must look at the answers and evidence all around us in detail before we risk offending someone who makes a claim from a scientific direction, because it may give us the very substance we need to undergird our faith or possibly even recognize our answered prayers!" offered John.

Chris nodded and said, "Absolutely." Then he added, "But the conflict with Mr. Allen and others who do not ask is almost enough to make me want to just keep my mouth closed and not risk any conflicts which can get so loud!"

"Do you think the church will suffer or prosper if most of its young people take that line of thinking?" asked John.

"Well, it will probably involve less yelling and be a much more quiet gathering, but I think the church will suffer for it in the long run," offered Chris.

"How so, Chris?" continued John.

Chris then responded, "Well, I just think when honest beliefs or even honest wondering is stopped by those not even willing to consider what is being presented, it's like saying don't have a faith that includes a scientific notions in any time where technology scientific discovery promise so many things for the world. People trust technology and scientific enlightenment, but some people in the church make it seem like anything along those lines is evil just because they don't understand some of the discoveries being made—and which really might support what they believe. They just don't want to even deal with it. They just want science to be off limits. And no one that I know finds that very open or honest!"

"Do you imagine that science and religious subjects could ever be in conflict, Chris?"

"No, John, I don't think they really truly are. Maybe we don't understand everything from a scientific point of view, but I think that the God of the Bible is also the true Creator of science as well. And this must mean that there is no real conflict."

"Tell you what, my friend, can you do a little extra research for our presentation at the debate which shows to our brethren that scientific understanding is something which is not shunned in the Bible?"

"Something not shunned?" Chris inquired.

"That it is not evil. That reasoning and observation do not go against biblical faith," answered John.

"Where do you want me to begin, John?" asked Chris.

"Well, that's entirely up to you, Chris. Anywhere in the Bible, really. I just am curious to see what you will come up with on your own. I'm just looking for something that is straightforward and logical enough to make the point that science is a friend of a true Christian, not an enemy," replied John. "Perhaps you should begin in the Gospels and the recorded words of dear Jesus?"

"Makes sense. I'll do it!" said Chris, accepting the task.

"With that said, Chris, let me have a look at your bicycle!" said John. "But before we go, would you join me in a prayer for Mr. Allen and others like him, Chris? Oh, and I suppose we might ask the Lord about a new bicycle for you too!"

Chris grinned and nodded enthusiastically!

17

THE EXTENDED TIME WITH MRS. ORTEGA

Mrs. Ortega had offered Sam a beverage after their initial exchange, which he gratefully accepted. He wanted very much to tell Mrs. Ortega everything that he heard but didn't feel it was right for him to simply volunteer to describe the details until he knew what to do about his testimony. Now a bit more calm or maybe with a little bit of distance from the actual event, he thought that maybe his best course of action would be to go home and think about all that happened.

He got up from the kitchen table to leave and said to his hostess, "Thank you so much for telling me the story Mrs. Ortega. I'm so happy that your wonderful daughter is safe and sound. I probably should be getting back home now..."

"Samuel?" said Mrs. Ortega, smiling. "May I ask at what point did you arrive at John's cabin today?"

Samuel noted that that she was looking directly at him as she said this. Now Samuel knew that he was busted. And he wasn't about to lie about any part of this story ever! He had to tell her the truth in whatever he told her. Anything less would be wrong.

"Well, uh," he started to stammer. "I headed over there after school ended today."

"But when did you first arrive?" she continued her query. Just then she stopped and thought for a moment and then rephrased her question. "What did you first see when you got there?"

"Well, that's the thing, Mrs. Ortega, because the first thing I saw was the newspaper in the woods, so that's what I went after first." He thought quickly and then added, "Just like I see you doing all the time. It's necessary to keep everything there so beautiful."

Mrs. Ortega smiled again at this but kept her gaze. She then asked him, "But you said you saw the ambulance. Was it there then?"

"Oh no, not yet, Mrs. Ortega," replied Sam.

"So you saw it sometime after you arrived?" she asked.

"Yes, ma'am," said Sam.

Mrs. Ortega noticed a look of discomfort in Sam's eyes. So she decided she would ask only one more question for now. It also happened to be the right question. "Samuel, did you see what happened to Melinda after I ran up to the road?"

"Uh, yes, Mrs. Ortega, I did," replied Samuel.

"Would you tell me what you saw, Sam?" asked Mrs. Ortega, truly wanting to know.

"I saw a miracle, Mrs. Ortega," said Sam.

Mrs. Ortega's eyes widened at hearing this, and Sam felt that he should continue.

"Mrs. Ortega, after you ran up the hill, John prayed to God for Melinda. She was literally raised from the dead, Mrs. Ortega. He didn't do CPR or anything like that. He just took her hand and said something to her after he thanked dear God for answering his prayer."

"Samuel, are you saying that John thanked dear God *before* he took Melinda's hand?" she said amazed.

"Yes, Mrs. Ortega, that is what I'm saying," replied Samuel.

"Did he do anything else then?" she asked honestly.

Samuel thought for a moment, not sure how to describe what it was that John said. Finally, Sam replied, "Mrs. Ortega he said something after he took her little hand in his which I didn't understand. It sounded like another language."

"Do you remember the words, Samuel?" she asked.

Sam didn't even hesitate in answering because he knew he would remember those words for the rest of his life. "It was something that sounded like *talitha kome*."

"Samuel, why didn't you say something to me before now?" asked Mrs. Ortega, not quite sure whether or not to feel hurt. Any doubts she had about this evaporated in Samuel's simple and honest answer.

"Mrs. Ortega, this is the greatest miracle I ever saw. I know that dear God allowed me to see this for a reason. I don't know this reason yet, but I do remember that in the Bible there were certain times where dear Jesus didn't want news of His miracles spread around right away. I wanted to make sure about why I was shown this before I started telling everyone." Samuel paused for a moment and then added, "I want you to know that when I got home, John called me to make sure I was all right since he didn't see me at the normal time. I told him the same thing that I told you at first. Then I came over to see you and Melinda right away."

Again Mrs. Ortega smiled, pleased at the boy's honesty, as well as the fact that he was sincerely trying to be a good steward of what he had been blessed to see.

"So John doesn't yet know that you saw this miracle?" inquired Mrs. Ortega.

"Well, I certainly didn't tell him directly, but…" Sam stopped.

"But what?" asked the young mom.

"I was just thinking, Mrs. Ortega. John prayed aloud. That's how I could hear him. I wonder if he really knows already that I was there."

"As strangely wonderful as this day has already turned out," Mrs. Ortega began, "I wouldn't be a bit surprised."

"Do you think John is an angel, Mrs. Ortega?" asked Sam honestly.

Her answer surprised Sam. "I don't know, Sam. He seems to be a human being who is amazingly gracious. His faith is paramount in his life, and dear God has answered his prayer miraculously for my baby. I heard a rumor just recently about him being much older than he looks!"

Sam had almost forgotten about that. "Yes, ma'am, I heard him say that he is older than Mr. Allen!"

"Well, that's odd, Samuel," said Mrs. Ortega. "He doesn't seem to be more than his late forties or early fifties to me."

"Mrs. Ortega?" Sam continued.

"Yes, Samuel?" she replied.

"John said he was 'quite a bit older' than Mr. Allen but didn't tell me how much. He also told me that he wasn't comfortable with talking about his age," said Samuel.

"Well then, Samuel, we mustn't bother him with so many questions," concluded Mrs. Ortega. "John asked dear God for a miracle concerning my baby, and his request was granted. I am forever grateful!"

Samuel noticed that all through their conversation, Mrs. Ortega spoke of the Lord as "dear God" just as John had shown Samuel by example. It sounded nice in his ears.

Samuel stayed just a little longer to say his thank you to Mrs. Ortega and his good-byes to both her and Melinda. He then headed home. He didn't want to be late and wanted to have enough time to think about everything still. He hoped he would have time tonight to use the computer to answer some of his own questions about John. One thing was for sure in his mind was that if John wanted to share with him the knowledge of the miracle, he should at least spend some time trying to understand the details of what he was so graciously shown.

18

A DISCUSSION OF DAYS

"Well, young gentleman," John began to address the two boys, "we come to the question of the biblical use of the word 'day.' I think it's fair to say that much of the argument against 'science' by some of our brethren comes down to the length of time that is given to the age of the Earth according to the Bible in contrast to what they believe scientists are saying about the same time frame. But I say to any person looking into this topic to be careful that you do not read anything into the Scripture that is not necessarily there. In other words, we each must ask ourselves if we are absolutely certain when it comes down to giving time absolutes here according to the Scripture. So to get us started. Do either of you have any thoughts with regard to the matter of time?"

Samuel was the first to speak up. "Well, John, doesn't the Bible say that 'a second is like a thousand years in the eyes of the Lord' or something like that?"

John nodded and said, "That is correct Samuel, in Psalm 90:4, it is written, 'For a thousand years in your sight are like a day that has just gone by, or like a watch in the night' according to the New International Version of the Bible. If you read the verse in the Contemporary English Version, it says, "...but a thousand years mean nothing to you! They are merely a day gone by or a few hours in the night.' And the King James Bible renders it as, 'For a thousand years in thy sight are but as yesterday when it is past, and as a watch in the night.'

"Did you also know that our dear brother Peter wrote in 2 Peter 3:8, 'But do not forget this one thing, dear friends: With the Lord a day is like a thousand years, and a thousand years are like a day.'"

Now it was Chris's turn to chime in. "John, does that mean we simply do not know for sure how to measure each of the six days of creation?"

"What we know, Chris, is that we are given a record of what the Lord accomplished in each of the six days of creation. That is not in question. We know that a day to our understanding is measured as approximately twenty-four hours in length, but what is that actually based upon?" said John, looking at each of the boys in turn.

Samuel responded again. "It is based upon the daylight and evening cycles of the sun, John."

"Yes, Samuel, according to our modern-day understanding, a single day is the time it takes for one full rotation of the Earth on its axis, giving us a period of daylight and a period of darkness. In fact, the Bible states very clearly that there were evenings and mornings associated with each of the respective days of creation it describes," said John. "So am I absolutely sure that each of the days is twenty-four hours long?"

"No, John, not necessarily," said Chris.

"Why ever would you say that, Chris?" returned John, smiling.

Chris replied, "Because the sun as described in the Genesis account is only first mentioned on the fourth day." He scrambled to pick up the open Bible before him and turn to the Genesis account. Reading from Genesis 1, verses 14–19, he read aloud the Bible passage:

"And God said, 'Let there be lights in the expanse of the sky to separate the day from the night, and let them serve as signs to mark seasons and days and years, and let them be lights in the expanse of the sky to give light on the earth.' And it was so. God made two great lights—the greater light to govern the day and the lesser light to govern the night. He also made the stars. God set them in the expanse of the sky to give light on the earth, to govern the day and the night, and to separate light from darkness. And God saw that it was good. And there was evening, and there was morning—the fourth day."

"Thank you, Chris. That was the right thing to do if you're are going to reckon what the Word is saying—go to it and read it!"

"But, John," Samuel asked, "dear God created day and night on the first day too, didn't He?"

"Yes, he did, Sam. So what does that tell us about the days?" John asked.

"It says that they may not be tuned to twenty-four hours cycles of the Earth's rotation," said Chris.

"Yes, but it also doesn't say that it is *not* tuned to twenty-four hour cycles either," replied John. "Remember, we must be careful about reading things in to what the Scripture is saying in addition to not reading what it says in the first place!"

"So where does that leave us about the Earth's age being 4.55 billion years old or about 6,000 years old?" asked Samuel.

"Well, that is a very good question. It is a question that has a very elaborate answer as well," said John. "Since the Lord's Crucifixion and Resurrection, after the church was established on the Day of Pentecost, it might be fair to say that most Christians did not involve themselves in academic discourse about natural science. Academic discussion at that time centered on demonstrating that dear Jesus was the Messiah as was predicted in the Holy Scriptures. Instead, I believe an honest study will determine that the early Christians were rather firstly concerned about fulfilling the Great Commission and spreading the Gospel among the nations, all the while struggling in various hostile environments to stay alive. When we get to the time of Augustine, however, born in AD 354, the philosophical exposition of the Bible had now gotten underway. Examining the Genesis account, he came up with something very different indeed. According to Dr. Davis A. Young in his book *Christianity and the Age of the Earth*, 'Augustine initiated the view that the first three days were not ordinary days. He said that these days could not have been ordinary days because they were not marked by the rising and setting of the sun.' Davis went on to quote Augustine as having written, 'What kind of days these were is difficult or impossible to conceive.'

According to Davis, Augustine maintained that the events described in the first two verses of the Bible were not a part of the six days. In other words, Augustine's own writing actually allowed for an Earth much older than six thousand years!

"Now through the years, different ideas emerged from the study of the Scriptures by different people at different times. In fact, as scientific investigation and discovery began to take hold in the world, paradigm-shifting ideas also began to emerge. The point to remember is that we are concerned about the ideas of Christians within the church and their ideas about what the Word of God was actually saying."

Samuel and Chris both looked at John seriously until Samuel broke the silence.

"So, John, what is the right view of a Christian today? Did I have it right or wrong when Mr. Allen got so angry at me?"

"The funny thing was, Samuel, you weren't even making a claim about the age of the Earth as I recall. Your concern was that he had utterly condemned the big bang theory as blasphemy, thus rendering you a blasphemer! In fact, the wider implication was that all scientific work, discoveries, and theories of any field which do not maintain the literal six-day-creation event and relatively short history of the Earth are worthless, sinful, and evil," said John.

"That's exactly what I felt, John, but couldn't put into words," replied Sam.

"So what do most Christians believe today, John?" asked Chris. "And what's acceptable?"

"Well, since that is the core question of the debate," John said. "I can tell you that today, generally, most views fall into one of three camps. These are the 24-Hour View, the Day Age View, and the Framework View. Each of these were summarized by David G. Hagopian in the introduction to a book titled *The Genesis Debate* in 2001. According to Hagopian, 'The 24-hour view holds that God created the universe and all life in six sequential natural days marked by evenings and mornings. According to this view, God created the universe and all life in approximately 144 hours and in the sequence presented in Genesis 1.' The team of authors defending this view included J. Ligon Duncan III and David W. Hall.

"Hagopian defined the 'day-age view' as related by Hugh Ross and Gleason L. Archer as agreeing 'with the 24-hour view that the events recorded in Genesis 1 are sequential. The day-age view, however, parts company with the 24-hour view regarding the length of the creation days. According to the day-age view, God did not create the universe and all life in six 24-hour days but in six sequential ages of unspecified, though finite, duration.'

"Finally, Hagopian describes the framework view as holding 'that the days of Genesis form a figurative framework in which the divine works of a creation are narrated in a topical, rather than sequential, order.' This view presented by Lee Irons in consultation with Meredith G. Kline 'holds that the picture of God completing His work of creation in six days and resting on the seventh was not intended to reveal the sequence or duration of creation, but to proclaim an eschatological theology of creation.'

"In fact, six proponents of each of these views came together to collaborate on the book where the two proponents of each of the views collaborated on a summary of their respective view, critiqued the collaborative summaries of each of the other views (while theirs was also critiqued), and, in the case of all three teams, each team finally responded to the critiques presented to them of their own view by the other teams."

"Now that seems like a pretty fair arrangement!" said Sam. "Were they all Christians writing?"

"Well, that's the encouraging news about this volume boys, because *all* of the participants were described in the foreword of the book written by Norman Geisler, as each holding a 'a high view of Scripture affirming both the infallibility and inerrancy of Holy Writ.' Geisler goes on to state something very basic that we must make sure we bring out in our debate, 'the creation-day debate is not over the *inspiration* of the Bible, but over its *interpretation*. Each participant holds firmly to the full inspiration of Scripture.'"

"But we do hold to that, John!" cried Chris. "It has never been about doubting the inspiration of the Scripture!"

"I know that, Chris. Both you and Sam made that very clear to me on the first days of meeting together for our preparation for the debate," said John. "All I'm doing is reminding you that neither you nor Mr. Allen can look at the other and cry 'Heathen!' or some such colorful term."

Both boys giggled at this.

"And that brings me to the second point that Mr. Geisler made. In his words, 'At best, the creation-day debate is not one of evangelical *authenticity* but of evangelical *consistency*.' He goes on to reaffirm this by saying that 'the maximum charge that should be leveled by one proponent against another is that his view is not consistent with Scripture or the facts of nature, not that it is unorthodox.' Does this make sense to you, boys?"

"Yes, John, we're talking about looking for a best-fit interpretation, right?" asked Samuel.

"Exactly right, Sam! We are interested in spending our lifetimes as Christians examining all things in order to find the truth. Our faith will only be enhanced by Truth and can never really be threatened. But believe me again when I tell you, searching for and living by the truth is a lifetime vocation. We will spend our lives doing this and constantly be fine-tuning our understanding of many things on many levels. Our faith in Christ is based upon the acceptance of the Truth of the Gospel, which God will enable you to see if you are willing to see. Once saved, always saved. However, be careful to remember this. Once saved, we must constantly work toward evangelism that will bring others to salvation, including ministering to them in effective ways so that they do make a good decision for Christ Jesus... If we are not mindful of our particular witnessing to an individual..."

"Then he or she may never see the light from where he or she is standing!" said Sam.

"Very good, Sam! We must do our utmost to give an honest seeker a chance to accept Christ," replied John. "If we fail to reach them meaningfully, then there may not come another opportunity for them later."

Now it was Chris who contributed, "And that would be the real tragedy, John. How many scientists will not be saved if we aren't thinking about their personal points of view or difficulties with an interpretation of Genesis which they feel they cannot accept let alone entertain and which may not even be correct!"

"And that will be the lesson for everyone who partakes of our debate!"

Suddenly, the boys and John now moved forward with an appreciation of their personal responsibilities in the debate before them. They didn't want to "force" their own views on anyone in the church any longer, but at the same time they insisted on the right to pursue their own personal investigation of the truth *based upon* what was revealed in Scripture as so many others had, with different results. And they realized that whatever conclusions that they each personally arrived at would affect the way each would present the Gospel to individuals they would encounter in all walks of life in a dying world.

CHAPTER 19

SAMUEL TALKS WITH CHRIS ON THE PHONE ABOUT THEIR MYSTERIOUS NEIGHBOR, JOHN

It was already pretty late, just before Samuel's bedtime. He asked his mother if he could call Chris to ask him something quickly before he went to sleep, but she refused at first. After seeing the earnest look on her son's face however, she made the call herself, explaining to Christopher's father that it was to settle Samuel down for the evening, and probably in conjunction with this, Christopher as well. Chris's father laughed in agreement and then put his son on the phone with Samuel.

"Hi, Chris," began Sam. "I just wanted to ask you about something before I went to sleep."

"Sure, Sam, go ahead," his young friend replied.

"Well, I don't know how to tell you this, but the other day I saw something over at John's store that I think was a miracle," said Sam.

"What kind of miracle, Sam?" replied his friend.

"A very big one, Chris, which I might not believe if I didn't see it myself!" said Sam excitedly.

"What did you see?"

"Melinda had drowned in the lake, and she couldn't be revived by her mother," Sam went on.

"Oh, Sam, that can't be… I just saw her this afternoon when my mother was driving us home!"

"Yes, you only saw her because John raised her from the dead."

"What?" asked Chris incredulously.

"Please believe me, Chris, I saw him pray to God after he sent her mother up to the roadside to direct the ambulance when it got there. He then took her by the hand, and she got up!"

"Are you serious?"

"Yes, Chris. I wanted to share it with you because I am wondering if John is an angel."

"An angel?" asked Chris. "Why not just a disciple in the present day?"

"What do you mean?" asked Samuel honestly.

"Well, I don't recall stories of angels raising people from the dead in the Bible, but only of faithful followers of the Lord who did that. But now that I think about it, I think of John as a faithful follower of the Lord."

"Well, I suppose I can ask Pastor Greg tomorrow. I have an appointment with him at the church, but I just wanted to let you know what I saw just in case other people find out first."

"Well, thanks, good buddy! That sure is cool news! I got to go now, but I hope to see you tomorrow."

"Good night, Chris!" Samuel hung up but now felt satisfied that he had shared an essential bit of news with his friend. After all they were partners in the faith and in the truth. And this truth was very big truth, which because of the current situation, he didn't feel comfortable keeping to himself!

CHAPTER 20

SAMUEL HAS A MEETING
WITH THE PASTOR

"So, Sam, how's the preparation for the debate going?" inquired the kindly pastor.

"Fine, Pastor," Samuel replied.

"I understand you wanted to see me. So what's on your mind, young man?" the pastor continued.

To this Samuel responded, "Well, Pastor, I was just wondering if you ever have seen an angel?"

Not expecting this at all, the pastor looked down at Samuel, still smiling, but with his eyebrows arching in response as he said, "Excuse me, Samuel?"

"I want to know if you have ever seen one of dear God's angels," Sam further clarified.

"Well, if I have, Samuel, it is possible that I wouldn't have realized it at the time of the actual visit."

"Why not?" responded the boy.

"Because as the Bible says in Hebrews 13:2, 'Be not forgetful to entertain strangers: for thereby some have entertained angels unawares.'" He paused for a moment and then asked Samuel, "Do you think you have been visited by one?"

Samuel looked back at him squarely and said, "I don't know, Pastor. Dear God blessed me to see a miracle, and I was wondering if an angel can do a miracle."

"You witnessed a miracle, Samuel?" asked the pastor, truly interested in what Samuel was saying.

"Yes, sir," replied the boy.

"You say that so certainly, Samuel. I believe you, but so many people I have counseled over the years when they come to talk with me about something they have seen usually have great questions about exactly what they were reporting!" He paused. "Can you tell me what it was that you saw?"

"Well, at first, Pastor, I didn't want to tell anybody about it until I could think about the reason that dear God blessed me to witness it." He paused and thought. "I thought that dear Jesus sometimes didn't seem to want people openly talking about things after He had done something great for them. Because of that, I wasn't even sure what my responsibility would be," Samuel replied. Before the pastor could say anything, Samuel continued his response. "But I also believe in my heart that dear God would let me ask you about anything this important!"

At this Pastor Gregg genuinely smiled. "Thank you for your confidence, Samuel! But most importantly, I thank dear God for His allowing me in on this confidence."

"I'm glad to be here, Pastor. When I went to John's house three days ago, I arrived and saw that little Melinda Ortega had drowned in the lake—"

"What, Samuel?!" the pastor interrupted.

"Oh, you don't have to worry, Pastor. Melinda is fine now," Samuel quickly added.

"Well, I'm glad to hear that!" said the pastor as he sighed. "I guess she gave everyone there a scare but was able to be revived by CPR or something?"

"Oh no, Pastor, Melinda was definitely dead. Mrs. Ortega was not able to bring her back with CPR, and John called the ambulance," explained the boy.

Now Pastor Gregg felt a combination of anxiety and concern welling up inside of him, as well as something else that was hard for him to put his finger on. All he was able to do then was prod the boy on for the rest of the testimony. "Please continue, Samuel."

"When John asked Mrs. Ortega to go up to the top of the driveway to make sure the ambulance could get to where Melinda was, as soon as he was alone with Melinda, I heard him pray," continued Sam. "After he prayed, he thanked dear God. Then he took Melinda by the hand and said something to her. She then opened her eyes and got up!" Sam took a breath. "I first wondered if John might be an angel, Pastor, but my friend Chris said that he only knew of faithful followers of the Lord who did that in the Bible—and we both believe that John is a faithful follower of the Lord."

Pastor Gregg could barely contain himself! He now had so many questions, but yet wanted to make sure he carried himself with the right measure of dignity that the scene in which he found himself demanded. "Did you hear what he said to Melinda, Samuel?"

"Oh yeah, it sounded like *Talitha kome*," replied the young boy.

At this, inwardly, the pastor gasped. He recognized the Aramaic term used in the fifth chapter of Mark. The funny thing about it was that this passage always called his attention to itself whenever he read it, even for the first time as a teenager. Even the previous day he had mused about this event when he was preparing a list of notes for the next Sunday sermon! Incredible timing or dear God's economy? He smiled again as he realized that John Barzeb's own reference to the Lord as "dear God" was becoming his own natural reference to the Almighty. Now he just wanted time to sort this out completely for himself. Fortunately, Samuel was still there so he could perhaps get some more information connected to this event to facilitate his complete understanding.

"Samuel," Pastor asked the boy, "did John see you there?"

"Oh no, Pastor," replied Sam. "I was lying down on the ground ever since I had come around the back of his house and saw Melinda laying there dead. I don't think he saw me, but then why did he pray out loud, I wonder."

"That also is a good question, Samuel." He paused. "Anything else?"

To that Samuel said, "I guess not. I was just wondering if John might actually be an angel?"

"Well, Samuel," began the pastor, "I believe you were definitely blessed to have been witness to a real miracle, but my sense of angels is that they play more of a subtle role in their duties when they are performing them on Earth. I tend to regard them as making their presence known in more 'fleeting' ways, and I've had the pleasure of knowing John for going on two decades." The pastor paused. "But who's to say for sure. Maybe he's a special kind of angel. Keep contemplating what you saw in your heart and ask dear God for clarity and understanding."

This made sense to Samuel. "Thanks, Pastor. I now feel better about it inside. But I will ask the Lord for clarity and understanding like you say. Thanks so much for listening, Pastor Gregg!"

"You're welcome. I guess that's all then, Sam?" asked Pastor Gregg.

"I also have the name of the lake where John grew up," said Samuel.

"Yes?"

"The lake where John grew up is Lake Genesareth. I looked it up and it could be in Oakland County, Michigan, or in Ontario Canada. There was another reference for it in the *Catholic Encyclopedia* referring to the Sea of Galilee also, but I figured that one might just be a bit too far away!"

Upon hearing this last geographic location, Pastor Gregg took a breath and paused again. He'd have much to think about this evening himself for sure. All he could blurt out to young Samuel was, "Very interesting, Samuel, but let's not rule anything out too soon. Any other details you can tell me about with respect what you've learned about our friend?"

"Not that I can think of at the moment…oh, wait…there is one other detail that I heard and that I really don't understand," said Sam.

"And what is that, Sam?"

"John said that he had a stepmother and a mother."

"Why is that so strange, Samuel? I can think of quite a few instances where that is true."

"Yes, Pastor, but he said that his parents were not divorced and were still living together in a different place. John said that she was a very special woman whom his dearest friend had asked him to watch after when he no longer could."

This also caused Pastor Greg to pause and even close his eyes for a moment.

Concerned, Samuel asked, "Pastor Greg, are you okay?"

"Oh yes, Samuel, but I believe the Lord is ministering to my heart even as we've been speaking to each other."

"Really, Pastor? That is so cool!" replied Sam.

"In fact, just in the last few minutes I have gotten some wonderful ideas which are already blessing this church and the ministry here," said the pastor, this time appearing more at ease and smiling. "In fact, I think I'll spend some time following up with a little research now."

"Okay, Pastor Greg. I hope to see you again soon!"

"Until next time then, my young friend!" said the pastor.

CHAPTER 21

ALONE WITH HIS THOUGHTS, PASTOR GREGG IN CONTEMPLATION

Pastor Greg placed his Bible directly in front of him on his desk and then turned in his chair and turned on his computer. Young Samuel had given him many things to think about and more than one meaningful clue about John's background. Pastor Greg had known John for nearly fifteen years he reckoned, and he had been actively involved in the church ministries there at Grace Church. He was well-liked and always involving himself in helping people, usually at critical times in their lives he now recalled.

This business with Mr. Allen at first seemed so uncharacteristic of John; but after considering the discussion that had gone on in the very office he was now sitting in between John, Mr. Allen, and himself, he felt a sort of peace in the new communal direction that John had literally put them on. At the same time, if he was being honest with himself, the pastor felt a strange wonder over what he learned about John at that very first meeting. He was much older than he appeared, had lived with the personal agony of a martyred brother, and that he was a practiced Hebrew scholar. The other stunning thing was that he handled the Scriptures with a scholarly facility when it came to reviewing problems in the church community and where an appropriate reference could be found for remedy and direction.

Personally, he also had been privately concerned with the numbers of young people not returning to the church after beginning studies at university. John had been absolutely correct in that observation. At the same time Pastor Greg would not compromise his genuine faith in the Word of God and offer to "compromise" on so-called scientific details that he truly believed in his heart were misleading just so he could stem the tide of shrinking membership! Real ministry had to be more than about numbers after all. He wanted to reach out to them, but really didn't know how to do it.

After that initial meeting, he had explored the Scriptures to which John made reference and, combining these with what he said (and had done with respect to Mr. Allen!), found himself in agreement with the wisdom shared by the fisherman. The fisherman.

And that was just it. Where would a fisherman obtain such knowledge and wise application thereof?

At first, he thought that maybe John had been a pastor who had retired to run a fishing store. But John did not appear to be retired at all. If anything, it would seem that John had come from the actual fishing industry. He still supplied the local market and was even schooled in fishing techniques—exotically old ones, in fact. He appeared to be every bit involved in local commerce as any other business person was. Yet at the same time he had managed to fire up the entire church—and even town—community where people suddenly were interested in the Bible, what it actually said, and how it would ultimately change their church brethren and local population. From the standpoint of the church, he loved the "Berean" atmosphere! He himself was again delving into his first love, and he couldn't be happier. He truly felt that the Lord was directing him now for his own personal growth as well as edification of his church!

Then there was the fact that John was Jewish! How had that escaped his notice in a decade and a half? John was a real Hebrew Christian who had been blessing his church and community for going on two decades!

And now came the report of a miracle! Not merely a healing or rescue from an accident, not that those would be any less formidable testimony of the wonders associated with the man. This miracle involved the raising from the dead of a beautiful little girl whom he personally treasured. *Praise God*, he thought. Then he rephrased himself, *Praise dear God!* Wow, this fisherman could really set an example!

Samuel had shared with him many wonderful details surrounding their mysterious neighbor. The pastor felt an internal obligation to find out more about his familiar but elusive church member.

After scrawling down a quick list of the items he needed to investigate, Pastor Greg began with his usual search engine and typed in the word *talitha*.

CHAPTER *22*

SCIENTIFIC ANALYSIS APPROVED, BUT IS IT LAMENTED FOR STOPPING SHORT OF UNDERSTANDING?

As Chris was reading at the table with Samuel and John, he came across Luke 12:54 through 56 in the New Testament, "He said to the crowd: 'When you see a cloud rising in the west, immediately you say, 'It's going to rain,' and it does. And when the south wind blows, you say, 'It's going to be hot,' and it is. Hypocrites! You know how to interpret the appearance of the earth and the sky. How is it that you don't know how to interpret this present time?"

"John?"

"Yes, Chris?"

"I found a passage in the Bible where the Lord Jesus talked about interpreting the signs of the weather... You think this would indicate that he appreciated science and learning how to use it to live on the Earth most effectively?"

"You mean Luke 12:54–56? Yes, Chris, I think that is an excellent observation! In fact, it is a statement that the Lord gave as a basis of 'common sense' to those holding him up to close scrutiny. In Israel, wind which came from the west blew from the direction of the Mediterranean Sea, but if it was from the south, it came from the desert. People would use this knowledge to do basic weather forecasts!

And see how dear Jesus uses this fact in the point he is making… It is as if He is saying, you can do this one thing well with respect to your understanding of natural law, so why don't you open your minds to other, even more important signs!"

Samuel paused from his own reading to listen to the exchange between John and Christopher and then think about the implications of what was being discussed. He found it fascinating to hear the evidence that the Lord actually seemed to encourage science and logical observation!

"And, Chris," John continued, "you will find where dear Jesus made a similar point in Matthew chapter 16 verses 1 through 3."

Both Chris and Samuel each quickly flipped open Matthew and found the passage:

"The Pharisees and Sadducees came to Jesus and tested him by asking him to show them a sign from heaven. He replied, 'When evening comes, you say, 'It will be fair weather, for the sky is red,' and in the morning, 'Today it will be stormy, for the sky is red and overcast.' You know how to interpret the appearance of the sky, but you cannot interpret the signs of the times. A wicked and adulterous generation looks for a miraculous sign, but none will be given it except the sign of Jonah.' Jesus then left them and went away."

"This one seems to be a little different because it talks about the appearance of the sky rather than the direction of the wind," said Chris.

"Well, the two passages are not the same instance. In Luke, the Lord was speaking to a large crowd, but in Matthew's Gospel, He was speaking to the Pharisees and Sadducees."

"John?" asked Samuel.

"Yes, Samuel?" John replied.

"I see that sometimes in the Bible some things are repeated in the different Gospels, but some things are not," Samuel said. "Why is that?"

"Well, Samuel," John answered, "that's because each writer was blessed by dear God to write according to his own witness, his own experience. Each writer observed, experienced, and was particularly impressed with the Gospel unfolding before him in very special ways unique to their own perception."

"You mean unique to each witness's own perception?" inquired Samuel.

"Yes, Samuel, dear God can train up each one of his children to bring forth something very special according to the child's special walk with the Lord. In the case of His witnesses who wrote the Gospel accounts, they would ultimately write according to His Holy Spirit but would also be able to communicate special characteristics, details, or events which He wanted to emphasize in their respective accounts in order to meet the needs of the listeners who would hear what dear God would say to His people."

"Like spiritual gifts, John?" asked Samuel again.

"Yes, Sam, their observational powers and abilities to clearly recall details we trust were especially enabled by the Holy Spirit to bring us the infallible Word of God. But what I'm emphasizing now is that their own particular backgrounds and their own unique walks with the Lord enabled them to include very special details to which they were especially drawn."

"That is even more amazing, John," Samuel said, dreamy look evident in his eyes. "Can you tell me what are the special details which makes Matthew different from Luke or Mark from John or Matthew from John, you know what I mean?"

"I think I understand what you're asking, Samuel," John replied. "Well, for starters, I suppose we can describe Matthew's Gospel as being directed to the Jewish people, concerned with showing the Lord Jesus as the Holy Messiah promised to come to them from the lineage of King David. Mark, on the other hand, is widely regarded as presenting our Lord and Savior as the Suffering Servant. Luke was a Gentile physician who travelled with Paul. His Gospel account, based upon careful investigation rather than the personal eyewitness testimony of Luke himself, is concerned with showing that the Lord is the Son of Man, beginning his account with the Lord's descent from Adam!" John paused for a moment. "Because Luke was a doctor, he included in his good account medical details which actually have much bearing upon the death of our Lord. In fact, Luke's writing in the New Testament actually includes more medical observations than does the Greek writer Hippocrates!"

"No way!" Samuel exclaimed.

"That's amazing!" said Chris.

"Yes, indeed it does, my young friends!" replied John, smiling now and enjoying the wonder of his young students.

"John, what about the Gospel which has your name?" asked Samuel. "How is this one different from the others?"

John paused for a moment and then began. "Well, Samuel, this last Gospel was written after the others and at a point just prior to the destruction of the Temple in Jerusalem in AD 70. The other Gospels had already been written, and the early church had been establishing their community for years. In fact, there was great hope in Jerusalem among the believers that their example of love in the community would be a powerful witness to their countrymen. And actually, it was."

"So why did John write his testimony if they already had three?" Samuel asked.

"Well, I can give you two reasons, Samuel," John answered. "The first is that the apostles had endeavored to maintain their relationship with the risen Lord. They devoted themselves to witnessing for Him and spent much of their time in prayer. John perceived that it was important to add his testimony to the others to serve as a guide and as a written witness to his verbal testimony. Remember, John was getting older and he wanted to make sure that his witness was written down as a service to dear God to be used as a guide to the young church."

"That makes sense," young Christopher offered. "What was the other reason?"

"The other had to do with the perverse teachings which were beginning to grow up from outside the church. These are collectively known today as the Gnostic 'gospel' teachings, and they seemed devoted to disrupting the initial understanding and testimony of the brethren. In fact, they seem to have been part of a collective effort to disrupt the proclaimed consistency and prophetic fulfillment between the Tanakh and the revelation of Jesus Christ. In fact, some of their leaders even went so far as to say that dear Jesus didn't have a physical body, that he didn't even leave footprints! And, of course, this was in direct contradiction to the Resurrection of the Lord in the flesh! Oh, just the thought of it was enough to make anyone who had witnessed Thomas's experience and proclamation concerning the Lord after that first day of His Resurrection filled with righteous anger."

"John, I love how you do that when you teach us about the Lord," offered Samuel.

"What do you mean, my friend?" queried John.

"Well, you make it seem like you were really there, always making it an extra special experience for me!" Samuel laughed.

At this a horn sounded in the driveway. It was Chris's mother who had come to pick up her son. Their family was heading out to a barbeque that night, and he had to leave the debate preparation a little earlier.

After they said their good-byes to Chris, John continued, "Well, I'm glad my own testimony comes across as a living witness to you! It was always our goal to be effective witnesses for the Lord rather than to establish some kind of creed or new 'religion' as did the Gnostics."

"Our 'goal'?" asked Sam.

"Me, my brother, and a small group of missionaries who years ago became determined to extend the Gospel to the world in the most meaningful ways possible!"

"Your brother James?" asked Sam.

"Yes, my dear brother James," replied John. "He and I wanted to be the most effective missionaries the world would ever see! Actually, just as did our mother hope for us!"

"John, I am truly sorry about your brother. I can't imagine how horrible it must have been to lose him, especially if he was like you, John," offered little Samuel truthfully.

John smiled warmly at this genuine offering of comfort from his young friend. Then still smiling broadly, he said, "Thank you, Samuel, for understanding my feelings. But now on a lighter note, I would like to show you something that I think you will find pretty cool!"

Samuel looked up, again in wonder, but smiling nevertheless. He just knew it would be something good!

CHAPTER 23

JOURNEY TO A NEW PART OF A FAMILIAR HOUSE AND FINDING A TREASURE

Samuel followed behind John as he walked to the garage out in the back. As he brought out a key ring, he turned to Samuel and said, "I noticed that you seem to enjoy cars, Samuel."

Samuel looked up at John and said, "Yes, John, I love cars!"

"What's your favorite car, Sam?" asked John.

"That's easy. The Corvette, John! It's the coolest!"

John smiled and then said with a wink, "I actually already knew that was your favorite, Sam. Your collection of die-cast cars makes that very clear!"

To this Sam replied, "Oh yes, John, the Corvette is my favorite car ever. And there have been so many cool ones since it first came out in 1953!"

"Do you have a favorite year in particular, Samuel?" asked John again.

"Yes, John, I like all of the Corvettes, but my favorite year is a 1969."

"That's the version with the long pretty nose and curvy sides?"

"Yes, John, it actually is very close to the 1968, but it was slightly different in a few ways… It also was the first of the long ones with the word 'Stingray' on its sides."

"I thought that they had used the word 'Stingray' before, Sam?"

"Yes, John, they used the name on the Corvettes from 1963 to 1967 but not as one word, as two words 'Sting' and 'Ray.'"

"You certainly know a lot about Corvettes, young Samuel! Do you know where the styling change came from for the Corvette in 1968, Samuel?"

"I'm sure they were trying to follow one of their prototypes for a new style."

"Right again, Samuel. Have you ever seen a picture of the prototype?"

"No, John, never," replied the boy.

They had stopped in front of the garage door out back and continued talking.

"It was a 1965 prototype show car called the Makoshark II, not to be confused with the Mako Shark from 1961. It was very unique in its bold design with its wavy curves... I bet you can guess the reaction when it was first unveiled to the world beginning in Paris, since they went with it after some slight refinements..."

Samuel was now caught up in the story and essentially forgot where they were standing. Looking up at John, he asked, "Could you show me a picture of it, John?"

John then inserted one of the keys he had on the ring into the lock. He then gave it a turn. Then he pulled on the handle and slid the door to the left side. As he did so, he said to Samuel, "I'll do better than that, Samuel. Samuel, meet the Makoshark II."

Before them was a car hidden by a blue drop cloth. Samuel could see the aggressive but beautiful curved lines showing from under a covering sheet. John walked up to the front of the car, reached out for the edge of the sheet, and pulled.

Samuel's mouth dropped open. Before him was sitting the most beautiful car he had ever seen, Corvette or otherwise! He noticed how similar it appeared to the 1969 shown in the photos he had collected. There was something very exotic about the different spacing of the hidden headlamps as well as a more accentuated curve on either side of the hood bulge than on the 1969 model. On the center rise of the hood were chrome letters and numbers "MARK IV 427."

As John turned on the garage lights, Samuel gasped at the shining finish on the car. It was a deep navy blue on top of the roof and hood, but somehow faded to a light blue before going to light gray along the lower six inches of the body of the car nearest the ground. The entire car was polished to a gleaming shine on every surface. Even the wheels were special, each with three small "shark-like fins" coming off of a raised center cap that rose up from evenly spaced ribs splayed to the edges of the wheels. They appeared to be either chrome or polished aluminum and were very impressive.

"John, that's the most beautiful car I've ever seen!" said Samuel.

"Well, thank you, Samuel!"

"Why do you have it, John?" asked the dreamy-eyed boy.

"It is used as part of a ministry run by somebody I know. I'm keeping it for him until it is needed in the near future," replied John.

"It's used in ministry, John?" asked Samuel incredulously.

"Yes, her name is Ronwyn. She was built to be used primarily to encourage mostly men and young men at first, I suppose. Now she can be used to reach women as well, I'm told. She is a message to people that their own lives are very valuable indeed to God, despite any unfortunate experiences that they may have gone through in their own lives. In fact, they now can be even more useful to the Lord because they have gone through some very tough experiences. She's used as an example to show them how dear God can take anyone who's gone through very difficult times or who in some way became 'worthless' in the world's eyes—in whatever way or for whatever reason—and turn them into a fully functional, extremely valuable, and integral part of a greater cause or vital ministry!"

"Wow, John. Does that mean that she was once—" Samuel stopped.

"Yes, Sam, she was. A total wreck, for that matter, literally destroyed in a one-car accident with a telephone pole after a great many years of neglect. Prior to the wreck she had been abused for years by someone who saw very little intrinsic value in her as she got older. I understand that the previous owner was happy, even relieved to walk away. That's when she was purchased from the insurance company for a few hundred dollars. The people at the insurance company figured that there might only be some residual parts that could be resold for restoration or replacement purposes on other cars. But for all intents and purposes, she was presumed to be too far gone to be restored herself. Now, after all of the special work, modifications, and testing that has been done to her, she is valued conservatively at over one million dollars. She's a rolling allegory for the Lord's redemptive plan for humanity!"

Noticing the wheels, Samuel said to John, "Wow, those wheels are really cool! I love those shark fins in the middle!"

"Those are called 'knock-off' wheels, Samuel… You can unbolt the wheel using only the center piece beneath the three-pronged spinner. They are rare in and of themselves!"

Samuel noticed similar wheels hanging on the wall of the garage. "Hey, John, why do you have extra knock-off wheels for Ronwyn?"

"Well, Samuel, if you look closely, those wheels are not actually authentic knock-off wheels hanging there. They only look like it with a simulated look of a spinner in the center of the hubcap. They actually get bolted on like most any other wheel, instead of through one center point… The mounting positions are simply camouflaged beneath the large hubcap!"

"Oh, I see, John. Why do you have extra wheels anyway?"

"Actually, Sam, they were a gift from someone who was trying to help with the construction. They had found the wheels at a shop down in Florida and thought they would serve well for the ministry project."

"Too bad they couldn't be used at all," replied Sam.

"Oh, I wouldn't say that Sam. I can think of a very vital use for those at the right time and place." John smiled at Samuel as he said this.

Samuel returned the smile and said, "I bet you can, and I bet you will! Is she fast too, John?"

"She's been clocked in the quarter mile at under eleven seconds and her top speed was once estimated at 180 miles per hour," replied John.

"Wow, John!"

Samuel walked over to the driver's door and peered in through the window. He looked at the dashboard and center console and gasped again.

"John!" he exclaimed. "Her control panels seem like they are from the future! She looks like a spaceship cockpit!"

"Why don't you get in and see how she feels, Sam?"

"Really, John?"

"Yes, really, Sam!"

Samuel shyly reached out for the door handle and pushed down the silver metal opener at the top of the door. A smooth click was heard as the door sprung open a few inches simultaneously triggering interior lighting and the roof to begin tilting upward on a hinge toward the top of the back of the passenger compartment. At this the boy squealed with delight! Slowly, he opened the door the rest of the way and could now smell the clean leather interior. Everything was apparently silver-colored leather.

As Sam positioned himself in the driver's seat, he couldn't help but make engine noises as he gripped the beautiful wood-rimmed steering wheel, which made him for some reason think of a speedboat... After a moment he couldn't resist feeding his insatiable curiosity and excitement with a question or two.

"John, what do all of these buttons on the center console do?"

"Why don't you press that first one, and we'll see?"

Samuel reached for the first button and pressed. As his little finger depressed the button, a small mechanical whine was heard as a rear spoiler began to rise out of the back of the car just below the fastback rear window. Samuel turned and got out of the car for a moment to follow John's pointing finger and saw the raised spoiler.

"That is so cool!" he exclaimed.

And so began Sam's introduction to the Makoshark II. After about a solid thirty minutes of inspection, including a trial of the various subsystems with lots of questions and answers, Sam seemed satisfied, at least for the moment. John looked at his watch and asked Sam what time his mother would be coming to pick him up, since he and Chris had both been dropped off that day.

Sam replied, "Oh, she said she would be by at around 5:30 p.m."

John then made a suggestion to Sam. "Why don't you call her and tell her that I'll bring you home this evening?"

"Really, John?" asked Sam. "She doesn't have any problem picking me up."

"Well, unless you don't want a ride home in Ronwyn?" replied the smiling fisherman.

Samuel nearly fainted with glee at the suggestion! At John's suggestion he took his cell phone and made the call home as fast as he could dial! He surely didn't want to risk even giving his mother a fractional chance of her already having started out on the short drive to pick him up! In fact, he did more than that: he told his mother to have his father and sister waiting outside to mark his arrival without telling them exactly why!

John was pleased to see that the boy's enthusiasm and exuberant behavior was always governed by his better decisions to restrain himself for a better result. Pretty impressive for an eight-year-old boy!

When Sam hung up, John asked him just one more thing. "Samuel, would you like another small edition to your collection?"

Samuel looked up at him with inquiring eyes.

From behind his back, John brought forth a small compact box which had a return address on it marked "Mint Models" from "Latham, New York." Samuel excitedly opened the box, but with deliberate movements so that he would not drop it. From inside the box, he then pulled out and unwrapped a beautiful small-scale replica of the Makoshark II in its own clear plastic display box.

The little boy gratefully accepted the gift, saying, "Thank you so much, John! This is now my new favorite for today and all time!"

John smiled back and said to the happy lad, "Just one more thing, Samuel. Do you think that we could we keep this time a secret between us at least until after the debate? Not including your family, of course!"

Samuel replied directly, "Yes, John, of course!" Samuel thought that John probably didn't want to make Christopher feel badly for having missed out on the unveiling of the Makoshark II. *How considerate of John*, he thought.

Gripping his new prize with special care, Samuel got into the car and left with John, smiling all the way home! The only pause came when Officer Raymond Jackson waved at them and gave a big thumbs-up as they headed through town. John pulled the Corvette over to the side and greeted the kindly officer, saying, "Well, Raymond, I think we've got a future Corvette owner here!"

"Well, I'm delighted to see another car enthusiast with good taste!" said Officer Ray.

Samuel, still ecstatic over the transpiring events, lifted up his miniature and said, "Look, Officer Ray, isn't this the coolest! I especially love the knock-off wheels with the three-prong spinners!" At this he pointed enthusiastically to the miniature rendering on his die-cast replica.

Officer Ray nodded back and said to him, "I've have heard it said that those with class drive fiberglass!"

Samuel nodded enthusiastically, knowing that Corvettes had been one of the few cars made in America that actually had been made out of fiberglass at its very beginning in 1953. Of course, so was the Makoshark II. When they arrived at Samuel's house, his mother and father must have taken a thousand photos of young Samuel and the Corvette, all to be future treasures and the compliments to many stories, Sam was sure.

CHAPTER 24

PASTOR AND JOHN: SETTING UP SOME PRE-DEBATE PROTOCOLS

The pastor looked up from his work at the computer that had gone on for nearly four hours already! Adding this to the fact that it had been many weeks since young Samuel's visit and the pastor had been hard at work many hours each day just trying to get to the bottom of the enigma of his fisherman neighbor.

Was that a knock I heard? thought Pastor Gregg. "Come in," he ventured to say just in case.

To his partial surprise, in walked John Barzeb!

"Hello, John!" the pastor said most enthusiastically. "What can I do for you, my friend?"

John warmly smiled at the pastor and nodded his head just slightly. "Well, Pastor Gregg, I thought we might talk a bit about the protocol of our debate tomorrow evening."

"That would be not only fine, but a good idea to boot!" replied the pastor cheerily.

"Since my two young debaters are as young as they are dedicated and have each come quite a long way in their own spiritual quests of inquiry, I thought that we might modify traditional debating rules in order to facilitate their own presentations as well as give the members of the audience a chance to ask questions," offered John.

"That sounds like it would be to the benefit both of the debaters as well as of the community listening," replied Pastor Greg.

"I also thought that both you and I might be given 'intervening status' to help explain, extend, and summarize the points being made by either side. Certainly, that would be good for Sam and Chris, but I thought Mr. Allen might appreciate it as well," offered John.

"Yes, yes, that also will be good to keep things flowing and make it easier for the participants to communicate freely with less stress on them," agreed the pastor. "Do you have any other good ideas, John?"

"I think that's it for now, Pastor, but I'll let you know if I have anything more to share," replied John, smiling again.

"John, I err, uh?"

"Pastor?"

"John, for the sake of my own spiritual walk, I just wanted to acknowledge all that you are doing and say that I am both honored and thrilled at your involvement here in our church and the community!" said the pastor almost shyly. "I just had a question for you which I now believe could only be answered by you, not including, of course, dear God's intervention."

"Yes, Pastor, please ask me anything you wish," replied John.

"Well, Samuel mentioned to me that your dearest friend asked you to watch over his mother and that you actually refer to her as your stepmother?" asked the pastor.

"Yes, Pastor, that is true," replied John.

"May I ask whether you were able to continue watching over her in your household from that point forward, John?" asked the pastor.

"Well, Pastor Gregg, there was a time when, because of my job, I had to go away on an extended trip of sorts. In that case my only means of contact with my stepmother was written correspondence," answered John. "But others stepped in to look after her needs in my absence."

"Would you say that she is in good hands now?" asked the pastor earnestly.

"Yes, although that was long ago, Pastor Greg. She is well and back with her son," replied John.

"Perchance was that trip you were forced to take somewhere in the Greek islands?" asked the pastor.

"Why, yes, it was. More specifically it was on the island of Patmos," answered John.

"Is it possible that at least some of this correspondence is within the reach of, say, the brethren of the church today?" inquired the pastor.

"I would say that it is within the reach of both the brethren as well as many outside of the church today," answered John again. "But if you really want to know the truth, why don't you take Chuck Missler's good advice and 'read through the Second Epistle of John from *Mary's* perspective, and see what the Spirit confirms to you,'" responded the wise fisherman. "That's really all that I can tell you right now."

Pastor Gregg's breathing was now approaching hyperventilation. "I am indeed familiar with what Dr. Missler has written about that book... Then one more question, please, if I may, John?" asked Pastor Greg.

"Sure, Pastor, like I said before, anything."

"I understand that at one time prior to your friend's passing that you went with your friend and two other associates, one of whom was your brother James and climbed a mountain to witness a grand event which I can only try to imagine. I also know that the other associate who was not your brother also had a younger brother who was not among you. Can you tell me why he was not included, since as I understand things, he was involved with the same ministry from the beginning?" asked the pastor.

"That is a very good question, Pastor, but please be careful not to read too deeply into the lack of Andrew's presence. Remember, that the Lord's ministry included so many people of whom different things were asked and accomplished. Do you remember about my writing about the man born blind?" asked John.

"Yes, in John 9:1–5," replied the pastor quickly.

"Very good, Pastor Gregg." John continued, "'As he went along, he saw a man blind from birth. His disciples asked him, 'Rabbi, who sinned, this man or his parents, that he was born blind?' 'Neither this man nor his parents sinned,' said Jesus, 'but this happened so that the work of God might be displayed in his life. As long as it is day, we must do the work of him who sent me. Night is coming, when no one can work. While I am in the world, I am the light of the world' as recorded in John 9:1–5. Don't think that he was excluded because of something bad he did Pastor.

John continued, "Andrew's not being there should not be taken as a negative factor in his discipleship. So many things were to be accomplished at that time and he was vitally needed elsewhere during that event."

"John," the pastor began hesitantly, "could you tell me how things are going here? If you can…" He then added quickly, "But if you cannot, that's fine. I just am concerned about things in general, and especially the events that led up to the debate."

"Dear Pastor Greg, the Lord knows your heart. Keep following Him closely, as you have been doing, and you will feel his pleasure in all that you do. He appreciates your good service and looks forward to giving you your reward." And with those words, John smiled.

Hardly able to speak, Pastor Greg just managed to get out the words, "Thank you, John, or should I say 'Boanerge'?"

"One of two, my pastor, at your service," John said, again smiling brightly. And with that, he left the office.

Pastor Gregg's face had tears streaming down it.

CHAPTER 25

PRE-DEBATE WITH
FATHER RICHARD

The night of the debate finally arrived. Samuel felt superlatives of excitement and dread simultaneously as his mind alternated between the potential outcomes he could envision. On the one hand, there was the possibility of, hopefully, once and for all, competently proving that what the Bible said did not necessarily exclude what the discoveries and theories of modern astronomy, geology, physics, and science in general were putting out there for all the world to enjoy and consider. On the other hand, however, if they failed to make their points well enough to make a difference in the minds of their listeners, then there might never be another opportunity to state a good case for the scientific witness of the Lord and show how science pointed to Him all throughout His miraculous creation. Oh, that this latter possibility would never happen!

Just as his thoughts were about to compel young Samuel into another terrible episode of self-doubt and vanquished confidence, a knock was heard on the door of the dressing room. Silently, Samuel walked over to the door and opened it. Greeting him was the smiling face of Father Richard from Our Lady of Grace Church a few blocks away from Pastor Greg's church.

Looking up at him, Samuel said, "Hello, Father Richard," making sure to address him with the title Father out of respect.

"Hello, young Samuel!" said the kindly priest. "I wanted to come by and wish you, Chris, and John well tonight!"

"Thank you, Father Richard," said Samuel.

Studying the look on his face, the intuitive priest said, "Are you a little nervous, my young friend?"

Samuel smiled and said, "I guess I am, Father Richard. I don't want to say anything wrong or be disrespectful to our opponents. I kind of feel badly when I think of how people always seem to start taking sides as soon as anything about science is brought up!"

Just then John walked up behind Father Richard and gave the kindly priest a hearty pat on the shoulder.

"Hello, Father Richard" said John. "I'm sure glad you had time to come tonight!"

"I wouldn't miss it for the world, John! Thank you for inviting me," said the father. "I'm so glad you have given people a time to pause and think about what they believe about our Lord and His Word and how science relates to their faith. It's more than about time, I think! And if I know my friend John, your opponents are going to have their hands full this evening!"

John smiled and then said, "Well, to be sure, our goal certainly is to at least try to engage them in several ways they might not have given much thought to before!"

"I'll say, John," replied Father Richard. "If they know their Bible one tenth as well as you do, they would already have PhDs in biblical studies! Add to that your knowledge of natural science and I think the show will be dazzling!"

"Thank you, Father," replied John.

"John knows all about chemistry and quantum physics too," chimed in an excited Christopher, the admiration streaming from his eyes!

"I hope you both are not overestimating me just a tad." John laughed. "Our main hope tonight is to awaken people to connect the dots, to arouse in them an interest in science, study, and an appreciation of the Lord's glorious Creation...to awaken a desire to begin to explore its relationship to the Holy Word of dear God. If they truly believe that dear God created science in addition to the Earth, his footstool, I hope they will use the opportunities that will be made available to them after tonight to continue to explore the connection, examining all the exciting discoveries being reported by scientists nowadays in light of the Scriptures."

"Such a noble ambition, John, I cannot thank you enough for raising this issue. I am planning on a series of homilies in my own church to address these very concerns. Too many of my parishioners have not had their consciousness aroused by such thoughts, and it's high time they started resolving their two distinct notions of faith and science, instead of keeping them in 'separate silos,' so to speak," said Father Richard.

"I see where you are going with this, Father." John smiled. "You want to make sure they confront the evolution issue among others in their own minds with respect to their faith in the Genesis account of the Torah."

"Yes, John," replied the priest. "Not only this, but that they pursue this issue actively in their lives in order to resolve it! Far too many have not tried to figure out what they are willing to believe in light of the claims of a godless beginning by too many atheists masquerading as scientists."

"For the non-Christian left unchecked, I believe that any subconscious animosity toward our Lord will ultimately lead them to risking their own destruction if they seek to separate science from faith in order to confine their concept of 'reality' only to science," added John. "After all, how can one hope to love the Lord and worship Him in spirit and in truth if you regard truth as being separate from the Lord's own account of the truth! Perhaps tonight we'll be able to give those in the audience some pause before accepting such a view, or better yet, a new attitude and direction toward seeking the truth!"

"Amen to that, my friend!" replied the priest. "May the Lord be with you three tonight!"

And with that, the friendly priest turned and hurried to the sanctuary in order to make sure he had a good seat.

John looked at Samuel, noting the puzzled look on his face. "What's the matter, Samuel?"

Samuel looked up and then said, "John, I don't believe in all the same things that I know that the Catholics believe in. It's hard to feel the unity of spirit knowing that we're so different on so many things."

"Hard to feel it or afraid to feel it because you think you are compromising critical beliefs?" asked John. John smiled and then said firmly, "Now hear this, my young friend. Father Richard does indeed have a somewhat different perspective than you or I have about a few things, but he also is our brother in the Lord. Why is this? Because he believes in dear God and in His Son Jesus Christ and in the Gospel message of the Lord coming to Earth to die for our sins, being buried, and then being raised to life on the third day for our justification. This means he is our brother in Christ. Plain and simple."

"But I've heard people say all kinds of things about Catholics and how they believe in the pope as Jesus's representative on Earth and how the wafer and wine during Communion actually become the body and blood of the Lord."

"Samuel, have you yourself looked in to any of these matters to understand why you believe what you believe in and why they believe what they believe in?" replied John.

"Oh no, here we go again!" said Samuel a bit sheepishly.

Smiling, John shook his head slowly from side to side. He then quoted Proverbs 18:13, saying, "Remember what King Solomon gave us: 'He who answers before listening—that is his folly and his shame.' I want you to also remember this one to go with it as well, 'It is not good to have zeal without knowledge, nor to be hasty and miss the way' (Prov. 19:2, NIV). You know they just might have a point to make in each of these matters, Samuel. No matter what they believe outside the Gospel, it's up to us to learn what it is, understand it as the Holy Spirit empowers us to understand it in the light of the Scriptures, and then to decide what we will do about it in our own lives. But if you sense that a brother in the faith has an anointing from the Lord, it is essential that you don't undermine him. Remember what the LORD said in Psalm 105:15, 'Do not touch my anointed ones; do my prophets no harm.'"

"But, John, what if I determine that they really are not believing the right things?" asked Samuel earnestly.

"Samuel, as long as they believe in the Gospel, they will be raised up with us by the Lord. One day we will be able to see much more clearly and know fully just as we will also be fully known ourselves. Don't let an error that does not lead to death destroy a brotherhood or a friendship, especially in the family of Christ...and whatever you do, don't put needless stumbling blocks in the pathways of those who do not yet know the Lord—if in fact you think that they truly do not know him!"

"But John, how did they make so many mistakes?" Samuel continued.

"Samuel, these perceived mistakes you are referring to may be the result of an error on either their part or our parts. As long as the Gospel is intact in their hearts and souls, they will be saved and we will be saved. They can undergo sanctification just as we can."

"But what about the big differences, John?" Chris asked emphatically. "You know the praying to statues and praying to Mary?"

"Chris, it's what I have already said. Investigate the reasons for what they believe and do. Don't you remember the parable of the weeds?" said John.

"Weeds?" queried Chris.

"Yes, it's in Matthew 13, the parable of the vineyard with the weeds that were sown by an enemy."

"Oh yeah, I remember, John," said Samuel.

"What did the Master of the Vineyard say when the workers offered to pull up the weeds?" asked John.

"He forbade them to do it," replied Chris this time.

"Why?" continued John.

"Because some of the good crop would be destroyed in doing that," answered Samuel.

"So why should we pursue vehemently the so-called noncritical doctrinal differences between Christians which do not snuff out the vital Gospel message nor take the church along a path that is truly destructive?"

"I guess then that we shouldn't risk alienating anyone from Christ," answered Samuel.

"*Exactly* and well said, my young friend," replied John happily. "We also don't want to discourage our brethren wherever they may be by coming down hard on them at every turn! My dear young friends, you may be surprised to discover that many times people who argue such 'fine points' may not even be saved themselves. They think they are putting on a good show for the Lord, but still leave themselves out of making any personal decision for Christ and accepting His forgiveness. Worse, they leave themselves out of Christ's inheritance and then risk confusing or preventing others from trying to enter into salvation. If either situation is true, then why should you and I happily feed these peculiar chest-beating sessions? If we strike up discord and someone's soul does not benefit from this, it is of no benefit and a poor use of our time!

"And besides, have you ever considered the possibility that different groups of believers who have so-called doctrinal differences from what you find comfortable in your own faith, but which do not impair the Gospel message, might just also be the beneficiaries of certain people sent to their communities by dear God with special gifts meant to build up the Body of Christ in that particular area of true believers? Let's always be loving, always be careful, and always be vigilant."

"But, John?" shyly continued Samuel.

"Yes, Samuel?" replied John.

"I think I'm only comfortable with what I believe, not that I want to change others from something 'non-critically' different," said the boy.

His friend Christopher was nodding in agreement as soon as he heard it.

"That's only natural, Samuel," said his mentor. "But that is where healthy, respectful discussion comes in. You must seek to dialogue without needlessly forcing the issue into a destructive, argumentative realm and without generating hostility if at all possible. You may just find that this practice might actually start to enhance your own knowledge and faith, not to mention love, as well as their own, making you and those with whom you have contact more faithful followers of the Lord in the long run."

"I'm not sure I fully understand all of these things, John," replied Samuel.

"Okay, as a real-world example, let's say our brother Mr. Allen actually begins to listen to some of the things you have in mind with regard to the big bang theory. He might just actually find during an honest, non-combative discussion that his fears of an anti-biblical viewpoint on your part are actually unwarranted and that the possibility of supporting the biblical account by this theory is actually interesting. Or at least he might soundly determine that you are not an 'enemy' waiting at the gate of the church to destroy the Bible or compromise what it says... In this way, he would potentially become less odious in his rapport with his fellow brothers in the Lord who do not necessarily view things as he does. In other words, his personal walk with the Lord as well as alongside his brothers and sisters in Christ might just improve!"

"Oh, I think I'm starting to get it, John...thanks a million for your patience," replied the boy.

Chris had been listening to the entire exchange and, once it was done, smiled and nodded his head at John.

"Yes, thank you, John," replied Chris. "It really does make total sense when you explain it that way!"

"You're welcome, my young friends!" replied the elder.

John walked to the door and then turned to the boys. "Before we pray for the success of tonight's debate for everyone in the room, regardless of which side 'wins,' I just want to share with you two some things. First, I am so pleased with you boys, your dedication, and how hard you have worked to make this effort for the Lord a success. I am very protective of your following the Lord's leading in each of your own lives and cannot abide someone's thwarting this, whether or not the resolution was well intended." John continued, "As you may well know, my basis for concern is in fact derived from the Bible in Ephesians 6:4 and Colossians 3:21. You can look up the quote in Ephesians, but Colossians 3:21 says, 'Fathers, do not embitter your children, or they will become discouraged.' I don't want either of you to ever have this happen. Please always fight the good fight for the Lord!

"Secondly, although we have a strong position to take to correct and prevent any needless and unfortunate 'embitterment' of the type which Mr. Allen nearly provoked in Samuel, at the same time, we must also be sensitive to Mr. Allen's needs too, regardless of how he acted toward Samuel. In 1 Timothy 5:1, our dear brother Paul told Timothy, 'Do not rebuke an older man harshly, but exhort him as if he were your father.' He further instructed him to 'treat younger men as brothers, older women as mothers, and younger women as sisters, with absolute purity' in 1 Timothy 5:2. Our attitude is vital along with the message we want to share. So please, my good friends, guard yourselves in your witness and in your ways. You each have so much to share to build up and extend the Body of Christ. So let's do it and let's do it well with dear God's help! Now let us pray."

The three bowed their heads and then prayed.

26

THE DEBATE: THE TEAMS, THE RESOLUTION, AND THE INTRODUCTIONS

The sanctuary of the church had already filled up fifteen minutes before the debate was to begin. The upper level toward the back of the room was also filling up and more seats were being brought in behind the last row of the pews on the main floor. It seemed like the whole community was turning out. In a sudden inspiration of thought, Pastor Gregg had advised his technical support staff to make videos of the event available for anyone who wanted to purchase one. That way people could re-watch it, of course, but also any who were unable to make the event or who were not able to be seated because of the very full sanctuary would also be able to see it! Some people might just want to have a record of the debate, possibly using it for future instruction of some type. A sign had been made for interested people to sign up, and for the cost of five dollars, they could have a DVD sent to whatever address they directed.

At last Pastor Greg walked out onto the platform behind the altar where Communion was held during worship. As if on cue, people clapped their hands in greeting. Rather enthusiastically, he thought. That was good, because that is how he himself felt inside. After his experience with John, a feeling of excitement and hopeful expectation seemed to permeate his entire soul, replacing all of the apprehensive feelings that had been building prior to their exchange. He picked up the microphone from its stand, cleared his throat, and said, "Good evening, ladies and gentlemen. We are delighted that you came to share in what we hope will be a truly edifying event for those gathered here tonight. When I say edifying, I mean both for the church and the community together!"

Again more applause erupted from the spectators.

The pastor continued, "Tonight we are going to share in what we hope will be a constructive discussion surrounding the timing of the events of creation recorded in Genesis, the first book of the Bible."

With this came more applause, but this time with a few select shouts of commentary from the gathered spectators. They curiously hailed from different viewpoints.

"Finally, we'll put an end to the apostate path misleading our children in the school system once and for all!"

"Faith and science go hand in hand!"

"Selective Editing ends in a twisted story!"

"Adam didn't hunt dinosaurs"

"The Bible says what it says!"

The pastor signaled for silence. As the crowd quieted down, he stated simply, "Now while I appreciate your excitement, enthusiasm, and commitment to proclaiming the truth, I want to lay down some ground rules here for the benefit of tonight's presentation. First, we are modifying the rules of debate in order to give a better experience to all. We have two young boys and their mentor John Barzeb, a respected Sunday school teacher to our children and young adults here, and we have Mr. Allen, also a Sunday school teacher, to our adults and young couples. I'm Pastor Gregg, I am the local pastor here. None of us, I assure you, is an experienced debater in the usual sense of the word 'debate.' However each of us has strong convictions, nonetheless, and wants to bring our considered points out in full view for all to consider and advise." In a moment of inspiration, he then quickly added, "Perhaps like the Bereans might have reacted to the Apostle Paul so many years ago, to make sure that the Scriptures were upheld in any new teaching they experienced. I assume many of you are pursuing similar sensibilities as well this evening and we want to encourage you here."

"Here, here!" someone shouted, bringing the pastor's attention to the area of the room from which it came.

"Although I encourage you to applaud at the appropriate times," he continued. "That is, when you approve of something after it has been said, I still want you to be respectful so that we may all hear each of the things being said by the actual debaters. There is to be no mocking of any of the speakers here this evening."

At this, there seemed to be some hushed murmurs of agreement.

Continuing, the pastor said, "In order to facilitate each of the presentations to be given, John Barzeb and I have agreed that once the presenter or presenters have finished giving their arguments, we will reserve the right to help clarify the meaning of what was said, up to and including relevant additions to help each of them, as needed, in order to help them communicate each of their respective points of view. After all, each of us have worked with our respective presenters and hopefully have a good idea of what they are trying to convey to you. Of course, they have the right to refute any errors on our parts if they find it necessary!"

At this there was some laughter at various places around the sanctuary.

"Once we have finished any clarifications or additions to the respective arguments of each of the presenters, then we move on to the next session. John and I have agreed to give each side a limit of two questions prior to the rebuttal in the interest of time."

More softened murmurs of agreement were heard.

"After the arguments of each team are presented, we will move onto the rebuttals and summaries by each of the respective teams. After giving them time for rebuttal, we then reserve time for any relevant questions by the presenters first. Depending upon the time, we will not limit this session to two questions. After the presenters finish their inquiry of each other, we invite the audience to present any questions they may have or clarifications they wish to have done by any of our presenters. After this the audience will then vote on whether or not the proposition was in fact proven to them or not, that is whether or not it was carried in the entire interchange of the evening. Your vote is to be recorded on the paper, which each of you were given when you entered the sanctuary. The resolution will either be upheld or refuted by a simple majority of the votes collected."

At this point, there seemed to be no objection from the audience, so the pastor proceeded to ask the Lord to bless the nights proceedings. "And with that, let's pause for a word of prayer. For any who are attending who do not want to pray, we ask you to use your time for silent meditation or thought or whatever brings you into focus. Please, we ask that cell phones be silenced. Since we will be taping the debate, you are welcome to purchase a DVD recording of the event. The disk will then be mailed to whatever address you designate for receipt."

The pastor turned and then said, "Ladies and gentleman, may I introduce to you the debating participants according to their respective side for tonight. Mr. John Barzeb, Mr. Samuel Bodden, and Mr. Christopher Smits, representing the affirmative of the proposition, and Mr. Allen and myself, Pastor Robert Gregg, on the opposition side or 'negative' of the proposition."

The other debate participants now promptly joined Pastor Gregg up on the platform as he called their names and took their positions at the respective alternate sides of the stage to the enthusiastic, welcoming applause of the audience. John, Sam, and Chris were on the left side of the stage while Mr. Allen, and soon Pastor Gregg joining him, would be on the right.

Pastor Gregg continued, "Tonight's proposition or resolution is 'The Use of Science Is an Acceptable Means to Gain a Clearer Understanding of the Biblical Record given in the Book of Genesis.'" As he recited it, Pastor Gregg was deeply grateful that the resolution had finally been worded in a simple, yet effectively worded way, acceptable to both sides.

Now the sanctuary filled with enthusiastic applause again at the announcement of the topic. Suddenly, out of the corner of his eye, Pastor Gregg saw a local newscaster with her equipment team quietly narrating what was about to take place. He turned and began to open his objection when he caught John's eyes looking at him, followed by a very slight shake of his head, no. He smiled, gave him a quick nod in agreement, and then settled back to the matter at hand.

Looking at all of the seated spectators Pastor Gregg continued: "And since we want to examine and understand the Biblical account of Creation according to Genesis, it is most appropriate for us to hear it first. One of our own deacons, Mr. Russo, has volunteered to read the account of Creation for us now. Mr. Russo?"

Mr. Russo a kindly and compassionate church member now stood up and walked up to where the Pastor was standing, his NIV Bible in hand. He opened to the Book of Genesis and began to read:

"In the beginning God created the heavens and the earth. Now the earth was formless and empty, darkness was over the surface of the deep, and the Spirit of God was hovering over the waters.

"And God said, 'Let there be light,' and there was light. God saw that the light was good, and he separated the light from the darkness. God called the light 'day' and the darkness he called 'night.' And there was evening, and there was morning—the first day.

"And God said, 'Let there be an expanse between the waters to separate water from water.' So God made the expanse and separated the water under the expanse from the water above it. And it was so. God called the expanse 'sky.' And there was evening, and there was morning—the second day.

"And God said, 'Let the water under the sky be gathered to one place, and let dry ground appear.' And it was so. God called the dry ground 'land,' and the gathered waters he called 'seas.' And God saw that it was good.

"Then God said, 'Let the land produce vegetation: seed-bearing plants and trees on the land that bear fruit with seed in it, according to their various kinds.' And it was so. The land produced vegetation: plants bearing seed according to their kinds and trees bearing fruit with seed in it according to their kinds. And God saw that it was good. And there was evening, and there was morning—the third day.

"And God said, 'Let there be lights in the expanse of the sky to separate the day from the night, and let them serve as signs to mark seasons and days and years, and let them be lights in the expanse of the sky to give light on the earth.' And it was so. God made two great

145

lights—the greater light to govern the day and the lesser light to govern the night. He also made the stars. God set them in the expanse of the sky to give light on the earth, to govern the day and the night, and to separate light from darkness. And God saw that it was good. And there was evening, and there was morning—the fourth day.

"And God said, 'Let the water teem with living creatures, and let birds fly above the earth across the expanse of the sky.' So God created the great creatures of the sea and every living and moving thing with which the water teems, according to their kinds, and every winged bird according to its kind. And God saw that it was good. God blessed them and said, 'Be fruitful and increase in number and fill the water in the seas, and let the birds increase on the earth.' And there was evening, and there was morning—the fifth day.

"And God said, 'Let the land produce living creatures according to their kinds: livestock, creatures that move along the ground, and the wild animals, each according to its kind.' And it was so. God made the wild animals according to their kinds, the livestock according to their kinds, and all the creatures that move along the ground according to their kinds. And God saw that it was good.

"Then God said, 'Let us make man in our image, in our likeness, and let them rule over the fish of the sea and the birds of the air, over the livestock, over all the earth, and over all the creatures that move along the ground.'

"So God created man in his own image, in the image of God he created him; male and female he created them.

"God blessed them and said to them, 'Be fruitful and increase in number; fill the earth and subdue it. Rule over the fish of the sea and the birds of the air and over every living creature that moves on the ground.'

"Then God said, 'I give you every seed-bearing plant on the face of the whole earth and every tree that has fruit with seed in it. They will be yours for food. And to all the beasts of the earth and all the birds of the air and all the creatures that move on the ground—everything that has the breath of life in it—I give every green plant for food.' And it was so.

"God saw all that he had made, and it was very good. And there was evening, and there was morning—the sixth day."

Pastor Gregg thanked Mr. Russo and then addressed the audience: "And now it is my honor to bring up Mr. John Barzeb to lead us in an opening prayer," he announced and then joined Mr. Allen, sitting next to him in the adjacent chair.

Now it was John who stood up, warmly smiling at the pastor. He walked over to the lectern and picked up the mike from the stand. "Ladies and gentlemen, please stand and join us in a moment of prayer.

"Dear God in Heaven, King of the Universe, Maker of Heaven and Earth, we beseech thee to grant us wisdom in tonight's discussion. We ask this for the presenters and the listeners here tonight, as well as for those who will one day view this presentation at a later time. Please give us each a discerning spirit and proper understanding of your Holy Word so that we may properly glorify your Holy Name in spirit and in truth now and forever as we seek to learn the truth and live by it always. We ask this in the name of our Lord and Savior Jesus Christ. Amen."

John now addressed the audience. "By a flip of the coin, it has been determined that Mr. Allen representing the negative side, will make his presentation first. So let us begin tonight's debate, 'Resolved, The Use of Modern Science Is an Acceptable Means to Gain a Clearer and More Accurate Understanding of the Biblical Record given in the Book of Genesis.' Mr. Allen, sir." And with that said, John, still smiling, gestured to Mr. Allen.

Mr. Allen rose from his chair and, smiling also, walked up to the lectern now moved out to the center of the platform by John. He shook John's hand, after which John promptly sat down next to the boys. Mr. Allen then placed his notes on the lectern, put on his glasses, and then looked out at the audience. Smiling at the crowd, he began with a humorous statement.

"Wow, if I had all of you come over at the time of my harvest, I'd be done in less than a day!"

The audience returned the jovial offering with hearty laughter so that Mr. Allen continued, somewhat feeling more reassured now.

"Let me first say that I have been a Christian now for many years and have trusted in the Bible ever since I first made my decision for Christ. I have been disturbed by the recent trends which seem to ignore what the Bible says about things in general, but especially what it says about how the Lord created the Earth in Genesis. The Good Book says that the Lord created the Earth in six days and also gives details about what was created during each of these six days. It is there in black and white, end of story. Now I can tell you that I work as a farmer, very basic work maybe, but contrary to what many may think, I pay attention to science, to biology, and to genetics in particular. I am not afraid of science at all. It has its place in our world for sure. But it also seems to me, however, that when science is used in the wrong place or is incorrectly used, that suddenly, without any real justification, we are told that the age of the Earth is moved back to billions of years in direct contradiction to what the Scripture actually says. Scientists today seem to tell us every day that the process of evolution created life, so that, therefore, anyone who believes in the Bible and the story in Genesis is primitive and anti-science by implication. They are essentially saying to us all that there is no need for God and that any life we see has simply evolved into its current form from simpler forms in the past as part of a natural process.

"It turns out that this seems to be a shared view by many scientists with regard to the structures we see in the Earth's rocks. And they, the scientists, then give us their extended ages accordingly. But as I see it, the Bible says that with regard to what we experience on the Earth with our own senses, the biological diversity and geology need not require the extended periods of time that is insisted upon by so many of the scientists. Bringing it back to a matter of faith, my position is that the Bible speaks clearly enough without any extra work required on the part of the reader to believe it. In fact, some of the so-called scientific work that has been done has greatly harmed the proper understanding of what it is the Bible is trying to say. If one has faith in the Christian Gospel, one can trust the Bible without the need of additional science to clarify anything. Thank you very much." And with that last thank you, Mr. Allen sat down to hearty applause from the audience.

Now it was Samuel's and Chris's turn. The two boys had agreed that Samuel should lead it off, giving the fact that the original confrontation with Mr. Allen had actually led to the debate in the first place! John was up again and now would be calling Samuel up to give the introduction of their side.

"Thank you, Mr. Allen. And now, we will here from the affirmative side of the proposition, represented by young Mr. Samuel Bodden."

Samuel reached up both of his hands to his collar to make sure his tie was straight as he walked up to the lectern. Silently, he prayed, "Dear God, please help me to do a good job for you tonight. Please help me to remember to say all of the things I can say to help others see your glory. Amen."

After shaking John's hand, Samuel, now alone at the lectern, suddenly felt a calm come over him. He remembered to smile at the audience, and as he looked around to acknowledge the guests in front of him, he noticed little Melinda holding her Mr. Bunny in her lap, seated right next to her mother in the front row. He couldn't help but beam at her. So cute, so beautiful, so *alive*, he thought. And then he snapped his attention back to the task at hand.

"Good evening, ladies and gentlemen," he began. "My name is Samuel Bodden, and I have attended this church all of my life."

There was some amused laughter in the audience, but Samuel forcefully ignored it and proceeded.

"I am a Christian too and have been baptized for more than a year."

Again there was some muted laughter.

"I am up here tonight along with my neighbor John and my best friend Chris not to try to take anything away from the Bible, but to tell you how our love of science and learning things about the universe help us to understand it better and have strong faith in its message of salvation. We have noted that modern science in general gives a particularly consistent view of the Creation account in Genesis."

For some reason now, the countenance of the audience seemed to get more serious and, at the same time, the sanctuary atmosphere grew somewhat more hushed.

Now Samuel began to get even more concentrated in his mind, not really needing his notes in front of him.

"I have always loved learning about the amazing archaeological discoveries and research that has been done about many of the locations and historical periods of the Bible and have seen many forms of evidence which support the exact history recorded in the Bible. The work of Dr. Robert Cornuke alone has revealed so many wonderful things: what appears to be the true location of Mount Sinai, the actual anchor stocks which were cut loose into the sea from the Alexandrian freighter taking the Apostle Paul to Rome just before it was shipwrecked on the Island of Malta, and his more recent evidence presented for the correct locations of both the Jewish Temple in Jerusalem and the correct location of Golgotha, tying together so logically with the Gospel account according to Saint Matthew."

Samuel's use of the word "logically" embedded within the sophisticated wording of his introduction had many in the audience convinced he had been completely coached. Although unknown to Samuel, different parts of the room murmured negative conjecture that Samuel would soon be exposed in the argument and rebuttal parts of the debate. Nevertheless, their attention remained fixed on the message that the boy was trying to convey.

"Modern science also has made great discoveries which also lend support to the biblical record. For centuries so many non-Christian critics of the Bible preferred what was called the 'steady state' theory of the universe or the idea that the universe doesn't change, has always been here, and always will remain as it is. The Bible tells us something much different, that the Earth was created by God out of nothing along with everything else in the universe. And it was stunning to see nearly the entire world accept this fact after John C. Mather's work confirmed the big bang theory, showing that the universe did in fact begin at a single point in time! It was good that he was awarded the Nobel Prize in Physics for this in 2006, for his precise measurements of the cosmic microwave background radiation data collected from a satellite. He works for NASA at the Goddard Space Flight Center.

"The research and findings which good science offers us today really strengthens a Christian's position and does not harm Christianity at all. In fact, it can be said that science can help convince a skeptic that the Bible is an actual true record of events. And after a person is convinced of that, they might just firmly hold that the Gospel is a real message of salvation for those willing to believe it."

And with that, Samuel walked back to his seat and sat down. The audience was strangely silent for a moment and then applauded the young boy's presentation as loudly as they had Mr. Allen's.

CHAPTER 27

THE DEBATE: ARGUMENT, OPPOSITION

Samuel sat down next to Chris and saw his friend smiling at him. Chris whispered very softly, "Good job, Sam!" Sam couldn't help but smile back and knew in his heart that there was still much to go before they made a good case. The moment was then interrupted as both had their attention drawn to Mr. Allen as he made his way up to the lectern for the second time to begin the Argument session of the debate.

"If you go to the 'Answers in Genesis' website, you can find a quote which well summarizes what this debate is all about and the proper response to it. I will quote it now. 'The Bible—the 'history book of the universe'—provides a reliable, eyewitness account of the beginning of all things and can be trusted to tell the truth in all areas it touches on. Therefore, we are able to use it to help us make sense of this present world. When properly understood, the 'evidence' confirms the biblical account.' It seems to me that they here confirm that Genesis is actually an eyewitness account."

Mr. Allen paused allowing his words to sink in to the audience. Then he continued, "I also found on their website another quote, which I also wish to share with you tonight. 'We also desire to train others to develop a biblical worldview, and seek to expose the bankruptcy of evolutionary ideas, and its bedfellow, a 'millions of years old earth (and even older universe).' You see, they even recognize the harm, as do I, of 'reading things' into the record laid out for us so clearly in the Genesis account.

"As I stated before, I am not opposed to science, I simply maintain that it has no place in augmenting or detracting from the Genesis account of the Bible. I would now like to quote to you some of the ideas that have been put forth by Dr. Don DeYoung, physics professor at Grace College in Winona Lake, Indiana, author of twelve books on Bible-science topics. He is also a member of the RATE team of scientists. RATE is an acronym for Radioisotopes and the Age of The Earth. This team took a deep look into the radioactive age dates constantly being drawn upon by those who choose to change what is actually said in the inspired Text of Genesis. In his book *Thousands... Not Billions*, he states that 'the RATE team concludes that there have been episodes of major acceleration of nuclear decay in the past. This intriguing concept is directly related to the biblical, catastrophic view of earth history which Dr. DeYoung accepts. In other words, he has looked into the so-called 'science' behind these old dates and does not believe that they are accurate based upon scientific principles and the evidence in the rock record itself!" Mr. Allen seemed satisfied with having made this point and then moved on.

"In addressing the biblical text, Dr. DeYoung wrote in the 'RATE Conclusions' section that the findings of 'the linguistic studies of Genesis 1:1–2:3 likewise support a recent creation.' In this section he stated that 'research shows that biblical texts may be identified as either narrative or poetry with a high degree of confidence, based upon the Hebrew verb forms used.' After the sections involving the actual creation of the Earth were analyzed, Dr. DeYoung reports that after 'the distributions of finite verbs in the Old Testament narrative and poetic passages were analyzed,' and I quote, 'the Genesis creation story is found to be a narrative account describing literal historical events. This conclusion challenges all efforts to explain away the earlier chapters of Genesis as non-literal poetry, metaphor, or allegory.' And I quote again, 'the research also contradicts the currently popular idea that the Genesis account describes the big bang theory in pre-scientific terms.'

Allen

"You see my concern is that science doesn't need to be present for us to gain any 'truer' understanding than what is presented plainly in black and white. The idea of evolution even attempts to move us away from believing that God was involved in creating anything since, as I already stated, the development of organisms to scientists seems to be declared a natural phenomenon in the Earth. I guess if anyone believes that, they never were a farmer! This man I cited is a scientist and a practiced researcher and college professor. He confirms that nothing more is needed to better understand the biblical narrative. I say that anything that takes us away from the truth of God's Word and is hurtful to the Body of Christ, his church, has *no place* in His church! Thank you very much!" Mr. Allen then returned to his seat amidst some hearty applause from sections of the audience.

John at that moment walked to the lectern and turned to Mr. Allen, now seated, and asked, "Mr. Allen if I may ask you a clarifying question?"

Mr. Allen immediately replied, "Of course, John."

"I am familiar with Dr. DeYoung's book," said John. "His view seems to be a very straightforward and logical alternative explanation of radioactive isotope decay. Do you know if any of the studies he cited were able to focus on any extraterrestrial materials beyond those of the Earth?"

Mr. Allen looked at him quizzically and answered with a question of his own, "Extraterrestrial?"

John replied, "Extraterrestrial, meaning things not found to be a part of the Earth, like moon rocks and meteorites."

"Well, I know his theory applies to the universe, but I am not precisely sure what types of rocks were measured exactly," he answered.

"Well, for the benefit of our session here, let me just point out that in chapter 11 of his book there is a section entitled 'Challenges for the Future.' In the third point under it, he wrote, and I quote, 'the RATE project has been limited in its scope to earth materials.' He goes on to state in that same section that 'the youngest known lunar meteorite, found in Africa's Sahara Desert, is dated at 2.9 billion years by radioisotope methods.' He goes on to cite ages in excess of a billion years for 'meteorites found in Antarctica and elsewhere' and 'which appear to have originated from Mars.' He then states that 'to explain these additional observations, the concept of accelerated decay needs to be extended to include the solar system and space beyond.' In other words, the older ages have so far only been obtained at these 'excessive levels' for these rocks originating from outside of the earth and which also conflict with your own 'proper view' of what the Genesis record is saying." John paused for a moment and then continued, "Would you agree that this 'scientific study' is far from conclusive then as far as the entire universe is concerned?"

Mr. Allen appeared to be somewhat uncomfortable with the question and did not answer right away. After a moment, he gruffly stated, "I guess not since the study was confined to earth materials."

John turned and faced the audience and stated, "Please don't misunderstand me, ladies and gentlemen, Mr. Allen's citation is top-notch. Dr. DeYoung makes a good case for his position. I merely point out that it is a position that has not yet involved analysis of all of the materials it projects are much younger than has been reported by others. I recognize that the rocks of the universe may very well be younger than previously thought by mainstream science. However, I am unwilling to deem it a validated scientific concept at this time."

Now it was the pastor's time to speak up. "But, John, are you in fact conceding that it well may be a young earth and universe that will eventually emerge from such a study?"

"Of course I am, Pastor. I don't even need Dr. DeYoung for that. One of the first straightforward interpretations of the Creation Week is in fact that it was done in six twenty-four-hour days. That still remains a viable conclusion for anyone reading the biblical text. There are others, however, who believe that there may be more to the Creation Week that is not necessarily evident in the plain text, or should I say that may be 'hidden in plain sight' within the text." John paused and looked around. "Before we proceed to the next argument in favor of the resolution, I would also like to ask the boys a quick question of clarification about something that was just mentioned in Mr. Allen's testimony."

"By all means, John," said a curious pastor.

"Thank you, Pastor Greg." He then turned to Samuel and Chris. "Boys, Mr. Allen just remarked something to the effect that 'the idea of evolution even attempts to move us away from believing that God was involved in creating anything, since the development of organisms to many scientists seems to be a natural phenomenon in the Earth.' Is it then true that part of your argument about the age of the earth possibly being much older than the six twenty-four-hour days is only an attempt to find more time to fit creation into an evolutionary framework, explaining how life arose on the planet earth? Are you including within your argument the possibility of a longer time where evolution could then happen?"

Both Samuel and Christopher looked at each other and shook their heads no together and smiled. Chris then answered for them both.

"John, both Samuel and I told you during our weeks of preparation that we reject the explanation of evolutionary change in animal and plant forms on the macro scale, based simply on the great unlikelihood of so many beneficial random mutations needing to come together. We like to say that just because an organism finds itself in an environment that would be easier for them to inhabit with certain adaptations, doesn't mean that suddenly *and randomly* they get the very genetic mutations in their DNA for those very specialized adaptations!"

John then turned back to Mr. Allen and Pastor Gregg and stated, "The boys favor intelligent design over random mutation for explaining any specialized adaptations that an organism gets. In other words, they reject evolutionary theory based upon such unlikelihood. In fact, statistically speaking, we are all agreed that once you assume *random* mutations are behind the various specialized adaptations seen in organisms, you no longer have a means of explaining them since the timing required would be even more time than the 13.7 billion or so years projected by the big bang theory! Just think of how much time would be required for a human eye to 'evolve' with its more than two million working parts, not to mention what the 'competition' would look like in order for these traits to find exclusive expression in people? The only reasonable view in our estimation would be that the Creator gives the organism what it specifically needs in its DNA at the appropriate time. But for our debate tonight, we are *not* including a discussion of evolution. That would be better investigated after a careful reading of Dr. Michael Behe's various publications on the subject.

"So, Mr. Allen, can I assume now that we are clear that the affirmative side of the proposal tonight *does not* include any attempt at justification of the theory of evolution?" asked John. He paused, thought for a moment and then added, "In fact, it never has on our part."

"I suppose so, but I *am* glad that you qualified that, John," replied Mr. Allen. Then he added, "Very glad to hear that indeed."

"We are grateful to you and Pastor Gregg for allowing us to make that clear! Thank you, Mr. Allen. And thank you, Pastor Gregg," said John.

Mr. Allen nodded his head at this as did the pastor.

28

THE DEBATE: ARGUMENT, AFFIRMATIVE

John turned and faced the audience. "And now the Affirmative side will present their argument. We will begin with Mr. Christopher Smits at this time."

Christopher then stepped up to the lectern and began. Christopher now looked out at the audience from the point of view of a presenter.

"Good evening, ladies and gentlemen. John, Samuel and I are here tonight not to specifically argue that the Earth is 4.55 billion years old. What we are trying to do is explain that the biblical text may actually describe events to which modern science can also testify. We go to school to learn how to do reading and math and learn of historical events in our past. We also learn how to reason. And to us, that is what science is really. It isn't a body of knowledge that one memorizes. It is more a process. It is a process of conjecture and testing, observation and record keeping, of analysis and reasoning. Its goal is to establish existing theories of explanation so that we can better understand how things work. It is helpful in developing new drugs to treat diseases, new technologies for cellular phones, and for developing new spaceships to help explore the universe.

"We have found also that it may be helpful in giving us more details about the creation of the universe and the Earth also. At the same time, we have also recently discovered to our surprise that some believe that there is no place for such a reasoning process to be applied to the Creation account in Genesis, even if it affirms it! I think that we can all agree that a good place for us to learn what dear God thinks about the role of good 'scientific' reasoning is on our part would be to turn to the Bible."

Chris then opened the Bible he had brought up with him to the book-marked passage of Luke 12:54 through 56 and read,

"He said to the crowd: 'When you see a cloud rising in the west, immediately you say, 'It's going to rain,' and it does. And when the south wind blows, you say, 'It's going to be hot,' and it is. Hypocrites! You know how to interpret the appearance of the earth and the sky. How is it that you don't know how to interpret this present time?"

"Here the Lord Jesus talked about interpreting the signs of the weather and seems to affirm the good use of reasoning and encourages us to apply it to interpreting the times according to biblical fulfillment...some might just think that this indicates that he appreciated science and learning how to use it in our own lives on a regular basis. In other words, it is as if He is saying, you can do this one thing well with respect to your understanding of natural law, so why don't you open your minds to other, even more important biblical signs!

"Sometimes I think people forget to apply what they know to the new things which come up in their lives. This could be one of the reasons why the Pharisees and the teachers of the law could tell King Herod where the Messiah was to be born, but why too many of them, even with their vast knowledge of Scripture, could not discern that Jesus was the Promised Messiah who paid for their sins on the cross according to prophecy. Thank you very much."

Before the audience could give any applause, John quickly stood up and interjected, "And now Samuel will continue the rest of the presentation of the argument. Samuel?"

Samuel stood up and walked to the lectern. As he and Chris passed each other, their eyes met, and both nodded at each other. Again, Samuel felt a calm coming over him. He put his Bible and papers down on the stand and looked up at the audience. He was delighted to see that Melinda was again looking intently up at him.

He began, "I think most can agree that it is very important to understand exactly what the biblical text is saying in Genesis. Since the original language of the sacred text is ancient Hebrew, it might be helpful to point out some of the discoveries that we have come by in our studying the Genesis account of the Creation Week in the original Hebrew. According to Dr. Philip Moore in his book *The Messiah Conspiracy*, he writes concerning the creation:

> Many scoff at the biblical account of how the world began; however, the Bible does not really make such a simple claim—not to those of us who know the original Hebrew. In fact, there are two words in Hebrew for creation: *bara*; and *asah*. The first means to create something out of nothing—the true meaning of creation! However, the second means to create something from something else, in fact, to reconstruct something already in existence. There is also a third Hebrew word, which is located between creation and reconstruction; *tohu-va-vohu*... This word means 'chaos'; something beautiful and perfect that became obliterated into unorganized chaos... In our English Bibles the word *tohu-va-vohu* is translated as 'without form and void.' So what the Bible is really telling us is that: 'God created the earth and it was good...' in Genesis 1:1, and in Genesis 1:2, that it became *tohu-va-vohu*, which is the Hebrew word for shapeless and void in form, in other words, chaotic."

Samuel looked up at the audience and then said, "Dr. Moore wrote that it was clearly seen that in the time interval between the two biblical verses that a rebellion took place and that this first creation, *bara*, was original and occurred before the *asah*, a second creation described later in the book of Genesis. He believes 'that when Genesis 1:1 tells us that the original creation took place in the hands of God, it was millions of years ago, and in fact, did not include man or the modern life we have on earth today, but rather dinosaurs, mammoths, and other primitive animals."

Immediately, Mr. Allen raised his hand, practically jumping out of his seat! "Excuse me, I have a question if I may?"

John looked over at him and then Pastor Gregg and back to Samuel, who had turned to face him. "Samuel, just one moment, please. Yes, Mr. Allen, please ask your question."

"I've never heard of this before. You're actually talking about time even before the first day of Creation? And who is this Dr. Philip Moore?"

John then interjected, "Well, I can help you with the second question first and then Samuel will answer the first one. Dr. Philip Moore is an expert on ancient Hebrew, a former researcher for Hal Lindsey. He is more importantly a Hebrew Christian who loves our Lord with all of his heart, soul, and mind. He demonstrates a deep appreciation for the fulfillment of the Messiah's first coming in his book *The Messiah Conspiracy* from which Samuel has just drawn his quotes. In fact, many connections that are not common knowledge to Christians with regard to their faith may be found in his book. And as far as the idea of the 'time' before the first Day of Creation according to Genesis is concerned, Samuel?"

Samuel smiled and looked at Mr. Allen. "Yes, sir, well, I want to tell you that this was suggested by St. Augustine who was born in the year 354…" He then quickly picked up one of the papers on the stand and read, "According to Dr. Davis A. Young in his book *Christianity and the Age of the Earth*, he writes that 'Augustine initiated the view that the first three days were not ordinary days. He said that these days could not have been ordinary days because they were not marked by the rising and setting of the sun.' Davis went on to quote Augustine as having written that 'what kind of days these were is difficult or impossible to conceive.' According to Davis, Augustine maintained that the events described in the first two verses of the Bible were not a part of the six days of creation. In other words, Augustine's own writing actually allowed for an Earth much older than six thousand years!"

PAUL M. FEINBERG, PHD

Samuel looked up and saw that both Mr. Allen and Pastor Gregg were staring at him with their eyes wide open.

"Does that answer your question, sir?" asked the boy honestly.

"Yes, I guess… I just had no idea…please continue," said Mr. Allen, a little embarrassed.

Samuel then started to continue, saying, "There are also today other scholars who hold to different views of the events recorded in the Genesis account…"

Mr. Allen's hand shot up again and blurted out "I'm sorry, but I just need to ask one more thing if I may again?"

Now John answered back, "All right, Mr. Allen, we have no objection, but this will be the last time so that Samuel can complete a coherent argument for our audience. May I ask you to state your question?"

"We are here to talk about the account in Genesis according to the actual words in the account. I understand the point made about the ancient Hebrew, but I hope you are not now intending to take us to some wild theories which are not a part of the actual text. Am I right in assuming you will confine your argument to what those words in the sacred text actually mean?" asked the farmer earnestly.

"Well, Samuel? Can you respond to Mr. Allen's question?" asked John.

"Yes, John, I think so," replied Sam. He looked back at Mr. Allen. "Mr. Allen, I was just about to tell our audience about three different sets of scholars who believe in the *unchanging sacred text*. They're views all are concerned with the Sacred Text as a basic foundation of any credible view of the Creation Week and maintain that the words are the inspired Word of God. May I continue now?" asked Samuel.

"Yes, you may. I'm sorry, I just want to keep things on the level," replied Mr. Allen.

"Excuse me, ladies and gentlemen, before Samuel continues," interceded John. "Mr. Allen makes a very good point here, and I wish to underscore another factor which will be key in understanding the case being presented on the affirmative side of the resolution.

162

Samuel and Christopher could one of you summarize your view of the Scriptures for us?"

As if in chorus, both boys said together, "It is the inspired Word of God."

John asked then, "Meaning what?"

Now it was Samuel who spoke. "Meaning it is to be taken extremely seriously." He paused and quickly went through his small collection of papers again. He found the one he was looking for and then continued, "Our Lord said in Matthew 5:18 that 'not the smallest letter, not the least stroke of a pen, will by any means disappear from the Law until everything is accomplished.'"

"So you feel that the actual words are important, boys?" asked John.

Chris now spoke up. "As we always said in our preparation sessions, if anything is found that goes against the biblical text, it is to be discarded."

With this, Mr. Allen seemed to nod his head firmly in agreement and even offered a quick thumbs-up in acknowledgement! Even John seemed impressed, nodding his own head at Mr. Allen.

"Well, then, I think we can let Samuel finish now," said John. "Please continue, Samuel."

"Thank you, John," replied Sam. Sam then took a moment to think, then began, "We are concerned about the ideas of Christians within the church and their ideas about what the Word of God is actually saying to us. Today, most views fall into one of three camps. These are the 24-Hour View, the Day Age View, and the Framework View.

"As I understand it, the 24-hour view holds that God created the universe and all life on earth in six natural days with evenings and mornings, following the precise sequence given in Genesis and taking approximately 144 hours. Scholars who have this view include J. Ligon Duncan III and David W. Hall.

"The Day Age view differs from the 24-Hour View saying that the six days are of unspecified, but finite duration, meaning that we don't know how long they lasted in terms of time measured on a clock or calendar. The scholars who have this view include Hugh

Ross and Gleason L. Archer. Some here might recognize Gleason L. Archer as the author of the book *Encyclopedia of Bible Difficulties*, a book which has brought much scholarly support to those seeking to offer a defense of the faith when they find themselves bombarded with so-called 'higher criticism of the Bible.'"

Sam just happened to turn to look in the direction of Mr. Allen and Pastor Gregg and noticed his last point about 'so-called higher criticism of the Bible' seemed to have drawn approving nods from both Mr. Allen and Pastor Gregg!

"Finally," Sam continued, "there is the framework view which has the view that the days recorded in Genesis actually are used in a figurative framework in which the divine works of creation are given in a topical, rather than a sequential, order. This view was presented by Lee Irons in consultation with Meredith G. Kline. In this view, we have the idea that the account given by dear God of having completed His work of creation in six days and resting on the seventh was not intended to reveal the sequence or duration of creation, but to proclaim what in their view is an 'eschatological theology of creation.'

"So you see, ladies and gentlemen, there are in fact different views held by different Bible-believing, respected Christians. They give us some differences of interpretation to think about, but each view is concerned with the actual words of the Scripture. One of the biggest questions is about the length of each day, especially important because the first three days of the Creation Week, as St. Augustine noticed, apparently do not have the sun to help mark them. Are they still twenty-four hours long? They may be. Or you might remember what Peter wrote in 2 Peter 3:8, 'But do not forget this one thing, dear friends: With the Lord a day is like a thousand years, and a thousand years are like a day.'" Samuel paused, then continued, saying, "In Psalm 90:4 it is also written, 'a thousand years in your sight are like a day that has just gone by, or like a watch in the night' according to the New International Version of the Bible. The point is that these Scriptures do offer at least the possibility of a different interpretation of the time indicated by those seeking the truth.

"Now having shown the biblically-based possibility for a different sense of how to reckon time, how should a Christian insist on one biblical interpretation over another? If a scientific analysis helps us to more clearly understand the Bible by shedding additional light on dear God's Creation, then perhaps it should be welcomed at least for us to think about. Perhaps the scientific understanding might actually give us a better way of understanding the intended meaning of the Words. We believe that dear God created the universe, which includes natural law. We believe He established the natural laws by which things do function and by which we can learn to reason and understand other aspects of His miracle of creation. Perhaps we may actually learn more about what was written in the Bible by gaining a better understanding of dear God's creation and comparing it to the biblical record. Perhaps the scientific method can help move us to uncover even more biblical mysteries not even yet known if we apply it to a study of the Bible itself. This possibility excites us in view of all that we have learned about the Bible and science so far. Thank you very much."

As he finished speaking there was hearty applause all through the auditorium as well as pockets of contemplative silence. Samuel thought he had done the best he was able but stole a quick look at John before walking back to his seat. John intercepted his look and mouthed to him, "Remain for a moment, Samuel."

To this Samuel nodded his compliance. It was in that moment that he saw Pastor Gregg and Mr. Allen in a soft-spoken side-bar conversation that had the look of being "nonhostile" toward what was just presented.

CHAPTER 29

A REST INTERVAL,
A CLARIFICATION, AND A PEP TALK

After a moment, Pastor Gregg then spoke up. "That completes the argument portion of the debate, and we will move on to the rebuttals after a fifteen-minute break."

Immediately, people began to talk animatedly, to walk to the snack counter that had been set up just before the debate began, or to move quickly to the restroom. Soon Samuel noticed that even both Pastor Gregg and Mr. Allen had vanished off the platform to parts unknown.

Once the boys and John had departed the platform themselves, they walked to one of the empty classrooms not far from the sanctuary. After they closed the door, John then looked at his two teammates and said, "Well done, Samuel and Christopher! You both sounded like graduate students defending your master's theses!"

Both boys sheepishly beamed in appreciation of the kind words.

Samuel then asked John, "Why did you ask me to wait a moment, John? We already had reached the limit you set at the beginning for comments and questions."

"Well, really for two reasons. Because I think it is always better to politely wait and be ready for any possible comment or question from the audience," replied John. "If you immediately depart after rendering such a thoughtful presentation, you want to avoid giving the visual appearance that you don't 'own' what you said and will in fact stand by it to defend it. In other words, your body language should remain open, since you want to make the best possible case for the faith that is within you. This is also very important to remember whenever you have the privilege of witnessing to someone. Remember that you could possibly be their only opportunity to hear the Gospel, believe it, and be saved. Therefore, be ready—and patient—to make a case for your faith *and then* to receive any honest questions. If we believe that living by the Truth brings people into the Light, then make sure you stand ready to answer their questions to the best of your ability, helping them along by the grace of dear God with their own discovery of the truth—so that they can live by it and make the right decision to accept the gift of faith offered to them." John paused. "Sorry if I am sounding a little intense now, boys, but time is short, and there are many hidden opportunities here tonight. And, may I say again, you both are doing beautifully!"

Both boys smiled at John, truly feeling acknowledged by their wise mentor.

"It all makes very good sense to me," conceded Samuel.

"And to me too!" added Christopher.

Samuel looked at John and then asked, "What's the second reason you asked me to wait, John?"

John answered the boy with a question of his own. "Did you see the how the pastor and Mr. Allen were reacting to what you presented, Samuel?"

"Yes, I did, John. They seemed open somehow to what we had said."

"Well, you might have missed it otherwise!" said John.

"But how did you know how they would react to it?" asked Sam.

Looking at his watch, John answered, "All in good time, my boy. Now let's have a cold drink and have a little talk about our rebuttal strategy." John moved to the back of the room and produced a thermos of cold lemonade that had been sitting in a red picnic cooler filled with ice.

After pouring out three tall glasses of lemonade and handing one to each of the boys, John offered a brief prayer of thanks and said to the boys, "Okay, the rebuttal now faces us, and I think we need to be very careful of how we challenge, Mr. Allen."

"But how, John?" asked Chris. "He just wants to avoid science altogether and go by Scripture alone… I kind of understand it."

John then replied with a big smile, "Chris, to hear you say that shows me that you are truly striving with Mr. Allen to understand his point of view, which is *so very important* for our church brethren to learn how to do! How can we ever truly claim to love each other if we don't at least try to understand each other?"

"Yes, John, but what about our view. Isn't there any room for it also?" asked Samuel.

"Samuel, if I didn't think that, we wouldn't be here tonight. The point is that we must constantly seek to bridge the gaps we find amongst ourselves as Christians because we are to always love each other as part of a loving church family—as opposed to merely functioning as independent, insensitive, cold, dogmatic, and unapproachable components of some kind of intellectual society. We can have strong views, but if we fail to strive with each other in love, I think we are in direct violation of what the Lord Jesus commanded us to do when he said "love each other" the last time that the disciples were all together with Him before his Crucifixion." He paused, then said, "Just as I recorded it in the fifteenth chapter of John, verse 17!"

Both Samuel and Chris looked quickly at each other in puzzled wonderment at this last statement.

Quickly before the boys could say anything, John continued, "Samuel, you also must live while *always* being true to what you believe. Keep exploring, of course, and keep questing for the truth as it is revealed to you in your Scripture reading and in your life experiences—and in nature. Remember, all these were created by God, and they ultimately do in fact harmonize, even if we cannot see it just now. But also be patient with those real brethren who are at different places in their own journey of faith."

"But, John," Samuel began, "what if they are at a place that you know is not right? Should we then allow them to keep making that mistake?"

John saw the earnestness in the boy's facial intensity.

"Samuel, then you can reach out to them in love and then, if there is no change or response, simply and maybe silently agree in your heart to disagree with them on any point which lies outside the Gospel. Pray for them and yourself so that a resolution can be made. Perhaps it can be made. It is better to preserve the unity of the Body of Christ than to risk it on some non-essential point of contention which lies outside of what is required for salvation. But consider this as well. The truth which you bear witness to, whether or not it is rejected by some of your brethren, should not be suppressed by them either. You may find that you were called to bear additional witness to such things so that others may have an opportunity to hear the Gospel later, if somehow they can relate to you on common ground. In other words, you may open dialogues with others just because of your active witness to other components of the Lord's creation. I urge you both to seize those opportunities, boys! Salvation is just simply too important to not seize opportunities for their sakes!" John smiled again at them and then added, "And I know in my heart that you will both do just fine at it!" John looked at his watch again. The fifteen minutes were almost up. "Well, boys, let's go and do this rebuttal. Do you both feel comfortable with what we prepared?"

"Yes, John," the boys said in chorus.

"Okay, good. I will look for an opportunity to help Mr. Allen realize some things about which we have spoken. It may take our 'rebuttal' in a curious direction for you, but I assure you that it will bear good fruit if it does… Please be ready to chime in with anything either or both of you feel will help make our point in a respectable, loving way. Remember, Mr. Allen's relationship with the church is also vital to its overall health, both today and in the future. Let's make the best case that we can for him and our church family! Agreed?" John smiled again at both of them looking directly into their eyes.

"Agreed!" the boys chirped back to him enthusiastically. Both of them were secretly excited to learn just what "curious direction" might turn out to be.

And out of the room marched the refreshed trio prepared to make their good arguments.

CHAPTER 30

THE DEBATE: FIRST REBUTTAL AND SUMMARY AGAINST THE RESOLUTION

When John, Samuel, and Chris climbed up the platform and took their seats, Mr. Allen already stood at the lectern waiting to begin his rebuttal. The audience quieted, and he began.

"Ladies and gentlemen, tonight I bring forth the simple case that the Bible does not need to be qualified outside of itself by science in order to understand what it means. As I explained before, I am also a man of science, though possibly not a scientist in the usual sense of the word, but I do find it extremely useful to me as a farmer concerned with developing the best yield possible from my land.

"The two young boys and their mentor John have obviously done some very good research and have introduced some very interesting points to be considered. However, I still am not convinced that they really are necessary to find out what the Scripture is teaching us in the first book of the Bible. I am afraid that by including all of these interludes some people may muddy the proper interpretation of the text, distorting the record—in effect twisting it—until they make it read what certain scientists have convinced them it must be saying. Samuel, Chris, and John have made it clear that they have looked into the Scripture very deeply and have cited expertise in order to show that an interpretation of longer time is possibly involved in the

Creation week. Many of the things they presented were new to me, including some of the scholarly support of today. In my own defense, I have cited experts in science who are experts in radioactive age dating and who also believe as I do in an original, normal week of time. And as John acknowledged, they present solid scientific grounding for saying that the account is accurate as it is read in the plain text.

"I also take my view extremely seriously, deriving justification for it from Hebrews 10:23, 'Let us hold unswervingly to the hope we profess, for he who promised is faithful.' I know my Lord is faithful. It is certainly interesting that today certain scientists seem to be trying to make a bridge back to the Bible and faith, but I am most concerned that it is hopefully not a mistaken case alluded to in 2 Timothy 4:3 where the Scripture says, 'For the time will come when men will not put up with sound doctrine. Instead, to suit their own desires, they will gather around them a great number of teachers to say what their itching ears want to hear.' It is my great concern and I want to stand for what is right, and not only for my own good but for the spiritual health of the congregation as well. Thank you very much."

Some very hearty applause was then heard in certain areas of the sanctuary. Mr. Allen waved at the audience and then returned to his seat next to Pastor Gregg. Pastor Gregg immediately got up and took his place at the lectern.

"Ladies and Gentlemen," he began. "We acknowledge the fine research done by Samuel, Chris, and John on the affirmative side of the proposition that 'the use of science is an acceptable means to gain a clearer understanding of the biblical record,' but remain convinced that the biblical record is sufficient by itself for a proper and correct understanding of Creation and all related considerations. In fact, both Mr. Allen and I become very concerned about the addition of commentary by any scientist or biblical commentator, either in favor of or against the 'accuracy' of the Genesis account if it involves an 'interpretation' other than what is obvious in the words themselves. This is for the obvious reasons alluded to by the very appropriate Scripture quotes which Mr. Allen provided in his part of our rebuttal. Yes, there are some very interesting points made by the boys with regard to science and the actual Hebrew words used in the Genesis account. Mr. Allen himself brought up an equally interesting observation from the scientific realm. To be honest with you all"—now Pastor Gregg humorously lowered his voice and cupped a hand to the side of his mouth as if telling the audience a secret—"I am even determined to follow up on many if not all of the points brought up for my own edification."

At this, there was some murmured laughter among the audience. Then Pastor Gregg continued, "But now we still remain of the mind-set that the meaning of the Scripture is plain, it is written in black and white, and needs no augmentation by science to be understood appropriately. As Mr. Allen and I have discussed among ourselves and have seen here tonight in the actual testimonies of our three opponents, we are not in the least concerned about their love for Christ Jesus and His church. We do remain concerned, however, that augmentation of the Genesis account by scientific or any other finding invites misappropriation of the biblical texts by some who seek to destroy the church and replace the Lord God with science substituted in as a 'false god,' on the backhand so to speak. While we hold our opponents in the highest esteem and recognize their own wise views with regard to the theory of evolution and where it leads, this is certainly not the case for too many other individuals in the world. We are convinced this idea alone has resulted in a breakdown of moral absolutes, weakened modern society, and is even pulling apart our educational system here in this country. This insidious influx of apostasy must be guarded against with the highest priority for the health of the church body and for maintaining the strength and power of its witness which must never be adulterated by anyone, well intentioned or not. We therefore hold against the resolution. Mr. Allen and I both thank you for your attention."

The audience applauded Pastor Gregg and Mr. Allen then heartily. Enthusiasm actually seemed concentrated in several places within the sanctuary. Apparently, the negative side of the resolution had been quite convincing to many of the people who had come to observe and take part. No questions were even offered, leaving the impression that no challenges were found to be needed to their side.

CHAPTER 31

FINAL REBUTTAL FOR THE RESOLUTION, SOME LIVELY DISCUSSION, AND TALK ABOUT A GIFT OF DISCERNMENT

Samuel now stood at the lectern before the audience. Melinda stared up at him, tightly holding Mr. Bunny on her lap with a very serious look on her face.

"Ladies and gentleman," Samuel began, "tonight we have presented our case in favor of using science to help us gain an understanding of the Genesis account and hopefully have showed you that there are many individuals within the Lord's church which view scientific procedure as a friendly helper to understand the Bible record or, as some findings show, give us possibly a more insightful depth to our understanding of the truth as it is presented to us in the Scriptures. We recognize that Pastor Gregg and Mr. Allen want to protect the church and keep it free from corruption. We recognize that Pastor Gregg is the author of more than twenty-five articles on scriptural integrity and has made his life a testimony of the Bible's historical accuracy. We understand that a new article is even now being prepared to cover the topic in question tonight."

At this, Pastor Gregg smiled, but his face had on it an expression of "contained wonderment" on it, thought Samuel, noting the man's smile together with raised eyebrows!

Sam continued, "The Bible is not in dispute. Rather, Chris, John, and I have made the case from Scripture itself that the Lord seems to commend the use of scientific understanding in everyday life and seems to be disappointed that such common sense was not used by the Pharisees and experts in the Law when it came to seeing fulfilled prophecy.

"We have shown that the actual ancient Hebrew Words in Genesis may actually involve a scope of time longer than the twenty-four-hour days with which we are familiar and may involve even more time than the six days of Creation once the significance of *all* of the ancient Hebrew words are taken into account. This was seen by Augustine in the fourth century. We have cited Bible-believing Christians who take the Scriptures very seriously and who regarded their interpretation as extremely important for a Christian to adopt—and yet they do not all agree on how the time is to be precisely thought about. Finally, we have seen in our own research for the debate that Robert Jastrow in his book *God and the Astronomers* believed that the big bang theory put forth by Nobel Prize-winning scientist Dr. John Mather is actually what the Bible has been telling us all along.

"There are so many wonderful things which come out of a faithful reading of the Scriptures by those who seek to know the Lord and who want to live by His Truth…"

Just then Mr. Allen interrupted and finished the sentence for Samuel, "But we should not blind them to the Truth by adding needless conjecture…"

"*Excuse me*, Mr. Allen," asked John rather insistently. "And please excuse me also, Samuel. Samuel wasn't yet finished, but this is where I can perhaps lend my contribution to our rebuttal and closing arguments. I would like to ask you a clarification question in order that we may proceed to finish our rebuttal with all completeness. When you say 'needless conjecture,' are you assuming that all Christians must take the view you have supported here tonight in order to be most consistent with the Christian faith?"

"Yes, John, that is exactly what I am 'assuming' here," replied Mr. Allen.

"I see. Then am I correct in assuming that in your view there is no room in the Body of Christ for other, differing individual interpretations of scriptural reading?" asked John earnestly.

"Again, yes, John," replied Mr. Allen.

"But is that view consistent with what our beloved brother Paul the Apostle wrote regarding individual's and their individual views of days and which ones are holy?" asked John.

"I beg your pardon, John?" asked Mr. Allen.

Well, in the fourteenth chapter of the Book of Romans, Fifth verse, the Scripture says, 'One man considers one day more sacred than another; another man considers every day alike. Each one should be fully convinced in his own mind,' but you seem to think that somehow Christians need be identical in their regard for the 'true meaning' behind any Bible verse. Am I right in my assumption here, Mr. Allen?"

"Well, I am not familiar enough with—" He stopped.

John turned his gaze to Pastor Gregg. "Pastor Gregg, perhaps you can help us out here? Is it a correct assumption on the part of Christians today that everyone must be on precisely the same page so to speak with regard to their view of holy days?"

"No, John, the Apostle Paul was very clear on that in the very verse you are quoting. He insisted though that people should view individual days according to what they understand to be correct in accordance with their faith in order to be consistent," replied the pastor. "At the same time, I am not sure how much farther one should go with what the apostle said beyond a Christian's view of days and whether they should be esteemed with special significance."

"At this point, perhaps I can interject one or two examples from the record of the Apostle Paul's ministry, as recorded by Luke and as recorded by Paul himself," John offered.

"Please, John, do so." Noticing the quietness in the sanctuary, the pastor continued, "I think I speak for everybody when I say that you have our undivided attention!"

"Thank you, Pastor," said John before he continued. "In the book of Acts, Luke records at least two instances where the brethren urge Paul to stay with them or at least not to go up to Jerusalem. But

PAUL M. FEINBERG, PHD

this stands in contrast to what we read in the twentieth chapter, twenty-second verse where it was recorded what Paul said when he was at Miletus, 'And now, compelled by the Spirit, I am going to Jerusalem, not knowing what will happen to me there.' Then later, after reaching Tyre, it is recorded in the twenty-first chapter in the fourth verse that after meeting up with the disciples there, that 'through the Spirit they urged Paul not to go on to Jerusalem.' Later still, it is recorded in the same chapter in the twelfth verse, that after hearing a prophet named Agabus in Caesarea that Paul would be bound by the Jews of Jerusalem and handed over to the Gentiles, that 'we and the people there pleaded with Paul not to go up to Jerusalem.' In this case, the members of the Body of Christ acted in love toward Paul, but their urging and pleading was in a different direction than what Paul was actually doing by following the Holy Spirit. In other words, the many members of the church do not necessarily act in unison even when acting in love toward one another. Paul was compelled to follow in his own personal compliance with where he was being led by the Spirit while the brethren acted in love as a church, even urging him through the Spirit in Tyre, as it is written. Members of the Body of Christ, therefore, are not always seen to be acting in one accord. I dare say now that with regard to the church today, its very health may depend on relaxing what might be seen as 'needless rigidity.' And of course, by this, I do *not* mean lax discipline or scholarship!"

"But, John," replied Mr. Allen, "what if the person who is recommending the 'restriction' or 'rigidity' is only well-meaning in his intent for the health of the church?"

"I suppose you mean by that that they are not trying to be needlessly adversarial but only intend their advice for the good of the brethren?" asked John.

"Exactly, John," returned Mr. Allen.

"Well then, let me call your attention to Apollos mentioned in the sixteenth chapter of Acts. Since I know you are a very faithful and disciplined brother, I, without even hesitating, can affirm your confidence in the apostle Paul," replied John.

"You got that right, John!" replied Mr. Allen.

At this the audience laughed a little but still held their undivided attention to the conversation on display for their edification.

"Well, in the twelfth verse of the sixteenth chapter of First Corinthians, Paul writes, 'Now about our brother Apollos: I strongly urged him to go to you with the brothers.' Now Mr. Allen, I dare say that had you been there at the time, you would have probably taken a faithful stance with our brother Paul in this matter?" John said this time with the inflection in his voice, soliciting an answer.

"Yes, John, of course!" said the attentive Mr. Allen.

"Well, as much as I admire your strength of conviction and its undiminishing quality, we read in the remainder of the verse that 'He was quite unwilling to go now, but he will go when he has the opportunity.' I suppose that not only was this 'willfulness' tolerated by the apostle Paul, but that Apollos, not being excommunicated or banished or any such thing, was allowed or at least lovingly tolerated in his different direction, since his visit to the church as a strengthening or contributing member was also affirmed by Paul, but as coming at a later time in accordance with the personal direction of Apollos. So I guess, that the brethren can be seen in our precious Bible to have actually upheld their faith in ways that did not always appear with one accord," concluded John. "Wouldn't you agree?"

"I suppose so, John" said Mr. Allen a little dejectedly.

John smiled with compassion on the man then. "Mr. Allen, that does not mean that I or anyone else find your objections are without a holy foundation. Quite the contrary! Your voice is a crucial part of the dialogue that will keep the members of the Body of Christ on their guard against false teaching! This is critical, especially in these last days!"

Mr. Allen looked at John and considered what he had just said to him. He then simply nodded in acknowledgment.

John then turned to the pastor and said, "Pastor Gregg, do you believe it's possible that people can contribute to the understanding of dear God through their own special gifts?" asked John.

"Of course, John, that is what is behind the idea of spiritual gifts edifying the members of the church body," replied the pastor.

"So then is it possible that a spiritual gift just might include 'discernment' for an individual member and that by this gift, he or she might actually edify the Body of Christ?" asked John.

Thinking of his recent personal meeting with John, the pastor replied, "I have always thought so, John."

"Well then, is it then possible that Samuel and Chris are making a personal, spiritual gift-directed connection here which might in fact edify the entire Body of Christ?" asked John.

"Oh, come on, John! Are you telling us that science is a necessary spiritual add on in order for someone to receive the gift of faith?" interjected Mr. Allen, more forcefully this time.

"Oh, not in order for someone to receive the gift of faith but only that such academic discernment may add to one's experience and knowledge in studying the truth. This, of course, might just help a committed Christian to worship dear God in spirit and in an even greater appreciation of the truth," replied John. "In fact, it may help bring a deeper understanding to various aspects of the faith for their brothers and sisters in Christ where some might even increase what they already know well to a great degree!"

"I can't even imagine how," replied Mr. Allen.

"Well then, perhaps an example is in order?" John paused, then asked, "Mr. Allen, what day of the week did dear Jesus die, actually give his life for us?"

"Good Friday, of course!" replied Mr. Allen immediately. "What does science have to add about this that I already don't know?"

"A careful, thoughtful, and analytical reading of the Scripture, of that which appears in the precise wording of a Scripture passage, might just lead you to change or *enhance* your own conceptualization," replied John. "Such a thoughtful reading of the Scripture by Jack C. Deselms, seems to have done just this for many, I trust in the Body of Christ. In his book *The Great Christian Lie*, he makes a strong case that the Crucifixion took place on a Wednesday!"

"Based upon what?" asked both Pastor Gregg and Mr. Allen together.

"Based upon the Scripture and his knowledge of Jewish holy days is where this assertion derives," replied John.

Before either the pastor or Mr. Allen could reply, John continued his response, "In John 19:31, it is written, 'Now it was the day of Preparation, and the next day was to be a special Sabbath.' What does the verse mean by '*special* Sabbath'?"

Pastor Gregg responded while opening his Bible, "In Leviticus 23:5 the Scripture says, 'The LORD's Passover begins at twilight on the fourteenth day of the first month. On the fifteenth day of that month the LORD's Feast of Unleavened Bread begins; for seven days you must eat bread made without yeast. On the first day hold a sacred assembly and do no regular work.'"

John continued, "Jack Deselms writes simply that 'the Feast of Unleavened Bread was a high Sabbath, and the seventh day (Saturday) was a Sabbath' or what you might think of as a regular Sabbath. In fact, he points out that Matthew 28:1 is a wrong translation. 'Now after the Sabbath' should use the plural word 'Sabbaths'! Yet we know that the visitation to the tomb by Mary of Magdala took place on the first day of the week. This is why we celebrate our Lord's resurrection from the dead on Sunday. But how many days and nights did the Lord say that the Son of Man would be in the earth?" asked John.

Pastor Gregg spoke up again. "In Matthew 12:40, the answer is found, 'For as Jonah was three days and three nights in the belly of a huge fish, so the Son of Man will be three days and three nights in the heart of the earth.'

"So have you ever tried to get three days and three nights from just before Friday sundown, just before the Sabbath began, to early before sunrise on the first day of the week?" asked John.

Both Pastor Gregg and Mr. Allen looked at each other and smiled together. Pastor Gregg responded for them both, "So, John, you're showing us that a discerning Christian has now brought forth a clearer view of what took place?"

"That's exactly what I am trying to show you!" replied John. "And let me ask this, did it affect the Gospel message in any adverse way?"

"No, John, it strengthened the message, I think," replied Mr. Allen.

"So thankfully, by studying the Scripture and what surely probably amounted to reference materials regarding the celebration of the Sabbath, a deep analysis if you will, we have achieved a stronger framework for our understanding! In addition, we can now more effectively answer a skeptic, and better yet, we can now more effectively answer a skeptic's honest questions and help provide an even stronger basis for confidence in our faith for those observing us or possibly even considering accepting their own gift of faith," replied John.

The collective wonderment of the audience at the revelation of these points was beginning to be palpable to everyone in the sanctuary!

John continued, "I am getting the impression that people are starting to see the meaning behind what I am saying here. Ladies and gentlemen, we must never be afraid of knowledge or of living by the truth. In fact, I am firmly convinced that there is a very special message for us from the Lord in the Scripture from John 3:21, 'But whoever lives by the truth comes into the light, so that it may be seen plainly that what he has done has been done through God.' These words of our Lord inform me that I can be coming from a very obscure place indeed. But if I spend my life searching for, learning, and discerning the truth, in whatever starting point of life from which I am beginning, I will come to stand eventually before the Throne of dear Jesus if I always apply everything I learn to my own life and walk. It also means that a particular path of living by truth may actually begin or come through some very strange starting places."

"I'm not sure I am following you there, John," said Mr. Allen.

"Well, let's take a very specific case, Mr. Allen, although I can imagine very different variations on this theme. You have a scientist who is truly hungry to know the truth about dear God. As he studies things about dear God and His revelation, the Bible, he or she might just be in a special position, based upon his or her own research interests and knowledge learned up until that point in time, to appreciate the distinct and miraculous revelation of truth contained within its pages."

"Could you give me an example, John?" asked Mr. Allen.

"Sure, Mr. Allen," said John. "Have you ever heard of the equidistant letter codes discovered in the Bible?"

"I'm afraid not, John," replied Mr. Allen.

John turned toward the audience and briefly explained, "It has been discovered by meticulous research of the biblical texts through computer analyses that certain words will appear beneath the text, so to speak, if you count letters at discreet number intervals as they appear in the text and then put those letters together to see what words might emerge. For example, in his book *Cosmic Codes* Chuck Missler quotes Rabbi Moses Cordevaro of the sixteenth century saying that 'the secrets of the Torah are revealed...in the skipping of letters.' Missler goes on to say that 'In addition to the search for words at varying intervals, there is also the critical aspect of *clustering*: finding related words hidden *together, and in relevant places.*' For example, he goes on to show that beneath the plain text in Genesis 2:9, where dear God gives the trees which have fruit which yields seed as food to man, are encoded the words for all seven edible species of seed-bearing fruit in the Land of Israel as well as twenty-five trees delineated by Old Testament tradition!

"That is extraordinary!" exclaimed Mr. Allen.

"It most certainly is," added Pastor Gregg.

CHAPTER 32

MORE LIVELY DISCUSSION, GAMETRIA, AND A DEFENSE OF THE BIBLE BASED UPON THE VERY WORDS OF MARK

John looked at both Pastor Gregg and Mr. Allen directly and then said smiling, "It gets even more mysterious yet. We find that by studying the Bible closely and, in particular, learning about both the Hebrew and Greek alphabets, that the individual letters of each had numerical values. Gematria is the study of the usage of these values. By applying gametrical analyses today—either with or without a computer—there might just be even more good news to emerge for the Bible student who seems to be constantly bombarded by the claims of so-called higher criticism to discount the Divine Message or claim that it has been critically distorted somehow through the millennia."

Suddenly, John jumped down from the platform without using the stairs and went over to one of the pews.

"Excuse me, sir," he said to the man seated at the end, "would you mind handing me both of those Bibles on the back of the pew?" John thanked the man and then carried them back up to the lectern, this time taking the steps.

Placing the two Bibles on the lectern, John said to the audience as he opened each of them up to the last page of the Gospel according to Mark, "I have here two Bible translations used in many places of Christian worship today. One is the New International Version, or NIV, and the other is the New Living Translation, or NLT." Then taking the NIV first, John stated, "A note appears here in the NIV which states, 'The earliest manuscripts and some other ancient witnesses do not have Mark 16:9–20.' Similarly, the NLT being more subtle gives us two 'versions' for our so-called edification, one termed 'Shorter Ending of Mark' and the other 'Longer Ending of Mark.'"

John looked up and around at the people filling the sanctuary and then over at Pastor Gregg and Mr. Allen. Surprisingly, he now looked over at Samuel and Christopher, who were staring at him open-mouthed with anticipation. Obviously, this was not one of the topics the three had studied together in preparation for the debate.

Then without warning, Pastor Gregg chirped up, raising his hand politely, "Excuse me, John, I just want to say that I have always been bothered by the apparent disclaimer given about the last twelve verses in Mark! If you clear this up for me now, I'll give you my dessert tomorrow night after dinner!"

The audience heartily laughed at the humorous quip but then became intensely silent in waiting for what they sensed and hoped would be a most remarkable response—as had been experienced with the other things already presented.

"That's all right, Pastor Gregg, because I am happy to give everyone here a wonderful dessert for the mind right now to those striving to learn God's Word and who need to be encouraged with regard to its true integrity. First, let us remember what is written about dear God with regard to His Name and His Word in Psalm 138:2,

'I will bow down toward your holy
temple
and will praise your name
for your love and your faithfulness,
for you have exalted above all things
your name and your word.'"

John paused and then prayed aloud, "May dear God bless this to all of us at this time of learning. Amen."

"Well then, it always seems to me a bit disconcerting when someone casts doubt about the integrity of any biblical passage. In this case, I suppose since it's only twelve verses, how many significant problems could possibly arise with one of the Gospel accounts? Not much I suppose—unless you feel strongly about the included topics covered by those twelve verses—namely, the Resurrection, dear Jesus's final instructions, and the Ascension!"

Again the audience erupted in laughter while Pastor Gregg, Mr. Allen, Samuel, and Christopher all shook their heads in disbelief at such obvious nonsense.

John then continued, "Well, once again, I give hearty acclamation and lavish praise to the Koinonia House and to the late Chuck Missler in particular for raising this issue with a satisfying response for those thirsty for the truth! Now I'll leave it to you to look into the details of the history of the usage of the extant Greek manuscripts used for Bible translation and why these passages were claimed to have been added later. But for now, I just would like to add that as Chuck Missler reported in his article 'Additions or Deletions, The Last 12 Verses of Mark' available online at the khouse.org website, 'that Irenaeus in 150 AD and also Hypolytus in the 2nd century, each quote from these disputed verses, so the documentary evidence is that they were *deleted* later in the Alexandrian texts, not added subsequently.' But ladies and gentlemen, there is much more to be said about the authenticity of these verses here."

Rolling up his sleeves for effect, John hunched over the lectern and looked carefully from left to right at the audience as he spoke. "Now Chuck Missler was very thorough in his reporting of the comprehensive analysis that was done. I encourage all of you to go to the Koinonia House website https://www.khouse.org/articles/2000/201/) and read through all of the intricate details. To highlight some of what emerges, let me just say that the number 7 is seen in the Bible to be very unique. In fact, Chuck Missler reported that 'there are over six hundred explicit occurrences of 'sevens' throughout both the Old and New Testaments.' He went on to say that the

'Heptadic' or sevenfold structure found in the Biblical text is 'one of the remarkable characteristics of its authenticity.' In other words, it seems to be a very special number to our Lord. When those twelve verses are examined, some astonishing findings have been announced. Here are eight of them for your personal edification:

1) There are 175 (7 x 25) words in the Greek text of Mark 16:9–20.

2) These words use a total vocabulary of 98 different words (7 x 14).

3) The number of vowels is 294 (7 x 42).

4) The number of consonants is 259 (7 x 37).

5) The vocabulary of those 98 (7 x 14) words include 84 (7 x 12), which are found previously in Mark.

6) Fourteen words of these 12 verses (7 x 2) are found only here.

7) Forty-two (7 x 6) are found in the Lord's address (vv.15–18); 56 (7 x 8) are not part of His vocabulary here

8) Dr. Missler noted that Greek, like Hebrew, has assigned numerical values for each letter of its alphabet. Similarly, each word also has a numerical or 'gametrical' value based on its individual letters. The total numerical value of the passage is 103,656 (7 x 14,808). The value of v.9 is 11,795 (7 x 1,685); v.10 is 5,418 (7 x 774); v.11 is 11,795 (7 x 1,685); vv.12–20, 86,450 (7 x 12,350). In verse 10, the first word is 98 (7 x 14), the middle word is 4,529 (7 x 647), and the last word is 791 (7 x 113). The value of the total word forms is 89,663 (7 x 12,809).

"We can see from this a very definite pattern that defies coincidence! In his book *Cosmic Codes*, Chuck Missler cited these findings as deriving from the work by Dr. Ivan Panin, a Russian-born immigrant who ultimately came to the United States and studied at Harvard University. After graduating in 1892, he converted from agnosticism to Christianity. As Missler put it with regard to these 'numerical properties of the Biblical text,' 'these are not only intriguing to discover, they also demonstrate an intricacy of design which testifies to its supernatural origin!' In fact, he identified 75 heptadic features of the last twelve verses of Mark. If you don't appreciate exactly what that means in terms of design, Missler noted that 'If a supercomputer could be programmed to attempt 400 million attempts/second, working day and night, it would take one million of them over four million years to identify a combination of 7^{34} heptadic features by unaided chance alone.' It was Dr. Missler's considered opinion that these twelve verses demonstrate the Divine Fingerprint in their very existence! I'd like to point out that such scientific approach to studying the Scriptures here is as if the Bereans were here again, applying modern technology to their spiritual endeavors to know and understand dear God's Holy Word! I think it's fair to say that as far as these twelve verses in Mark are concerned, everyone here tonight has a renewed confidence in their being included in the Bible! Thankfully, someone bothered to do the scientific analysis!"

At that point, the audience now erupted with enthusiastic applause at this special form of encouragement!

John did not wait but proceeded to seize the moment. He smiled broadly and raised his arms and spoke. "So you see, my friends, courageous defenders of the faith like Pastor Gregg and Mr. Allen are actually aided in their assertion that the Bible has full integrity! Of course, it does! Their faith and solid standing against any attack is most encouraging and even admirable. But we are only showing everyone here tonight, that the Bible's integrity can actually be brought out in ways unimaginable by such righteous, holy, and committed studies of the Word, the universe, or whatever other work that is done by people living by the truth and which dear God led them to do! None of what we have presented came easily but came instead through the hard work, contemplation, and dedication of those who sought to study the Word or the created universe, and then made their results known. Since dear God is the author of the Bible and the Creator of the universe, should it really be surprising that we will continue to find a complete baseline of harmony between them?"

The audience applauded even more loudly now, if that was possible. Even Pastor Gregg and Mr. Allen could be seen nodding and smiling enthusiastically. Samuel and Chris sat mesmerized, both in awe at John's oration, the only visible difference being that Samuel's cheeks had tears running down them as he now felt fully vindicated in the hope he had maintained in his heart all along.

CHAPTER 33

FINAL REBUTTAL, PROVERBS 25:2, AND THE MENTION OF BOTH A MOVIE AND A SCIENTIST

Everyone was thoroughly amazed and caught up in consideration of these amazing facts. A wondrous murmur had broken out all over the room, and people seemed both enthused and encouraged.

Finally, the attention of everyone in the room became redirected to the debaters when Mr. Allen asked John, "But, John, why would one have to do all of this study to find out these wonderful connections? I mean, doesn't it seem like dear God would want to make these things relatively available to those who love Him and His Word?"

John smiled warmly at hearing Mr. Allen now refer to the Lord as "dear God."

"But, Mr. Allen," John replied most pleasantly, "we mustn't forget Proverbs 25:2, 'It is the glory of God to conceal a matter; to search out a matter is the glory of kings.' As I recall, this was also a favorite of Chuck Missler, who always seemed careful to point out the rewards which always seemed available to the diligent studiers of dear God's Word."

"Yes, indeed, we have heard some amazing things here tonight, John," replied Mr. Allen. "Personally, I must confess a renewed confidence in both the Genesis and Mark accounts by hearing what you had to say about the text itself! I guess my problem has always been more rooted in the rampant scientific disdain for dear God's Word."

"Well, Mr. Allen, I certainly can understand and appreciate that. But you might be interested in knowing something not widely recognized about someone who has been called 'the greatest scientist who ever lived,'" replied John.

"And just who would that be, John?" asked Pastor Gregg.

John now turned again to the audience and said, "I take it that many here have seen the *God Is Not Dead* movies?" he asked.

To this query, a fair amount of positive assent was heard.

"Well, just for anyone who has not seen them, in the first movie an atheist professor is debating with a student over the existence of God and actually holds up a certain scientist's seat at the University of Cambridge, as if the scientist who once held that seat is the ultimate rebuke against belief in God or in Christian faith in particular. That scientist's name is Sir Isaac Newton."

John continued, "The funny thing is, if the professor had only known some of the details about Sir Isaac Newton, what was written about him, and upon what the better part of his writings actually focused, he would not be the person to cite in your defense of atheism..."

The audience laughed gleefully now in expectation of the huge irony that they sensed would now be revealed. Samuel was surprised to spot even Mr. Edmund, his science teacher, sitting in the audience and even shaking his head in anticipation.

"I would like to read you some of the information and certain quotes uncovered by Dr. Philip Moore in his book *The End of History Messiah Conspiracy* with regard to Sir Isaac Newton. Apparently, Newton's own friend, John Craig, writing days after the man's death to John Conduit wrote that Newton himself...

> Was more solicitous in his inquiries into Religion than into Natural Philosophy [science per Phillip Moore]...he had written a long explication of remarkable parts of the Old and New Testament, while his understanding was in its

greatest perfection... But now it is hop'd [sic] that the worthy and ingenious Mr. Conduit will take care that they be publish'd [sic] that the world may see that Sr. Is: Newton was as good a Christian as he was a Mathematician and Philosopher.

"In fact, Dr. Moore goes on to quote Richard H. Popkin of UCLA in *The Books of Nature and Scripture*,

Newton was convinced that God had presented mankind in Scripture with certain most important clues about the future history of humanity. Newton's explorations of the problems involved in uncovering the text and discovering the true meaning of the text was carried on in private in the vast amount of unpublished manuscripts that he drafted for almost sixty years.

"Phillip Moore went on to quote Dr. Popkin further.

Newton's elaborate astronomical argument and his debunking of pagan chronological and historical claims aimed to show that the Bible was accurate in its history... And, assumed Newton, the message in the Bible was still of the greatest importance to mankind. The fact that the Bible was accurate historically meant that God had presented His message from the very beginning of the world through the history of the Hebrews and through the prophetic insights given to them."

John continued, looking around the room as he did so. "It has been noted by Philip Moore that Newton had concluded from his own study that the Jewish people would return to their own land in the twentieth century, but humbly admitted that he did not know by what means. Remember that this great scientist died in 1727!"

John paused then for a moment and then said, "Now after hearing these things, it is rather tragic to hear that when these papers were rediscovered in the twentieth century, it was suggested by one scientist that they be burned! But fortunately for us, another scientist, whose name you just might remember hearing somewhere, was tireless in his efforts to get them properly preserved! Yes, indeed, thankfully Dr. Albert Einstein worked as hard as he did to make sure that this record was preserved for posterity! Today, Newton's papers are available to see at the Hebrew University in Israel! In short, he seems to be hardly the person I would use in a defense of atheism! And from appearances at least, it seems that Albert Einstein also exulted in Newton's biblical studies, observations, and conclusions!"

After John finished, a murmur immediately broke out among the audience, mostly consisting of excited commentary, speculation, and some just plain old amazement! Then after a moment had passed and the murmur had begun to die down a little, another voice was heard above the din.

"I'll concede that there are well-meaning Christians who happen to be scientists, John, but I still think that there certainly are some scientists who do not in fact have our best interests in mind when it comes to the church and her individual members," said Mr. Allen. "And this is what concerns me the most—the deception which some actually seem to seek to foist upon innocent Christians who are open to scientific discovery but who also may be unsuspecting of less noble motives."

"But, Mr. Allen, if you seek to silence scientific learning because of certain scientists, then we miss all the special edification of the type with which we can build the church, or even defend it, of the type we have heard here this evening. And how do you know that certain scientists which contribute in this way haven't been especially chosen by the Lord to serve in this capacity?"

"Well, John, again I am willing to concede that scientists which contribute in a noble way do seem to be especially blessed by the

Lord to help edify the church…but what happens when bad teaching—like godless evolution—permeates through to the point of harming the body of Christ? What do we do then? How should we react?" asked the farmer earnestly.

CHAPTER 34

AN HONEST QUESTION ABOUT PROTECTING THE CHURCH, SPIRITUAL DISCERNMENT, AND HISTORICAL PRECEDENTS

"Mr. Allen," John began, "you ask an honest question now that is near and dear to my heart. You see, this debate tonight is in my mind, an opportunity to reawaken the church to many things, but also an opportunity to warn our brethren to guard against deception!"

At this, both Pastor Gregg and Mr. Allen leaned forward in their seats as if to be able to listen more intently. A corresponding silence also seemed to settle on the audience.

John then continued, "My encouragement to seek the Lord and magnify Him by learning and living by the Truth wherever it is made manifest should never be construed to be an encouragement for us to abandon the faith in the Gospel message. Quite the opposite! In fact, in my earlier years, I found amongst my family in Christ that apostasy was threatening the church by 'putting on sheep's clothing' and presenting itself as if it were an inherent part of the brethren. In reality, it was a vicious wolf, instead of a 'revelation' of inherent truth!"

John paused for a moment and closed his eyes as if dealing with a painful memory. Then he continued.

"Going back almost two millennia and studying the history of the early church, you may conclude that these false notions of Christ, even spurred the writing of the fourth account of the Gospel in order to clarify some of the inherent parts of the Gospel which were not previously recorded and which were needed to be brought into the light in order to counteract the gnostic cult which sought to destroy the early church. Thankfully, one of the twelve was still alive at the time!

"Remember, the Lord warned us not to be deceived! And consider this, what could have possibly happened if one of the prominent members of the church, gifted in hospitality and well-known amongst believers, both established and new, was suddenly perceived as endorsing one of these wolves by virtue of the fact that she or he had allowed them to visit and share with the brethren, not knowing the full extent of their message? This is where hospitality can be abused by those seeking to lure the innocent into destruction. It does not mean that those who offered the hospitality succumbed to such evil seduction, but it does risk the perception that any such contact 'validates' an enemy within the gates!"

John continued, "You may recall a letter written to 'the chosen lady and her children' warning them of the 'many deceivers, who do not acknowledge Jesus Christ as coming in the flesh.'

In fact, I specifically identified them individually by saying that 'any such person is the deceiver and the antichrist.' In retrospect now, I can tell you that it is absolutely essential to maintain such vigilance. However, you may ask, where do we draw the line between welcoming hospitality and hosting such imposters who seek to destroy?"

"Exactly, John," Pastor Gregg spoke up.

"Well, as I have advised in the past, I say again now, 'If anyone comes to you and does not bring this teaching, do not take him into your house or welcome him.' But this applies more when you are able to intercept them at the gate so to speak. Let us always, therefore, remember what our dear brother Paul wrote to the Galatian Church in the first chapter of Galatians in the eighth verse. It is our guide when it comes to keeping the faith in the face of such deception. 'But even if we or an angel from heaven should preach a gospel other than the one we preached to you, let him be eternally condemned!' That is how fiercely we must guard against accepting apostasy, my friends.

Remember what was written in the fourth chapter, in the first three verses of what is called First John, 'Do not believe every spirit, but test the spirits to see whether they are from God... Every spirit that acknowledges that Jesus Christ has come in the flesh is from God, but every spirit that does not acknowledge Jesus is not from God.' There is no other way of being saved except through dear Jesus."

Samuel and Chris looked at each other as they listened to these last few sentences of John's part of the rebuttal. Chris couldn't help whispering to Samuel, "Did you hear, Samuel? John just said that he wrote the letter of 2 John!, 'As I have advised in the past,' and then he follows with an exact quote from the New Testament letter!"

Samuel nodded excitedly and added, "And also where he said he identified the deceivers!"

Chris quickly, earnestly then asked Samuel, "Do you think Pastor Gregg caught it?"

Samuel thought for a moment, then responded, "He probably did, but if somehow he missed it, we can remind him later! I am very happy that they are recording all of this for the DVD!"

Just at that moment, the boys heard John say, "And on that note, I would like to request a ten-minute break to meet with my team!"

Chris leaned over and said to Samuel in a hushed voice, "I wonder if he heard us!"

Samuel responded, "Please, Chris, don't bring it up now!" just in time before John's gaze met his.

Pastor Gregg and Mr. Allen both gave their assent to John's request with good-natured nods, followed by Pastor Gregg's subsequent announcement that there would be a ten-minute interval as the teams paused to meet.

CHAPTER

35

A CAUTION FOR FOCUS AND A REMINDER TO APPLY WHAT WAS ALREADY LEARNED

As the three strode into their 'pre-debate' room once more, both of the boys exchanged glances.

Once the door was closed, John looked at the two boys and smiled. "Boys, we are about to close our argument fully, but I wanted to remind the audience that it is not right to close our minds in fear of learning something new about our world and universe. At the same time, I want to caution them not to simply 'accept' anything they hear blindly if it goes against our core belief…"

"John?" Chris began. "What if one of us has a great idea or discovery or made a connection and we wanted to share it so that it could be clearly understood?"

John looked at him knowingly and studied the faces of both boys. "To what kind of idea or 'discovery' might you be referring?" asked John, his eyes twinkling.

Samuel interrupted, saying, "I think this can wait for now, Chris. We are just about to finish our rebuttal and must make sure everything is understood clearly by everyone listening."

Before Chris could say anything in response, John replied to Sam's statement, "Yes, Samuel is right, Chris. We need to burden ourselves with the task at hand. Hopefully, you'll have a chance to discuss any revelations you've made in a little while. We must now finish the work to which we all have been called.

"John," added Samuel quickly, still concerned about starting a whole side-bar conversation about his references to the second letter of John in the Bible for which he knew that they didn't have time, "how should we tell our listeners here tonight to draw the line on ideas which are unworthy versus those which are worthy?"

"That is how I want to finish, Samuel, with that exact clarification! But I will need your help to get this across!"

"How?" the boys said in near unison.

"Remember our discussion after our brief meeting with Father Richard?" John replied.

"I think I see John what you're saying," said Samuel.

John looked at Chris who was still staring at him like he was more than a little preoccupied with another matter. "Is everything okay, Chris?" asked John.

"I guess I just have my mind on so many things right now and am struggling to concentrate," said Chris.

John responded, "Well, as understandable as that is, my boy, let's still try to focus now on our present task—that is to say, our final closing statements. Remember, we will still be responsible for answering any questions which the audience deems fit for us to answer. It will behoove us to strengthen our resolve to be excellent in this matter! Agreed, boys?"

"Agreed!" they responded firmly!

The three then returned to the platform.

CHAPTER **36**

A Firm foundation of Love, an Urgent Plea, and Various Constructions

Finally, John was back at the lectern. He then began, "Remember, my friends, that we as a church are supposed to be about love. Remember what the Lord told us the second greatest commandment is? To love our neighbors as ourselves. Of course, we still must guard the Gospel resolutely! And as Mr. Allen urged when he quoted from the twenty-third verse of the tenth chapter of Hebrews, 'Let us hold unswervingly to the hope we profess, for he who promised is faithful.' Let us also remember verse twenty-four, 'And let us consider how we may spur one another on toward love and good deeds.' Our Lord's great concern was that we maintain our love for one another as a sign of a healthy church family. Not provoking each other or thwarting each other because of the freedom we have as believers to follow the Holy Spirit as we trust we are being led. We must seek to use our freedom positively and even proactively—especially now! Our love also stands as a witness to those outside the church. And don't ever forget that dear God loves all of the people he created in the world too. Remember also what our dear brother Jude wrote in the twenty-second and twenty-third verses of his letter, encouraging his fellow believers to 'be merciful to those who doubt; snatch others from the fire and save them; to others show mercy, mixed with fear—hating even the clothing stained by corrupted flesh.' But we must remember in our Christian walk that dear Jesus has paid for the sins of nonbelievers too, but unless they accept Him, they will remain unsaved. Therefore, let us do our utmost so that they do accept His Lordship!

"If science, study, and careful illumination of both the Scriptures and the natural world can help, use them! Time is short! And don't forget, scientists need saving too! I hope my team and I have shown here tonight that during a believer's sanctification process here on Earth, as long as one endeavors to continue living by the truth, there may be more than one way that real Christians view what they are reading in Scripture, depending on where he or she is in their walk at a given time. Things not immediately related to the acceptance of the Gospel should *not* be used as stumbling blocks for people exploring faith in Christ. Do any of us think that the Lord should have done this to the dying thief when he was being crucified?

"We argue here tonight that if people continue to live by the truth throughout their individual lives, always applying the lessons they learn in order to be true to their individual walk, they will end up before the throne of the Lord—from wherever they begin that walk. So let us *not* hinder anyone! Some scientists who reject the Creationist interpretation of the 'truth' of the natural world for what they believe to be truly valid scientific reasons based upon their own knowledge, training, and experience at the present time are prevented from coming to faith in the fear that they will be committing intellectual suicide! As Davis A. Young put it in his book *Christianity and the Age of the Earth*, 'No non-Christian geologist is ever going to accept Flood geology or the young-Earth theory these days; the flaws and weaknesses are obvious to any practicing geologist.' In fact, he concluded, 'If acceptance of Christianity means accepting Flood geology, some might not want to become Christians.' My friends, the destination of hell is not a place we should ever take lightly—for ourselves or anyone else! So don't put such stumbling blocks to faith in front of others! Love them, just as the Lord told us we should. Don't do anything which will hasten them to that destination! Remember that loving our neighbor means doing what is in his or her best interests. Helping them escape hell should in fact be our primary concern! Or do you think that somehow they don't matter to our Lord?"

John looked out at the audience and saw that people were considering the various points brought up. He seemed satisfied that the murmur was positive, and then continued,

"Ladies and gentlemen, I want us to remember what our dear brother Peter wrote to us about our responsibility to witness to others. In the fifteenth and sixteenth verses of the third chapter of First Peter, he wrote, 'Always be prepared to give an answer to everyone who asks you to give the reason for the hope that you have. But do this with gentleness and respect, keeping a clear conscience, so that those who speak maliciously against your good behavior in Christ may be ashamed of their slander.' And please, ladies and gentlemen, let us *not* forget the gentleness part! Imagine how effective the apostle Paul would have been when he greeted the Athenians if he had begun by calling them 'lost and repugnant idol worshippers?'"

John then paused and allowed the audience's responsive laugh to actually foster his point.

"No, instead, we learn in Acts chapter 17 that he paid a compliment to them by noting that 'in every way' they were very 'religious.' Similarly, greet scientists, youths, and people just curious about the world in the same way…remove all needless stumbling blocks, and then you'll be best positioned to witness to them as the Lord presents that opportunity!"

At this point he turned to Pastor Gregg and said, "Pastor Gregg, I understand that you have been quite concerned about the youth of this church when they go off to college and do not return to the church until they are ready to get married. Is that correct?"

Pastor Gregg looked at John, smiled, and said, "Yes, John, it's quite disturbing to us that they remove themselves from the church during that critical period of their lives when they are just beginning to build a life, or start a career… It seems that the church has no place in their lives to help them with that phase of their lives."

John then replied, "Do you think perhaps that a more open approach of helping them reintegrate within the church by not provoking them with assertions which go against what many of them have studied in their collegiate pursuits might be a better plan?"

"I beg your pardon, John," returned the pastor.

John answered, "Well, do you think that certain things which are constantly being asserted and not directly linked to salvation, and which never seem open to discussion might actually be related to their nonattendance? That they are avoiding such unpleasant encounters until perhaps some 'future time' when they can assess them more completely?"

Pastor Gregg thought for a moment and then replied, "I never thought of that before, John. They in fact may be rejecting what appears to them a closed attitude on the part of the church which they don't feel will integrate well with their newly acquired awareness of the natural world."

"Precisely, Pastor," replied John.

"Well, I guess then that we'll have to be more considerate of them!" said Pastor Gregg.

Some jaws surely must have dropped when Mr. Allen's voice chimed in, "And I'll second that motion, sir!"

John smiled at Mr. Allen and held his gaze for a moment. "And, Mr. Allen, my brother, I deeply respect you for that, just so you know!"

For a moment, Mr. Allen seemed to almost choke up.

CHAPTER 37

LIVING IN AGAPE AND WORSHIPING IN SPIRIT AND IN TRUTH

"Now some may have come here tonight wondering who would give support or at least some voice to their strongly held convictions regarding dear God's Holy Word," began John. "And perhaps something was said which resonated with you. Perhaps nothing was said which did that. Perhaps you genuinely feel that some of tonight's debaters need some genuine 'course correction.' Well, to this I say, make your opinion known in a way that tries to convince and which is not afraid to engage in dialogue, but make certain it is born in love and delivered in love for the best effect!

"I can share with you from firsthand experience that I have known many people within the church who were quite honorably devoted to the Truth of which they had become convicted and have certain associated contentions which have come directly from those convictions. Even my two team members up here with me tonight, to their credit, are quite 'strict' in what they believe is the right way for a Christian to believe, or perhaps I should describe it like this: they are very firm about what they feel is not acceptable for a Christian to do when it comes to certain ways of living or even believing. Let me therefore give you seekers of the Truth this comfort and this warning from dear God's Word which I hope will both encourage and enlighten you: In First Corinthians, the third chapter, verses 10 through 15, our dear brother Paul wrote about people building on the foundation he laid as an 'expert builder.' He told the brethren in his letter that…

> …each one should be careful how he builds. For no one can lay any foundation other than the one already laid, which is Jesus Christ. If any man builds on this foundation using gold, silver, costly stones, wood, hay or straw, his work will be shown for what it is, because the Day will bring it to light. It will be revealed with fire, and the fire will test the quality of each man's work. If what he has built survives, he will receive his reward. If it is burned up, he will suffer loss; he himself will be saved, but only as one escaping through the flames.

So whatever it is you are contentious about, and if you see one of your brothers or sisters in Christ who have gone against what you believe to be the right way or practice, unless it goes against the Gospel, I strongly exhort you to bear with each other in love, patience, and constructive dialogue. No need for us to fret over the secondary things which separate us as members of the Body of Christ, though in no way do I dispute that many or most of you have solid reasons for believing a particular way. So whether it concerns infant baptism; baptism by immersion; the true Sabbath Day of the week; whether or not Mary gave birth to other children after she bore the Son of God; the wine and wafer celebration of the Lord's sacrificing of his own body and blood though Transubstantiation, Consubstantiation, or just in memory; belief in a prosperity gospel; believers speaking in tongues; belief in literal twenty-four-hour day duration for each of the Days of Creation; or whatever it is which has come to your attention and about which you may feel strongly, I assure you that the Truth will ultimately be known. Samuel, in the parable about the weeds, can you tell us what was the Master's response when his workers asked if they should pull up the weeds, even though the Master had admitted that an enemy was responsible for them?"

For the last time, Samuel got up from his chair and walked over to the lectern. Looking around the room at the audience, he then stated simply, "When the workers offered to pull up the weeds, the Master of the Vineyard forbade them to do it. He was concerned that some of the good crop would be destroyed in doing that. And in the same way, we should not so angrily dispute doctrinal differences between Christians which do not of themselves destroy the Gospel message. I believe that means also that we should never risk alienating anyone from Christ Jesus if we truly love them as our neighbor and as dear God would have us love them."

"Thank you, Samuel," John said. "An important conclusion to be sure!"

"And now, young Christopher." John now turned to the other boy. "Based upon your earlier contribution in the debate tonight, can you summarize for us the role that science can positively play in your view for the family of believers?"

Now Christopher rose and walked over to where John was standing. He pulled the microphone closer to his mouth in a most professional manner, causing the audience to respond with a soft, welcoming laugh of amusement, and which somehow encouraged young Christopher in its hearing.

"As I said earlier tonight, when we read about what our Lord said with regard to interpreting the weather based on the indicators in the atmosphere, this seems to me to indicate that our Lord appreciated science and learning how to use it in our own lives on a regular basis. At the same time, He also seems to be saying to us that we need to keep our minds open to other, even more important signs as they relate to the written Word of God. We remember that the Pharisees could tell King Herod where the Messiah was to be born according to the Scriptures, but they somehow failed to acknowledge or recognize dear Jesus as the Messiah. So as we study more and hopefully learn more, we must always remember to be as the Bereans were described in Acts 17:11. They studied the Scriptures daily in order to compare what Paul had taught them to the actual Scriptures in order to see if his teaching was true. And as I also stated before, if anything is found that goes against the biblical text, it is to be discarded."

"Absolutely, and thank you, Christopher," said John.

Now for a final time, John addressed the audience.

"In any contention that you hold, remember what our Lord said was the greatest commandment and what he said was the second greatest commandment. After loving God with all your heart and soul and mind and strength, make sure you are next prioritizing loving your neighbor, and making sure you do *everything*, and I mean *everything*, you can to give him or her the opportunity to hear, to believe, and to ultimately accept the Gospel and the personal Lordship of Jesus Christ our Savior, the only way to be saved. And that includes removing *any and all stumbling blocks wherever possible!* Remember that *time is short! No more needless dustups!* Reach others *through any means possible!* You may have to meet them in some very strange or peculiar places. Become like Paul said in First Corinthians, chapter 9, verses 19 to 22,

> Though I am free and belong to no man, I make myself a slave to everyone, to win as many as possible. To the Jews I became like a Jew, to win the Jews. To those under the law I became like one under the law (though I myself am not under the law), so as to win those under the law. To those not having the law I became like one not having the law (though I am not free from God's law but am under Christ's law), so as to win those not having the law. To the weak I became weak, to win the weak. I have become all things to all men so that by all possible means I might save some.

Remember what you have learned here tonight about the early church and the differences which ultimately *did not destroy* the church! *I will say it again—Time is short!* Thank you for your time and attention, my friends."

And with that, our neighbor John smiled, extended his right arm, and waved to everyone in the audience, and then left the lectern. His departure was not without what would be considered by anyone to be huge applause from the audience. John returned to his chair on the platform and then, leaning over first to Christopher, John shook his hand warmly and said to him, "Thank you, Christopher, for all of your hard work and contribution this evening! You were integral to a very successful testimony! Well done!"

To this Chris simply replied, "You are very welcome, John. Thank you for including me! I learned so much and hopefully will be able to apply all that we've learned!"

John now looked over to Samuel and shook his hand next. As he did so, he said to Samuel, "Your love of the Lord and love of the church is very refreshing, young Samuel! Your diligent work in preparation for this debate as well as your delivery will be remembered. Thank you, my young friend!"

Samuel then stood up and hugged John affectionately and said, "Thank you, John, for everything! I cannot believe what you did for me. So many blessings everywhere! For me and the church and hopefully even the world!"

John looked straight at Samuel and said, "I am very pleased that you see the bigger picture here Samuel! You will certainly always be welcome among the sons of Thunder!" He then bent closer and whispered in Samuel's ear, "And there are still many more things to do!"

Not fully understanding what that meant, Samuel looked back at John and said, "I look forward to doing whatever it is the Lord wants me to do, especially if I can work with you!"

John smiled and replied simply, "That sounds just about right, Samuel!"

CHAPTER 38

CLOSURE AT LAST BUT AROUND A CENTRAL QUESTION

Pastor Gregg now stood and walked up to the lectern. He first paused at John's seat, shook John's hand warmly, followed by the hands of his two acolytes, and then continued to the podium to address the audience. Before Pastor Gregg had uttered even the first word to the listeners, a sudden sound came from Mr. Allen's chair as the farmer stood up quickly and hurried over to John and the boys. He also then warmly shook each of their hands. A warm feeling spread throughout Pastor Gregg's entire being as he turned and then finally addressed the audience, "Before we adjourn, I think that it might be a good opportunity to open up the floor for any questions directed to any of the presenters."

A polite murmur among the people proceeded at that point, but suddenly was broken by the sweet sound of a little girl's voice.

"Excuse me," said little Melinda stepping out into the aisle away from her mother, still holding onto Mr. Bunny, "I would like to ask a question please."

The pastor looked down and smiled at the little girl dressed very nicely and noticing the big flowers in her hair that matched the pink fur of the stuffed animal. "Yes, Melinda, why don't you be the first! Who is your question for?"

Melinda replied, "My question is for you, Pastor. Can you tell me which way I need to believe so that I will go to heaven?"

At hearing this, suddenly the wisdom that had been offered by John overtook the pastor all at once. Suddenly this little girl was worried about her salvation. Salvation depended on the Gospel and not on human wisdom, not on esoteric matters that always seemed "part and parcel" to faith to so many Christians. The pastor was greatly shaken anew by the simple question and probably more so by the fact that it came from one of the little ones who believed in Jesus. She was "thirsty," and he now was determined more than ever to give her the cold cup of water that her soul craved. He therefore listened very carefully as the little girl continued to speak.

The little girl then said, "I saw a movie about 'dear Jesus' in Sunday school, and I was wondering if the dying thief next to him believed the right things about the creation of the Earth, I mean whether it was actual days or longer days?"

John, from his vantage point to Pastor Greg, watched the exchange intently between the pastor and his little church member. This was something the pastor needed to honestly answer and in the clearest of ways. He silently prayed, waited, and hoped.

The pastor looked lovingly at the little girl and spoke into the microphone for the benefit of all those listening, "Well, Melinda, I think I can answer that."

Melinda looked up at him with her big brown eyes and nodded.

"Melinda, our Lord Jesus came here to Earth to seek and to save the lost. The apostle Paul tells us in 1 Corinthians chapter 15 that we are saved when we believe the Gospel and hold firmly to the word as he originally told it to us. As the apostle Paul said, the Gospel of our Lord is that dear Jesus Christ died for our sins according to the Scriptures, that he was buried, that he was raised on the third day according to the Scriptures, and that he appeared to Peter, and then to the Twelve. After that, he appeared to more than five hundred of the brothers at the same time, most of whom were 'still living,' though some had 'fallen asleep.' So, Melinda, when we accept His precious gift of faith in this Gospel, we are sealed with the Holy Spirit and no one can ever take us from Him. One day, we will go to be with Him, inheriting eternal life through Him. And while we are waiting for Him, He will make changes in us if we continue to live by the truth, addressing the various things which come into our lives during our own lifetimes on Earth. His gift of faith in the Gospel is not dependent upon anything we can do. Just believe in the Gospel and continue to believe in it."

"So even if we don't understand everything the way we should in the rest of the Bible, we won't lose our salvation?" said the little girl.

"We won't ever lose our salvation if we believe in Him. When we believe in the Lord Jesus Christ and accept His Lordship in our lives, we are sealed with the Holy Spirit."

"Even if I make a wrong mistake in believing about the Creation week?" she continued.

"Yes, Melinda, if you don't understand everything in the Bible, even after being a good Berean, you don't lose your seal of the Holy Spirit. But I would hope that you will always keep in mind to check on your actions of love and faithfulness as you serve the Lord and make sure that you are bearing spiritual fruit in your walk with dear Jesus. He loves you and will always help you if you seek His counsel and companionship. Don't forget, even after dear God gives you your Salvation, He wants you to be sure to earn a reward. The Lord needs His overcomers ready for action now and in the future millennial kingdom and beyond."

Once again, John smiled at the pastor's use of the term *dear* in front of the Lord's name.

CHAPTER 39

ENDING THE DEBATE, SOME ENMITY, AND ADDING A NEW MEMBER OR TWO

After the pastor's response to Melinda, the sanctuary grew silent. People seemed suddenly lost in contemplation. The pastor moved over to the speaker and cleared his throat and addressed the people directly, "Ladies and gentlemen, unless there are any more questions, I think this is a good place to end our debate this evening." When no other questions were brought forth, he then stated, "This concludes the debate this evening. I do hope that our discussion helped to provide each of us with a better framework by which we may sort out our understanding, knowledge, and faith issues with regard to the creation week and how it pertains to our Christian lives. In our initial discussion about having this debate, John had suggested it on the basis of giving all of us a chance to emulate the Bereans who were constantly concerned about checking the apostle Paul's teachings with regard to the Scripture. I think that the resulting interchange we have just experienced this evening was well worth the efforts of the two presenting teams as well as your time. May I suggest that you don't forget to order a DVD on your way out?"

A round of amused laughter followed this last comment.

Pastor Gregg continued, "Now all that's left is for each of you to vote either 'for' or 'against' the resolution we stated at the beginning. 'Resolved, The Use of Modern Science Is an Acceptable Means to Gain a Clearer Understanding of the Biblical Record given in the Book of Genesis.' Be sure to place your voting slip in the boxes located next to each of the exits of the sanctuary. On behalf of the presenters, our thanks to each of you for coming!"

The pastor was then treated to thunderous applause by all present, even the newscaster he had seen at the beginning of the debate, and, to his surprise, by his co-presenters John, Samuel, Christopher, and Mr. Allen themselves. He felt a lump in his throat when he heard above the joyful din John say, "What a pastor! Just the kind my Master is overjoyed to have!"

As the applause subsided, people began to gather together in groups as they prepared to head home. Some others present, however, approached the debating teams. Before anyone could greet the presenters, Mr. Allen, who had reseated himself after shaking John's, Samuel's, and Christopher's hands, stood up again and walked over to John, Samuel, and Christopher again.

Mr. Allen looked first to Samuel and then to John. "Samuel and John, I'm so sorry for what I said and how I said it. I was just afraid that—"

Samuel finished for him, "Mr. Allen, you were just afraid that someone was going to disrespect the Lord!"

Mr. Allen stopped and looked down at the earnest blue eyes looking up at him so concerned for him and with such empathy and genuine concern for his well-being. "Thank you, Samuel, for realizing that. My intention may have been good, but my method was not very kind and not very loving. For that I do apologize and want you to know that I believe that you are a very faithful young man who is being called by the Lord for great things in the church and who knows where else indeed, hopefully somewhere fascinating in science as well!"

"Really, Mr. Allen, do you think I should really try to become a scientist?" asked the little boy in wide-eyed wonder.

"Well, I guess I will put it to you the way the Apostle Paul said it in Romans 12 verses 3 to 8,

> For by the grace given me I say to every one of you: Do not think of yourself more highly than you ought, but rather think of yourself with sober judgment, in accordance with the measure of faith God has given you. Just as each of us has one body with many members, and these members do not all have the same function, so in Christ we who are many form one body, and each member belongs to all the others. We have different gifts, according to the grace given us. If a man's gift is prophesying, let him use it in proportion to his faith. If it is serving, let him serve; if it is teaching, let him teach; if it is encouraging, let him encourage; if it is contributing to the needs of others, let him give generously; if it is leadership, let him govern diligently; if it is showing mercy, let him do it cheerfully.

So maybe your gifts and interests are leading you just to the place dear God wants you to be!" Mr. Allen concluded.

John thought for a minute, nodding slightly as if he was hearing a confidential suggestion from someone unseen, and said to Samuel, "Samuel, how important is what the Bible says to you when it comes to trying to understand the history of the Earth?"

Samuel looked up at him and said, "It is everything to me, John. There is no truth that can be different from its Truth."

John looked at him and then said, "Why do you say that, Samuel?"

Samuel replied again, "Because dear Jesus said in Matthew 5:18 that 'not the smallest letter, not the least stroke of a pen, will by any means disappear from the Law until everything is accomplished.' That means everything is very important in the Bible. You can't ignore it and be right."

"That is a very fine answer, Samuel," said Mr. Allen, smiling broadly. "I couldn't have given a better reason myself." He paused, looking still somewhat remorseful, but in peace. He paused only a moment more and said to Sam, "Thank you for forgiving me, son."

Samuel smiled and looked up at him and said, "That's okay, Mr. Allen. I know you only wanted to defend the Truth and were brave enough to speak out for what was right in your heart. I wish more men were as brave as you!" With this, the little boy who had proven so mature before the entire audience a moment ago opened his arms and gave Mr. Allen a genuinely warm hug. Mr. Allen hugged him right back and quickly wiped away a tear that had started to escape down his own cheek.

And just at that moment, the perfect one for that matter, a man made his way through the clusters of people that had aggregated to various places inside the church as people sought to talk, vote, and even just express their excitement over all that they had experienced together. Samuel recognized him immediately. It was Mr. Edmund, the science teacher from the school. He first reached out and shook John's hand, then Mr. Allen's, Christopher's, and finally Samuel's.

"A most impressive debate by all parties," he said. "It has certainly given me much to think about! Is your pastor around? I'd like to thank him also."

Samuel pointed to Pastor Gregg, deeply involved in a conversation with the pretty newscaster he had noticed at the beginning of the debate. He could just make out the pastor saying to her, "Yes, I think a class in 'ethical journalism' would be a wonderful idea for our church Sunday school. I think that the students will line up to get a real Christian television journalist's perspective too! And yes, we would be happy to accept you as part of our fellowship here! Perhaps we could find some time to discuss everything in greater detail over lunch on the Wednesday afternoon after you return from your assignment, say 12:30 p.m.?"

The newscaster smiled brightly and nodded, saying simply, "Yes, I'll mark that down in my calendar." She then shook the pastor's hand and walked over to her crew, giving each of them a membership information booklet that she had just received from the pastor.

Mr. Edmunds strode up to Pastor Gregg, just as the newscaster moved away to her crew.

"Pastor Gregg, thank you for such a wonderful debate this evening! I can't remember the last time I felt so engaged in a topic! Even my own master's thesis defense!" began the science teacher.

"Well, I'm so glad you enjoyed it Mr., err—"

"Edmund. I'm a science teacher at Sam's and Chris's school. I'm afraid that I wasn't very encouraging to young Samuel about this debate a while back."

"Well, I think you would find yourself not alone in that regard, Mr. Edmund."

"Regardless of where I may have been in terms of my attitude then, after hearing the things discussed tonight, I realize that your church is the kind of place I need to be so that I may explore Christian faith with an open mind and not be derided for my preoccupation with science," said the now jovial science teacher.

"Well, we certainly would want you to feel welcome, Mr. Edmund, and, of course, would want you to make your best decision for Christ without any prejudice induced from a church without compassion!"

"From what I witnessed tonight, I dare say that I don't think that will be a problem here, Pastor."

"Well then, Mr. Edmund, please feel free to come to services here tomorrow and I can introduce you afterward over some coffee and cake to some of our members and the head of the welcoming committee. We have many wonderful programs here and are always open to new suggestions for other ones as well!" replied the earnest pastor.

"As you might say, Pastor, Lord willing, I'll be there! By the way, do you have any programs in your adult Sunday school which seek to identify the wonderful discoveries in science which correspond so well with what the Bible is saying?"

Pastor Gregg nearly blanched with excitement at hearing this from the local science teacher. "Like I said, Mr. Edmund, we are always open to such good suggestions…"

Just then, Mr. Russo, the deacon who had read from the Genesis account at the beginning urgently came up to Pastor Gregg and addressed him, "Excuse me, Pastor Gregg, I'm so sorry to interrupt you and the gentlemen, but we have a final count for the vote on the debate resolution."

"By all means, please announce it," said Pastor Gregg, gesturing to the microphone.

He didn't know it, but Mr. Edmunds was inwardly impressed and pleased that the pastor urged the announcement to be made without inquiring about what it was beforehand. *Quite an ethical gentleman*, he thought.

The deacon climbed up to the lectern and pulled the microphone closer so that his announcement could be heard clearly by the many people who had decided to delay their departure so that they could hear the results of the voting.

"Ladies and gentlemen, we have the final results of the vote over the resolution of tonight's debate, 'The Use of Science Is an Acceptable Means to Gain a Clearer Understanding of the Biblical Record given in the Book of Genesis.' After counting all of the votes, the resolution is accepted with a final vote count of 499 to 0."

Suddenly Pastor Gregg spoke up and said laughingly, "I thought we had 500 voting slips printed up!"

Suddenly, little Melinda burst through the cluster of people between her and the edge of the platform so that the deacon could see her. She tried to speak as loudly as she could without actually yelling, "I forgot to give you mine!" And with her voting slip in one hand and Mr. Bunny in the other, she charged up the steps to the platform and handed her vote to Mr. Russo.

Without batting an eye, Mr. Russo looked at the slip, then back to the audience and around the room, and said simply, "Make that 500 to 0 in favor of the resolution."

Once again, the applause was thunderous!

CHAPTER 40

FINAL GREETINGS AND
JOHN DEPARTS

John stood there with Pastor Gregg waving and wishing well to all as the last of the people left the sanctuary after the announcement had been made, the DVDs were all ordered, and both short-term and long-term plans in which church members and spectators involved themselves were set up. Although the evening was still clear, some distant thunder could be heard, giving notice to a forthcoming summer thunderstorm. The pastor was very pleased to see that the "church" in these people continued with them as they left the church for the evening. He turned to John and smiled.

"John, thank you for all that you have done for us and our community. I suspect its scope is even larger than our town at this point. I'm sorry to have ever questioned your motives."

"Oh, Pastor, you didn't really question my motives as much as you sought to reestablish peace and love among your usually 'quiet members'!" John countered.

Pastor Gregg couldn't help himself and laughed openly. "You can say that again, John!"

"The important thing is that we have invigorated the Body of Christ here and hopefully awakened the members to higher priorities. I can see that you even added some new faces just this evening by putting focus on the right kinds of things with which they were personally concerned," said the experienced fisherman.

"Is that the way it was when you were with the Master, John?" asked the pastor, if just a bit shyly.

"We could always tell when people had been touched on a personal level. The joy just seemed to bubble up exuberantly when their deepest needs were addressed. Of course, we had the benefit of traveling with the most Wonderful Preacher of all time in the beginning. But the same kind of things could be seen in our work after dear Jesus ascended on High. We just have to remember that people are still people who can respond emotionally and even joyfully when they find their own needs touched in loving ways by Our Master's own servants' work. Fortunately, He empowers us in the performance of that work when we let Him," said John.

"I just can't believe that I have known you for so many years and have missed out on getting to know you at this level until just now!" said the pastor.

"Pastor Gregg, you have been faithful for many years and have treated each of your members with love and respect. I certainly have no complaints and neither do any of your members for that matter. It has been a pleasure being part of this community and being able to become involved at this critical time when mistakes which threaten the church body in so many places today actually were now threatening to become a dividing force here. That is why I was sent here."

"So what will you do now?" asked Pastor Gregg, a little apprehensively since he feared John would move on to something else which might remove him from the church.

"Whatever the Lord directs me to do, Pastor, of course" said John, smiling.

"Well, may His Will be done always, whatever it is," affirmed Pastor Gregg, reaching out his hand to shake that of the apostle. "Please tell Him I send my love."

"Sure I will, Pastor Gregg, just as you do every day!" The knowing fisherman smiled. "It has been a pleasure, sir, from one fisher of men to another!" At these words, Pastor Gregg walked over and embraced John warmly.

"Thank you, dear Boanerge, I truly enjoyed the thunder this evening!"

"It was our pleasure, Pastor Gregg! We hope the accompanying rain this evening will bring in a truly extraordinary harvest!"

And with those words, our neighbor John departed to the parking lot of the church.

CHAPTER 41

A STORM, A PARTING GIFT, AND NEWS OF A TRAGIC EVENT

The next morning the sun rose bright and beautiful against a magnificent blue sky. By ten o'clock, Chris began to stir in his bed and soon awakened with a satisfied smile, thinking of the previous night's event and how it seemed to be received so positively by everyone present. His mother and father greeted him as he strode into the kitchen, telling him that although he had slept much of the morning away, his timing was perfect as the power had just come back on since the previous night's thunderstorm. To this report, all Chris could say was, "Really?"

Chris recalled how the night before seemed so perfect as people had begun to depart from the church after the successful debate, with many stars twinkling overhead as they walked to their cars in the church parking lot. But by the time he and his parents had gotten home, the sky had clouded over and before long a storm appeared, complete with loud thunder, streaks of lightning, and a driving rain. Because Chris had gone directly to bed, he was sleeping deeply before even the first peal of thunder had sounded. Though his parents were surprised over his not having heard any of the storm, Chris was completely oblivious.

After he had finished his breakfast, his parents were curiously still lingering in the kitchen, apparently waiting for him to finish his meal. His father looked over at his mother, who then said to Chris.

"Chris, there seems to be something for you on the porch we discovered only this morning. Do you want to go see what it is?"

Curious, Chris replied, "Sure, Mom, but why did you wait until just now to tell me?"

His father answered for her, "Probably because your mom wanted you to eat first before you became too excited to see what was brought for you!"

At this Chris hopped up from the kitchen table and ran to the front door. Opening it fast but making sure not to let it slam into the front hallway, he pushed through the storm door and let himself onto the porch. In less than two seconds his parents, still walking to the porch, heard the joyful exclamation of their happy son.

"No way! Mom, Dad, you gotta see this!"

As the three of them gathered on the porch together, there before them was a beautiful new bicycle with an envelope attached to an invoice marked "paid in full" on it. The invoice indicated it had come from Jay's Cycle Center of Westfield, New Jersey, apparently ordered June 28 that same summer. Glancing over the invoice, Chris couldn't believe his eyes.

"A Specialized Hotrock with eight speeds, a front suspension, black with silver trim, with rechargeable lights…and a bell, a Jellibell-Twist," he read aloud.

His father then asked, "Chris, isn't that the same model and equipment you always say is the 'equipment of choice' for a bicycle? Please tell me you didn't somehow manipulate this gift from someone—"

"No, Dad, I promise. I did talk about such a bicycle with John a while back during one of our lessons, but only as an example of an answer to prayer. I would never have even thought of dropping any hint, strong or otherwise, about John or anyone else buying such an incredibly expensive bicycle for me."

His parents then looked at each other and nodded to each other.

His mother then said, "Honey, don't worry, we believe you."

At this Chris smiled, almost in relief, but ultimately he and his parents had a good relationship that was never pockmarked by lies.

Chris then opened the envelope and carefully read the note inside.

"For my young friend, Christopher, I hope you will enjoy this small token of my friendship and affection! You worked hard for our presentation tonight, and I hope this bicycle will commemorate our triumph for the Lord, yours, mine, and Samuel's, at least in this small way! (I'll also be happy to know that now you'll have working brakes!). With warmest wishes, always, JBZ."

"Mom, Dad," began Christopher, "it's from John! But I promise, I didn't—"

His father quickly put a hand on the boy's shoulder and then, squeezing slightly, said while glancing at the boy's mother, "Enjoy it, son! You certainly deserve it in our opinion."

Chris was then out and about on his new bicycle in less than five minutes, the time it took to remove both the invoice and envelope carefully, put them safely into a desk drawer in his room, and then carefully bring the bicycle down the porch steps!

*****

Samuel awakened with a smile that morning also. Like Christopher, he had fallen into a deep, restful sleep before the storm hit, so was oblivious to the timing of his wakening. As he opened his eyes, he could see the die-cast car replica of the Makoshark II that John had given him. He couldn't help but smile to himself at the memory of riding in the actual vehicle with John all the way from John's shop to his home. He even laughed a little remembering what the policeman Officer Ray had said when they had stopped to say hello during their drive. "Those with class drive fiberglass!"

Mostly though, the wonderful feelings surrounding his adventure with the Makoshark II aside, Sam felt very happy on a deeper level. He and the team had delivered a strong defense of the use of science to gain a clearer understanding of the biblical record. Mr. Allen had apologized but, more importantly, appeared to be personally blessed with his new understanding of what Samuel had tried to appreciate himself and convey to others all along. And what's more, the entire audience seemed to agree.

Oh, God is so good! Samuel thought. Samuel then remembered that he would, going forward, have to be accountable for all that was presented and discussed during the debate. Actually though, he didn't mind. This was the right thing to do. And there was still so many more fascinating things to learn!

Just at that moment, Samuel heard his mother calling from downstairs. "Is our little biblical scholar up yet?"

At this Samuel almost leaped out of his bed and, while grabbing for his jeans slung over the chair, answered her, "I'm coming right now, Mom!" His total dressing time was about forty-five seconds, allowing him to be literally giving a good morning hug each to his mom and dad downstairs in the kitchen in just under one minute flat!

"Well, son, your mother and I are very proud to have been witnesses to your fine presentation last night in the debate!" said his jovial father.

Joining in, his mother added, "We were literally in awe of the amount of information that you, John, and Chris were able to present! You certainly have spent a scholarly and disciplined summer, young man! And very importantly, Samuel, your time helped many people there to begin their search for the Lord. What could be more important than that?"

"Thanks, Mom and Dad!" said their grateful son.

Samuel then glanced at the clock over the stove, which was blinking "00 minutes 00 seconds," and asked, "What happened to the clock?"

His dad responded, "Well, I guess you weren't bothered by the rather large thunderstorm last night, son!"

"What thunderstorm?" asked the boy, who was now eating a bowl of cereal.

His mother now picked up the thread of conversation and said, "You fell fast asleep as soon as your head hit the pillow last night, so no wonder you don't know!"

"Wow," was just all that Samuel could say in response, wondering how everyone in the town fared after going through a major storm like that.

Just as Samuel was finishing up his cereal, the phone rang.

His mother walked over to the phone and answered it. After only a moment Sam heard her say, "Oh!" and then heard the phone crash to the kitchen floor. His father ran over to his mother and immediately guided her to a chair to sit down and then scooped up the phone from the floor. He answered it. "Hello, this is Art Bodden, may I help you?" Some moments passed as Sam heard his father say, "Yes, I understand. That is quite a shock…especially after last night. Yes, I'll tell him. Thank you for letting us know." He then hung up the phone and paused for a moment with his head down.

Samuel knew his father. This had to be very distressing news for him to react like he did. He kept staring at his father and waiting for him to compose himself. Meanwhile, his mother had leaned over, supporting her head with her hands, sobbing very softly. After a few minutes, Samuel couldn't wait any longer.

"Mom? Dad? What happened?"

Now his father looked straight at him and said, "Son, I'm afraid that I have some very sad news to share. Our wonderful neighbor John apparently was killed in a car accident last night."

Samuel sat there dumbfounded. Those words seemed to suspend him from the universe as the meaning of the terrible words started to ground themselves in reality. He sat there wishing somehow that he had not heard them. He couldn't even speak, though he tried. After a moment he just ran up to his room, closed the door, and flung himself onto his bed.

Twenty minutes later, both his mother and father entered his bedroom and sat on the bed next to their son. His mother gently stroked his back while his father put his hand on the back of Sam's head affectionately.

"We are so sorry, son. We cannot imagine how you must feel about this," he said after a few moments.

His mother, clearly affected in her own way, added, "Now you must rely on dear God to bring you through this very difficult time."

Slowly, Samuel turned over and looked at them. "I will. How did it happen?"

"The policeman on the phone told me that they found the remains of the car he had been driving still aflame on one of the back roads leading to his shop."

"John wasn't in the car?" Samuel said with a last surge of desperate hope, trying to make its way up to the surface.

"Well, let me state it as the officer stated it, 'There was no recognizable remains left in the driver's seat.'

Samuel and his mother both gasped at hearing this.

"So what happened? Did his truck suddenly explode or what, Dad?" asked Sam confused.

"No, son, he wasn't in his truck. The officer said it was in that fancy Corvette that you and he rode home together in a few weeks ago. Apparently a tree came down in the middle of the road and forced the impact of the vehicle into another tree when it swerved to avoid it. Apparently the impact of the car was at very high speed. The only consolation according to the officer was that the driver would have been killed instantly."

Samuel now had to bare the shock of knowing that John had died in the Makoshark II. And now the car of his dreams was destroyed. And although this was an additional tragedy as far as Sam was concerned, his heart ached for John and he couldn't even open up now within himself to contemplate the loss of the vehicle at the same time. The best news in all of this seemed to be that John didn't suffer in the crash.

"It's just that I loved John. He means so much to me," said Samuel, openly sobbing.

"We know that, baby," said his mother as she continued to stroke his back. Then she added "And he loved you too."

"Do you think so?" asked Sam through his tears. "He took up this debate to defend me and that is what got him killed. He never would have been driving from the church at that time if it wasn't for the debate."

"Now, son, you mustn't view it that way at all. John defended you because of all of the right reasons which you, Chris, and he presented last evening. Many people were touched in that debate, son. The blessings from that debate are still yet forthcoming. And it wouldn't have happened without you and our wonderful neighbor putting everything together as you did! Believe me when I tell you that John took great pleasure in that debate," said his father. "I believe in my heart that he did it for the glory of God and that he was pleased to be a part of the greatest witnessing for the Lord God that this town has seen in more than twenty years!"

"And long before that debate, John took an interest in you and in our family. You mustn't ever forget that, Samuel!" his mother urged.

These words to him started to take effect slowly. Samuel smiled sadly and remembered. "I used to love it when he would come over, have dinner with us, and look through the telescope with me."

"He loved it too, Sam" said his father. "Try to think on those times along with all of the wonderful memories you have of John whenever his name comes up. It will be like salve to an open wound I can tell you."

"I'll try to do that, Dad."

"That's our brave boy," said his mother, who now bent over and gave her son a kiss on the forehead. His dad followed suit. Samuel tried to convincingly smile at them through his wet eyes.

And before long, the phone rang again.

Mr. Bodden walked over to the phone and picked it up.

"Bodden residence, good morning. Oh, hi, Pastor Gregg…yes, we just heard…yes, he knows…well, he's taking it very bravely… yes, I think he would…all right, about 2:00 p.m.? All right, I'll ask him and bring him by if he agrees…if not, I'll call you back. Thanks, Pastor Gregg."

Mr. Bodden hung up the phone. He then walked into Sam's room, where he found his son lying on the bed still in the same position when he went to get the call. The only difference was that this time his son wasn't crying, just lying on the bed, staring up at his die-cast car of the Makoshark II.

"That was Pastor Gregg, Samuel," said his father. "He was wondering if you could go over to the church at about 2:00 p.m. this afternoon."

"What does he need, Dad?"

"If you are willing, he'd like to share something with you and Chris about John."

"Chris is going too?"

"Well, that's only if Chris agrees. What about you?"

"Yes, Dad. Pastor Gregg has also been very wonderful to me the entire time."

"He has indeed, my son. I'm glad you want to honor his request."

"Yes, Dad, maybe we'll all feel better if we start to focus on those wonderful memories you asked us to focus on."

*****

At 1:45 p.m., just as Sam and his parents had closed their front door to get into the car, a police car pulled up to the house. Sam recognized Officer Ray immediately and, seeing that the passenger side window was already down, greeted him with the most cheerful voice he could muster, "Hello, Officer Ray!"

The kindly officer smiled and said, "Hello, Sam." Then looking at his parents, he said, "Good afternoon, Mr. and Mrs. Bodden. I was wondering if I could have a minute to talk to Sam?"

"No problem, Officer Ray. Do you want us to wait inside?" answered Mr. Bodden.

"Oh no, that won't be necessary, it'll only take a minute," replied the policeman. Then getting out of his car, he stepped over to the back door, opened it, and withdrew a rather large box. He placed the box on the hood of his patrol car and then looked at Samuel affectionately. "Sam, I can only imagine what you're going through now after hearing about John. I've been friends with him for more than ten years, before I even attended the police academy. In fact, he helped me explore that possibility as a career." He paused and tried to clear his throat. "Anyway, I talked it over with my wife for more than two hours so far this morning, and we decided that I should bring this over for you, at the risk of upsetting you a little. You see, one day, perhaps not today, but someday in the future, this may represent something positive and meaningful for you, which you will be glad to keep. And if I don't give it to you now, it will most likely become lost, probably irretrievably so for a variety of reasons."

Sam looked up at him and said, "Officer Ray, you brought something for me in that box?"

"Yes, son, I did. I recognize now may not be the right time, but I fear more that it may also be the only time…you see it's meant to give you a lasting memento of a positive memory of John."

Both of Sam's parents looked at each other, then back at Sam. It was clear that they didn't know quite what the officer was talking about, nor what they should say in response to him either.

Sam settled everyone down by saying simply, "Thank you, Officer Ray. I greatly appreciate your thoughtfulness. If you don't mind, I'd like to open it later, since I'm now heading over to meet with the pastor of our church."

"No problem, Sam!" The officer smiled, handed the box to Sam, and got back into his patrol car. "So glad to see you're making an effort to be up and about! Perhaps when you're ready, we'll talk about this little gift later. In the meantime, I hope your meeting goes well!" And with that, he saluted them and drove off.

Standing there, holding the box, Samuel felt that it was indeed something relatively compact and sturdy. Without opening it, he put it inside the house, closed the front door, and was soon in the back seat of his parents' car on his way to meet with the pastor.

CHAPTER 42

SOME RESOLUTION AND COMFORT AND A PEEK AT DEAR GOD'S MYSTERIOUS AND EXCITING WAYS

When Samuel arrived at the church, he found the church secretary practically waiting for him at the door. Seeing Samuel get out of his parent's car, she opened the door for him and ushered him into Pastor Gregg's office. As he hurried into the church, out of the corner of his eye, he noted a shiny black bicycle locked in the bicycle rack along the front path. When he entered the pastor's office, Samuel felt a little heartened seeing Chris already sitting there patiently waiting along with the Pastor for Samuel to arrive.

Pastor Gregg immediately got up and gave him a hug. "Thank you for coming here, Samuel. I know it isn't exactly an easy time right now for you." He then gestured for Samuel to take a seat next to Christopher. "Young gentlemen," Pastor Gregg began, "we have all just been through a virtual roller coaster of emotion. Last night, the debate had me feeling euphoric, leaving me in contemplation of our witness of dear God to our entire community. I don't know if you know this, but your science teacher Mr. Edmund, the newscaster and her crew, and who knows who else more are considering joining our church?"

Both boys smiled politely at hearing this but didn't offer any verbal affirmation. So the pastor continued speaking. "In light of all that has happened with regard to the events leading up to the debate, I thought you boys might be encouraged if I was now able, in view of the tragic accident, to put a little more light on what we've been through and how it might relate to us and our church community going forward. I am hoping that this would be all right with each of you?"

Again both boys smiled slightly and each nodded his head ever so slightly.

"Good then!" The pastor continued, "Our first big assignment is to figure out just what has been taking place here with regard to our favorite fisherman neighbor."

"What do you mean, Pastor Gregg?" answered Samuel a little defensively. "He died in a car accident, the very night of the debate he so wonderfully put together!"

"Yes, Samuel, but who was John?" pushed the pastor. "Who?" he asked again more firmly.

"I'm not sure what you mean by that, Pastor Gregg," said Samuel.

Suddenly Chris interjected, "Sam, I think he means he wants to know if you see a bigger picture about John."

"Exactly, Chris!" replied Pastor Gregg.

Samuel then said, "Oh, I see what you are asking. Well, at first, I thought John might be an angel, Pastor. But after talking with Chris and you, I thought he might be just a faithful follower of the Lord who had been blessed to do miraculous work."

Yes, Samuel. It is those kinds of things which we all have experienced that I would like to put together all at the same time. I began to do this after you came to visit me the first time Samuel. Later, I had the privilege of meeting with John in this same office right before the debate. He confirmed to me that my conclusion about him was correct!"

"Your conclusion?" questioned Chris.

"Yes, Chris, in the course of this entire debate including its preparation, from the conception of the plan, the day Mr.

Allen spoke so harshly with Samuel until the night of the actual debate, many evidences were provided which indicate just who was among us."

Both boys now leaned in toward Pastor Gregg so as to not miss anything he might say.

Pastor Greg began, "We learned early on that John had a brother James, a Christian, who was literally martyred by someone who thought he was doing a religious act for the Glory of God! He also claimed to be older than Mr. Allen by 'at least ten years' and with a working knowledge of ancient Hebrew, which he could read, speak, and write. We learned that he was Jewish. We learned that he had a stepmother, though he also had a father and mother who were still together at the same time."

Sam interjected, "He said that his stepmother was the mother of a friend who was no longer able to look after her." The Pastor looked at Sam and then added: "I also learned that his stepmother was well and now back with her son, John's friend!" All Samuel could say now looking off was "Really?"

The pastor then looked at the boys and asked, "Do you remember what was recorded in the Gospel according to John when Jesus was being crucified and his mother Mary and John were watching him?"

Chris immediately flipped open his Bible to the book of John and searched for the sections covering the Crucifixion. He scanned the page and found a passage in chapter 19 and began reading.

"Beginning in verse 25 it says,

> Near the cross of Jesus stood his mother, his mother's sister, Mary the wife of Clopas, and Mary of Magdala. When Jesus saw his mother there, and the disciple whom he loved standing nearby, he said to his mother, 'Dear woman, here is your son,' and to the disciple, 'Here is your mother.' From that time on, this disciple took her into his home."

"I found out from John in my own meeting with him that he wrote to his stepmother when he was on the Greek Island of Patmos. Boys, do you know what else was written on Patmos and by whom?"

Now Samuel spoke up: "The book of Revelation written by the Apostle John!"

Pastor Greg paused a moment to gather his thoughts, then continued, "Samuel reported seeing John perform an ancient 'net casting' technique, one used back in the Lord Jesus's time on Earth. This also reveals to us that he not only was a fisherman today, but one with knowledge that would fit right back in time two thousand years ago! Samuel learned that John had grown up with his brother James and learned this technique from his father on the waters of Lake Genesareth. I think we might have figured some things out sooner if he had used a different but more familiar name for the same body of water, the 'sea of Galilee!'"

Both boys sat openmouthed at all of these facts being listed simultaneously.

"Finally, boys, we have Samuel's testimony of the miracle of little Melinda Ortega being raised from the dead. Samuel told me that he heard John distinctively say 'talitha *koum*.' If you go into your Bible in the fifth chapter of Mark, look at what the Lord did for Jairus the synagogue leader when his daughter had died. Apparently, the meaning of these very words of the Lord when he awakened the little child and, as it is noted in the Scripture, is, 'Little girl, I say to you, get up!'"

Both Samuel and Chris uttered their surprise at this, but Pastor Gregg pushed on a little further asking them a question, "And do you know who attended the Lord Jesus when he healed the little one?"

Collectively the boys then asked as if one voice, "Who, Pastor?"

Pastor Gregg looked seriously at both of them and then said, "The Scripture notes that the Lord did not let anyone follow him 'except Peter; James; and John, the brother of James to Jairus's home.' The Scripture makes note that when they arrived and the Lord went in to heal the girl, he brought the disciples who were with him in addition to the child's mother and father. That would be Peter; James; and John, the brother of James."

"Our neighbor John is John the Apostle," said Samuel in a straight, matter-of-fact tone.

"But how can that be?" asked Chris. "I know that our neighbor was very special indeed even at times making it seem like he was actually present to witness the Biblical events or even was the writer of portions of Scripture which he often talked about, but how could it be that John was alive after all these many years?"

Pastor Greg smiled and said, "Well, boys, since that is such a great question and is in fact key to our understanding of what has taken place here, I'd like to read something to both of you from the Gospel according to John, if that is all right?"

In chorus both boys responded, "Yes, please do!"

"All right then," Pastor Gregg said as he opened up his Bible to John 21. He began reading from the twentieth verse,

> Peter turned and saw that the disciple whom Jesus loved was following them. (This was the one who had leaned back against Jesus at the supper and had said, 'Lord, who is going to betray you?') When Peter saw him, he asked, 'Lord, what about him?'
>
> Jesus answered, 'If I want him to remain alive until I return, what is that to you? You must follow me.' Because of this, the rumor spread among the brothers that this disciple would not die. But Jesus did not say that he would not die; he only said, 'If I want him to remain alive until I return, what is that to you?'"

"So there is a biblical basis or at least a possibility for believing that John lived among us even up to yesterday, right, Pastor?" asked Samuel.

"I certainly see what we have just read as that," said Pastor Greg. "And"—the pastor paused—"John essentially admitted this to me when we spoke in this room before the debate! And for certain, I do not believe that our neighbor John is or was a liar."

The use of the word "was" brought home to the boys again that John was no longer among them. However, inside they were just starting to feel very grateful to God for making it clear to them with whom it was that they had been so blessed to work. Nevertheless, they missed their mentor and friend more than words could say.

Pastor Gregg then tried to perk things up optimistically and said to the boys, "Well, boys, it seems that before John was to go home to the Lord, he needed to at least visit a local church, not even in existence at the time of Jesus's ministry on Earth. Perhaps his work here will play an important role in the revival that this land so desperately needs—that even the world so desperately needs. I'm also quite certain that you will recall stories and experiences concerning John for years to come which will both bless and edify the church in very special ways—the church here as well as the Body of Christ universally, the Holy Catholic Church. We have all been witnesses to a special miracle done in our midst! Our humble church has been mentored by John the Apostle, the disciple whom Jesus loved! How great is that? I hope that each of you will always feel free to share with me anything more because I would love to hear it all!"

Both boys perked up and smiled immediately acknowledging their very special privilege of participating in the work begun by John and as evidenced in everything that had occurred.

After a few moments, Samuel spoke up. "Pastor Gregg?"

"Yes, Samuel," replied the pastor.

"Did you learn anything else from John that you can share with us?"

"Actually, yes, but I would like to wait to reveal that later, while I ponder its implications for building up the Body of Christ. I hope you understand that sometimes the servant needs to take note of his blessings and spend some time in prayer and contemplation in order to help him find the right venue which he can later use to pass blessings to others. Everything in its right time! Is that all right, Samuel?"

"Yes, Pastor, it makes perfect sense!" replied the boy, who was now feeling better about the entire situation, not exactly sure why, but feeling it nonetheless. "Sometimes we must keep things close until such time as they are ready to be brought out as blessing."

"Thank you, Sam. You have much wisdom for one so young… actually, you both do." The pastor looked over now to Chris. "It seems that you both are being used by God as yet another blessing to our church community, which I hope to make known to you at a later time also," said the pastor warmly.

Then suddenly as if it occurred to him just at that moment in time, Pastor Gregg shared another personal note with the boys. "It was funny how I had known our friend for going on two decades but somehow missed the deeper significance of his presence. Even his name didn't provoke in me any clue!"

"His name?" asked Chris.

"Yes, sometimes there are characteristics about a name which reveal its origin. I didn't recognize 'Barzeb' as being Jewish," confessed the pastor.

Then, as if remembering something significant, but not quite sure of how to relate it to what the pastor said, Chris spoke up again. "He didn't even sign his name in the letter that came with the bicycle."

"What bicycle?" asked Samuel.

"Yes, what bicycle, Chris?" asked Pastor Gregg.

"Oh, I almost forgot to tell you. This morning my parents discovered a gift left for me on the porch by John!"

"That new bicycle outside, Chris?" asked Samuel, smiling.

"Yes, can you believe it? I remember that John was concerned about my old bike and even did a little mechanical work on the brakes to make it safer… We were talking about answers to prayer, and I used the bicycle as an example… I remember exactly when I said it because it was the last day of June, June 30. I actually said in my example to him that if I asked the Lord for a bicycle and received it a short time later, it would be a definite answer to prayer. The funny thing is that the invoice indicated that the bicycle had been ordered from a bicycle shop in Westfield, New Jersey, on the twenty-eight of June, two days before we were even talking about it—and with the exact equipment I specified for the 'ideal new bicycle'!"

"That's amazing, Chris!" said Samuel.

"And it was on your porch this morning?" asked the pastor, clearly in a state of wonderment. "He must have brought it over to your house right after he left me at the church," the pastor mused.

"Yes," replied Chris. "And in the note he signed it, JBZ."

"JBZ?" repeated Samuel.

"Oh! Boys, I can't get over this! Another blessing in our midst! The "B" then isn't part of the actual name! It stands for the separate word *Bar*, the Aramaic word for 'son of'! Somehow it didn't occur to me before hearing how John signed Chris's letter!"

"John, son of 'Z'?" asked Samuel.

"John, son of Zebedee!" declared the pastor, this time with tears running down his face. "Praise dear God now and forever!"

Seeing the pastor crying, both of the boys jumped up from their chairs and took positions on either side of their spiritual leader, their hands placed in loving support on the shoulder nearest to each of them.

"We do and we will, Pastor Gregg!" said Samuel. "We praise God for this miracle in our midst, which, once again, testifies for us that God is good all the time! And…"

Now it was Chris's turn, "And all the time, God is good!"

And now each of them began to feel the clouds of sadness lifting from around them to reveal a greater purpose and not simply a discordant, incidental tragedy. Each one silently felt a growing confidence coupled with joy within them that everything that had transpired concerning John had happened according to the perfect schedule of the King of the Universe. After all, there were no accidents in dear God's timetable! If dear God wanted to call John home after this last mission, so be it.

CHAPTER 43

SAMUEL FINALLY OPENS HIS GIFT AND MAKES A STUNNING CONCLUSION

Both of Sam's parents were very happy to see the rather remarkable and positive change in their son once they picked him up from his meeting with Pastor Gregg. There seemed to be a renewed positivity and sense of purpose in his demeanor, just as he had demonstrated during the preparation time spent with John and Christopher over the summer weeks. Sam even asked his mother what she was cooking for dinner that night! Upon hearing that question, his father smiled and said jovially, "Well, Sam, if your appetite is returning, I'm taking that as a good sign that there is healing going on in our special guy!"

Samuel laughed at this and added, "And if we could have chocolate cake for desert, I think the healing would be even faster!"

That it must have been a funny coincidence occurred to all three of them in the car, but just at that precise moment they were passing the bakery in town, but not so quickly that his dad couldn't put on the directional and pull into the side parking area. As he put the car in park, he said to Samuel and his mother, "Well then, let's make sure we get exactly the perfect kind of cake for the healing!"

Later after they had arrived home, Samuel noticed the box brought for him by Officer Ray. Asking his mother to borrow her scissors, he set about opening up the box on the kitchen table.

"What do you think it might be, son?" his father asked.

"I'm not sure, Dad, but it is pretty solid so it's probably not some kind of clothing," replied Sam.

"Would you like us to help you, dear?" his mom offered.

"No, that's okay, I think I got it now," Sam said as he succeeded in piercing with the scissor the last piece of packing tape that encircled and sealed the box shut.

He pulled back the four flaps of the large box and inhaled sharply at the image that came into view. Inside the box was what appeared to be one of the knock-off wheels he had seen with John the day he was introduced to the Makoshark II. Samuel put his hand onto the center of the wheel's hubcap to touch the three prongs that fanned out from the center, almost like a ninja dart in his mind.

Musing aloud, Samuel said to his parents, "This is one of the wheels' hubcaps from the Makoshark II, which I saw on the day John gave me the ride home. Along the way, John and I stopped to talk to Officer Ray and…" Suddenly, he broke off in mid-sentence. His parents watched him as he focused intently on the spinner of the hubcap as if he was trying to remember something. Just as suddenly, he turned to his mother and father and said, "Mom, Dad, could you drive me to John's shop now?"

"Why, son?" his father asked.

"There is something I have to see before it's too late," Sam said without further explanation.

Realizing that Samuel had seemingly made so much progress that day in adjusting to the loss of John, his parents agreed.

"Dad will drive you over while I start on our dinner, Sam."

About twenty minutes later they pulled into the parking lot of John's cabin store fishing supply shop. When Samuel saw John's truck there, he was momentarily struck by the feeling that everything was normal. He knew better than to get lost in remorse now, however, and decided to press on toward the goal for which he had enlisted his father's service.

As his father parked the car, he turned to Samuel and said, "Okay, son, we're here. What is it you want to see?"

Samuel looked at his father and said, "It's inside the garage."

As the two walked toward the garage at the back of the store, his father noticed that the door was closed and had a locking mechanism just above the handle. Before he said anything however, as they approached the door, he noticed that the key was actually still in the lock.

"Wow, Sam, it looks like John forgot to take the key with him when he last closed the door."

"It sure looks that way, Dad, but John never forgot things like that."

Standing at the closed door, his father decided that since they had no ill intent, it wouldn't be a terrible thing for them to take a look inside. Making his decision, he turned to his son and said, "All right, Sam, let's go have a look around since you and he were very close, and in a short while, things may end up disheveled as the curious come by!"

Samuel looked up at his father and said, "Thank you, Dad. This means a lot to me."

With that his father twisted the key, pulled down the handle, and slid open the door.

The two stood looking at the empty place where Ronwyn, aka the Makoshark II had once been parked. Everything else in the garage appeared to be the same as Samuel remembered it with one exception—the reason for Samuel's mission there today. Where once hung four hubcap simulations of knock-off wheels were only the empty hooks.

Samuel smiled, and his father heard him say, "I thought so!"

"Well, Samuel, what did you want to see here?" his father asked.

"I've already seen it, Dad, thank you so much for driving me here!" said his grateful son, almost enthusiastically.

"Is there anything you want to share, Sam?" asked his curious father.

"Well, Dad, maybe at the right time and right place, but for now I need to think this through," replied Samuel. Before his father could say anything, Samuel added, "I want to be sure of things before I say anything silly."

Seeming satisfied with his son's answer, he then said to Sam, "Well, son, on that note, let's return home and get ready to sample some of Mom's delicious cooking and that chocolate cake for dessert!"

At this Sam looked into his father's eyes and then hugged him tightly. "Thank you, Dad. With all the miracles that dear God has blessed me to experience, you are certainly one of them that I have had with me all of my life."

Looking back down at his son and clearly touched by what he said, his father replied, "And, son, you are one of my miracles with which the Lord has blessed me for over eight years!"

And with that, his father closed the garage door and returned to the car, this time holding his son's hand.

CHAPTER 44

LOOKING BACK FROM THE PRESENT DAY BEFORE LOOKING FORWARD, BLESSINGS ABOUNDING!

Samuel summarized the events as briefly as he could which had followed the debate given that summer at Grace Church in Bolton Landing, New York.

"The Saturday edition of the local newspaper printed a highly favorable record of the debate which had taken place. Over the next weeks, attendance grew steadily as Pastor Gregg's sermons seemed to really be drawing the curious inside. When the DVDs became available, they must have ignited a huge interest in and of themselves because requests poured in from all over the state first, and then later the rest of the country. Requests were then found to come from even outside the borders of the nation!"

Samuel smiled as he thought back. Then he wrote some more, "The newscaster ultimately joined the church, along with each of her filming crew, and later began a Sunday school class on ethics in journalism, which she still teaches to this day. Even Mr. Edmund joined the church, and later, after he was baptized, worked with the local outreach committee of the church in order to bring the good news to young professionals who craved meaning in their lives. As for Mr. Allen, he is now in his eighties and teaches a class on science and

Scripture in the adult Sunday school! He is a favorite leader of the children's ministry for taking the youth to science museums, even all the way down to New York City!"

Samuel continued to write, "Pastor Gregg was soon forced to sponsor a funding drive to raise money for expanding the church buildings. In less than two years he raised enough to expand the sanctuary to one thousand seats and to expand the adjacent twelve classrooms to accommodate a minimum of fifty students each at any given time! Most people were initially surprised when he later presented a proposal before the church committee to change the name of the church from Grace Church to Grace Church of the Apostle John. Members of the committee had become fully aware of the pastor's testimony about the events surrounding the debate and, not wanting to disregard the specialness of all that had happened, unanimously approved the expansion of the name!

"Mrs. Ortega, although greatly saddened when she learned of the passing of John from our midst, was soon surprised and simply delighted to learn that John had left his entire estate to her and Melinda. In fact, his business had been set up to smoothly pass into her hands, John having listed her as a partner. The business continues to this day. Her cousins did arrive later in the United States which turned out to be a huge blessing for them all, as they were quite adept at keeping the fishing supply business running in a healthy, robust way. In fact, they were able to expand the business to several other counties over the years. I still see Melinda and her mother on school holidays and vacations. Even at eighteen years of age now, Melinda still keeps Mr. Bunny in pristine condition! She's a very beautiful young woman now, and I'm sure that she probably has to work to keep all those pesky boys at bay. Rumor has it that she's in line for a scholarship at a prestigious school somewhere, although I confess I don't know which one yet.

"And about that hubcap, the gift from Officer Ray, and about what I had noticed, I had felt then that it was not meant to be shared—at least not at that time. My dad was very good about it, fortunately, but I wanted to be faithful to what I believed dear God was showing only to me during those events of the summer. I had remembered what Pastor Gregg had said to me only a short time earlier that same day when I asked him about any additional things he had learned from John. His reply seemed so perfect, 'I hope you understand that sometimes the servant needs to take note of his blessings and spend some time in prayer and contemplation in order to help him find the right venue which he can later use to pass blessings to others. Everything in its right time!' As I recall, I responded, 'Sometimes we must keep things close until such time as they are ready to be brought out as blessing.'

"Even now," Sam continued to write, "it is still not the time to share it in public but maybe one day soon. Quite honestly, however, there was deep significance in what I had observed that day."

Sam took a moment and looked up at the die-cast model car of the Makoshark II sitting on the shelf above his desk. He smiled to himself and then started typing at the keyboard once again.

"I'm so glad that John showed me those hubcaps on the wall that day we took the ride in the Makoshark II. Otherwise I would never have made the connection that I made that day. Officer Ray's gift, however thoughtful on his and his wife's part, did not come from the Makoshark II, which was assumed destroyed in the car accident and which everyone assumed killed John. The hubcap he gave me simulated a knock-off wheel only and had never been mounted on the car which John had showed me and in which we had both ridden together. The Makoshark II used real knock-off wheels, not hubcaps! I discovered that day with my father that the hubcaps which had hung on the wall were no longer in the garage. In fact, they had been removed by someone, before anyone had a chance to find them there or make the connection about what was retrieved from the smoldering wreck."

Samuel thought a moment more and then continued writing, "John introduced me to that car by myself, not in the presence of Christopher, Pastor Gregg, or anyone else. I trusted that the information I gleaned from my fabulous introduction was given to me for safekeeping for some reason at that time and continue to trust is still significant today. I suppose I have been waiting ever since to see where it will lead—so far even after fourteen years!"

Samuel now decided to end his writing labors for the time and put down his final thought.

"One day I hope to see John again. To work with him again. To pick up where we left off. I know in my heart that he is not dead, but instead waiting patiently for the Lord's timing, as I am also trying to do. At the moment we concluded our presentation at the debate that summer night, John said to me, 'And there are still many more things to do!' After I told him that I looked 'forward to doing whatever it is the Lord wants me to do,' especially if I could work with him, John smiled and replied simply, 'That sounds just about right, Samuel!' And if truth be told, everything sounded right to me too, especially in my personal estimate of where things stood then—and how they stand now for that matter!"

Satisfied that he had covered the essential points he had wanted to record from the beginning, Samuel saved his work onto the hard drive of the computer and onto a flash drive for back up. Just over twenty minutes remained until his debate at the school's main auditorium, plenty of time to walk there, greet a few friends, and settle into the moment.

As Samuel headed off to the college debate, he encountered a messenger who approached the dormitory building with a telegram. He didn't even know that telegrams could still be sent! Meeting Samuel's gaze, the messenger asked him if he knew how he could deliver his telegram to one of the students who lived there. Samuel asked, "To whom is it going?"

The messenger responded, "It is to be delivered to Samuel Bodden by 7:40 p.m."

Samuel smiled to himself. Apparently it was from another well-wisher from his hometown of Bolton Landing, New York, who wanted to encourage him, along with all the others who had been sending him messages all week through various means.

As Samuel opened the telegram, he gazed down at the slip of paper and read it aloud to himself, "My dearest Samuel, keeper of the secret of the hubcap, thank you for all that you do for our Lord! May tonight's debate be as special as one that took place on an August evening all those years ago! May dear Jesus bless you and keep you always. As our dear brother Paul might say, 'Keep on fighting that good fight!' only remember to do it with love in your heart, soul, mind, and strength and, of course, always in action! Love always, JBZ."

Samuel turned his head away from the messenger to find the privacy he needed to keep secure the tears that immediately welled up…accompanied by the surging of an inner strength he felt all through his body.

For the Son of Man is going to come in his
Father's glory with his angels, and then he
will reward each person according to what he
has done. I tell you the truth, some who are
standing here will not taste death before they
see the Son of Man coming in his kingdom.
—Matthew 16:27–28 (NIV)

If anyone is ashamed of me and my words,
the Son of Man will be ashamed of him when
he comes in his glory and in the glory of the
Father and of the holy angels. I tell you the
truth, some who are standing here will not taste
death before they see the kingdom of God.
—Luke 9:26–27 (NIV)

I tell you the truth, this generation[1] will
certainly not pass away until all these things
have happened. Heaven and Earth will pass
away, but my words will never pass away.
—Matthew 24:34–35 (NIV)

I tell you the truth, until heaven and earth
disappear, not the smallest letter, not the least
stroke of a pen, will by any means disappear
from the Law until everything is accomplished.
—Matthew 5:18 (NIV)

---

[1] Or *race*

ABOUT THE AUTHOR

Paul M. Feinberg, PhD has been an adjunct assistant professor of Geology at Hunter College, CUNY, since 2003. He earned his doctorate in Earth and Environmental Science at the Graduate Center of the City University of New York in 2006. He has also earned both BA (1983) and MA (1987) degrees in geology from Boston University as well as a master's degree in education (2009) from the City College of New York, CUNY. He has worked more than ten years as an environmental geologist and geological consultant.

Dr. Feinberg continues to be a member of the supporting science staff to Dr. Robert Cornuke of the Bible Archaeology, Search & Exploration (BASE) Institute, now for more than a decade. Dr. Feinberg has traveled with Bob Cornuke to Ethiopia; the Greek islands of Malta, Athens, Patmos, and Crete; the ancient city of Ephesus in Turkey; and, most recently, to Jerusalem. He has provided assistance with many of the past and ongoing projects at BASE, including the geological analysis of the rock samples from Jabel Al Lawz in Saudi Arabia, the ongoing sampling in Iran in the search for Noah's Ark, and the recent search for the location of Solomon's Temple in Jerusalem.

He is also a huge Corvette fan, is fascinated by Star Trek TOS, and is captivated by the naval and aviation history of the United States. A lover of Shetland sheepdogs, he still misses his baby dog Abigail Esther Peebles. He lives with his wife, Sofia, in North Plainfield, New Jersey.

feinbergpaul@yahoo.com

CPSIA information can be obtained
at www.ICGtesting.com
Printed in the USA
FSHW020921251020
75159FS